theivanai

Kala is the author of two books of poetry, *He Is Honey, Salt and the Most Perfect Grammar* (2016) and *Offer Him All Things, Charred, Burned & Cindered* (2018) and of *Mahasena*, Part One of the Murugan Trilogy. She lives in Bangalore with Paru, Gauri, Sathyavak and Totoro.

PART TWO OF
THE MURUGAN TRILOGY

theivanai

KALA KRISHNAN

First published by Westland Books, a division of Nasadiya Technologies Private Limited, in 2024

No. 269/2B, First Floor, 'Irai Arul', Vimalraj Street, Nethaji Nagar, Alapakkam Main Road, Maduravoyal, Chennai 600095

Westland and the Westland logo are the trademarks of Nasadiya Technologies Private Limited, or its affiliates.

Copyright © Kala Krishnan, 2024

Kala Krishnan asserts the moral right to be identified as the author of this work.

ISBN: 9789360458966

10 9 8 7 6 5 4 3 2 1

This is a work of fiction. Names, characters, organisations, places, events and incidents are either products of the author's imagination or used fictitiously.

All rights reserved

Typeset by Jojy Philip, New Delhi
Printed at Manipal Technologies Limited, Manipal

No part of this book may be reproduced, or stored in a retrieval system, or transmitted in any form or by any means, electronic, mechanical, photocopying, recording, or otherwise, without express written permission of the publisher.

*For
Gauri, the middle child
like your name: filled with light*

CONTENTS

The God's Test

1. Waiting — 3
2. Aambal is Brought to Pothigai — 5
3. The Battle Starts — 14
4. Garjana and Idaychi — 23
5. Krauncha, the Mountain — 37
6. Tarakan — 48
7. The Knots in Aambal's Memory — 55
8. Banukopan — 61
9. Singamugan — 67
10. Surapadman and Mahasena — 79
11. The Secret — 87
12. In the Aftermath — 105

The Poet's Victory — 111

1. A Sojourn in Mayilai — 113
2. Aambal Recovers — 134

3.	Pazhani Again	139
4.	The Wooing of Theivanai	153
5.	Paramkundram	167
6.	Akattiyan Reveals the Secret	190
7.	Theivanai Sends for Aambal	202
8.	Nakkeeran and the 'Plot'	216
9.	Everybody Prepares	230
10.	The Selection	237
11.	Confessions	260
12.	In the Aftermath	268

Acknowledgements   274

the god's test

1

WAITING

Ganesha looked out over the red sand of Chendur's beach into the turbulent sea. The rise and fall of his belly, in rhythm with his breathing, was slow, gentle. He was thinking of the events that had led to the impending battle between Murugan and Surapadman. And of Murugan's secret name, which neither he, nor the few others who knew it, could say out aloud. It was a name that had to remain unspoken until its owner solved the riddle it held, bringing to a close the game Murugan had agreed to play: Surapadman's great game. Ganesha shut his eyes, he counted out Murugan's known names: Kandhan, Kumara, Skanda, Karthikeya, Murugan and now, Chenduran, Senani and Mahasena. Even as the pleasing syllables of these many names rippled on Ganesha's tongue, he felt such an urge to say the other one out. His eyes swept the horizon, rose to the skies and came back to the waves. He closed his eyes and breathed deeply.

His mind went back to an earlier time, a time when Kandhan had demanded a story before he would take a bath. It sped over the tale and came to the conclusion, 'Kandha, of the many great Asuras, there is none as great as the mighty Surapadman. He has chosen when and how to go back to the Vast. And he has chosen you to aid him. He has devised a game, which you agreed to play before you took this form. You have accepted to forget and to solve the riddle, to unveil the secret of who you are and what you are known as, for the secret is in your name. One that I cannot speak, nor anyone else. And Suran will not return to the Vast till you recover your name. You know that, don't you?'

As he sat there recalling that moment, Ganesha's mind was filled, as it often was, with thoughts about language, of the act of naming; of how language gives the myriad forms of the universes a definite place and use. So, too, Murugan is what he is, but that form of his is hidden inside its namelessness. Only when he names himself can it burst out of its shell. Ganesha sighed. He was impatient. He wanted the battle to start and end, he wanted to be back on Pothigai.

2

AAMBAL IS BROUGHT TO POTHIGAI

There was a single, winding path up Pothigai's steep slope, hidden to all but the Kani whose home it was, and to those the mountain welcomed, like Akattiyan, or permitted, like Aambal's family was now. Ganesha waited at the head of it for the six Kani women and men and the Sage of Pothigai to return with the visitors: Aambal's paternal grandfather, both grandmothers, her parents. And, of course, Aambal, whom one of the six, most likely Chakki, would hoist on to their back and carry up. Perhaps the Kani would be subdued—Aambal would not be reciting her poetry, she could not see them. The visitors would walk up as easily as the Kani did, for climbing hills and mountains was habitual to all those who worshipped the God of the Kurinji.

But today, Ganesha thought, they would not be feeling worshipful. That god, who was supposed to guard their bodies and minds as faithfully as he sentinelled their lands and their language, had failed them: Aambal was unconscious and she was mute. Ganesha sighed. So much suffering. Poor Aambal, poor, poor Aambal. He felt a sadness that he knew was not necessary. Everything had happened as it should—this was part of Aambal's journey, this loss of voice and feeling, a necessary fracturing to mark another stage in her journey to the most important role of her life. He had only to look ahead to see what Aambal would become, or to look back to recall why she had been born. But still, he could only sigh and prepare himself to meet Aambal's family now.

The vetiver-scented, tree-sieved, soothing winds on Pothigai fanned Ganesha, and again he was thankful to be here on its restful slopes, where everything slowed down, slipping into a repose that was inexplicable: there was no saying why you felt unburdened as soon as you arrived here. You could have betrayed your little brother's trust, you could feel as if your heart had wrenched itself out of your ribs and followed your sibling as he strode away from his home, and from you, you could feel as if you were the most despicable creature alive, as he had, but when you came to Pothigai, it was as if the mountain held you still and swept you out, like it had done with him.

Ganesha was glad Akattiyan was here. The old man, once so restless that even the elements moved out of his way, and mountains quaked when he crossed them, had become, like Pothigai: kindly, still, motherly.

His mind turned to the great six-day battle on Chendur beach, to those who had died or been wounded, and to the final day, when Murugan defeated Surapadman. It was over now, and everything and everyone had played their roles, including Aambal, war bard to Mahasena. On that last day, to all appearances, she looked just as she had when the battle began. But those who knew the ways of such things said that what had a claim on Aambal would wait while she finished her duties, and then it would burst, like a seed from its coat, bursting with muscular stems that thrust into her mind and heart, feeding on her.

And that was how it had happened: Aambal collapsed only after she reached her parents' home in Chendur after performing the ritual songs with Thennan and the musicians in the closing ceremony of the battle, and then taking leave of everyone. She lay for days tossing, turning, leaping up in sweating terrors. Her grandparents drizzled the holy water from Velan's Hill onto her tongue and over her anguished body, to no avail. They called in the veriyattam dancers to dance away the affliction, but it didn't work, neither did the singing of the thousand names of the God of Hills, or the powders of the kadamba, so dear to that god, or the milk of the umatha, or anything else they tried. They became more and more afraid for her as the days passed. Just as they were considering sending word to Murugan, a visitor to their neighbour's house, a man of medicine, examined her and said to them, 'She has forgotten how to speak. Can't you see she's gasping not for breath, but for language?' And they realised that her mouth was not struggling to breathe, but to speak. This was far more frightening, for they knew that Aambal's life was planted in language. How could she live without poetry? What did she have if there were no words? No lines, no verses, no metre or rhythm? They did not even want to imagine it. She had given them all up and followed Murugan, the God of Language, and had become to herself, and to the world, 'Murugan's Poet'.

It was Aambal's grandfather who fought the dread that was settling over them. 'Aambal is Murugan's poet. She cannot be unlanguaged. It will all come back to her. This is her life, and it has not ended,' he said. 'Let us take her to the Mother of Tamizh, the muni on top of the great mountain where the Kani people have their home. Kindly Pothigai will heal her, and the muni will teach her to speak again.' So they travelled with Aambal in a bullock cart, and, at the foothills, found a group of Kani folk waiting for them, along with Akattiyan, who embraced each of them and spoke calming words. Chakki hoisted Aambal onto her back and climbed effortlessly, and the others followed, one behind the other, Akattiyan at the end.

Ganesha was waiting for them, and when they stood before him, weeping, clutching at his fragrant, cool body, tears flowed out of his eyes and he could not speak. It was Akattiyan who reassured everyone that Aambal would be herself, in time, at the right time. After a day, when he told them to go back home, he repeated his assurance, 'She has to win her words back, syllable by syllable. She has to regain language and she needs to wait, and to be alone. When that happens, she will begin to heal and she will be herself.' They returned to Chendur, their worry lightened but not gone, for they knew that, to people like Aambal, poets, oracles, bards, their words were their life-breath, and on Bhu, to live without breath is impossible.

Even on holy Pothigai, the days and nights continued to be fearsome for Aambal: images ambushed her, entering through the unguarded frontiers of her mind like marauding hordes, razing everything in their path. It always stopped at the same scene, the same terrifying form that tore into her dreams, and knocked her out of exhausted slumber into a maddening frenzy, neither asleep nor awake, her gaping eyes blind with fear, her voice unsounding in her quavering throat. The Kani women and men took turns to tend to her, holding her against their chests when the terror struck, repeating the name of the one whose name resounded to them from everything: Velan, Velan, Velan. Their fingers put food into her mouth, and held her lips shut till her throat pulsed open and let it slide in; they cleaned her when the wastes burst out of her where she lay; they poured into her resisting mouth the green sap of the leaves that to them was a cure for all ailments; they bathed her, rubbing her down with the soft mud beside the stream, greened by falling leaves; they lay her out on sun-hot rocks, over which they first ran their hands; they combed the knots out of her hair, and attended to her with care.

When one full moon had come and gone, and then twice five and another two days had passed, they saw that Aambal's eyes were looking at them—she could see them. Movement returned to her hands and feet, and slowly to all her limbs. Her lips moved, no longer contorted with her soundless screams, but now attempting to form the shapes of the words that had passed through them from a time when she could speak.

Akattiyan watched over Aambal like the matriarch of a large household watches a newborn baby, his feet unconsciously wending thatward to see how she was responding to the care being given to her. As the days passed and Aambal got better, the old one's shoulders seemed to straighten, and he and Ganesha began to smile again. Ganesha could not bear the sight of an immobile, voiceless Aambal. Whenever he thought of checking on her, his eyes filled with an image that made him retrace his steps: Aambal darting out from behind kanakambaram bushes, her child-voice praising a verse that had just been recited, her eyes shining, her face serious, her sturdy body standing with practiced erectness. And later, his little brother, stubborn, wilful Kandhan, overcome by a hesitance that was alien to him, stuttering and stammering to her a question that she had answered then, and would always answer, in the affirmative: 'Will you be my friend?'

When Aambal could stand, one or the other of the Kani, most often Chakki, who was around the same age as Aambal, led her around by the hand, pointing out and naming things in their language. They sang to her songs that they had always sung, the words of which carried the sounds of birds, beasts and the kind earth. Aambal could not say what it was they were singing, but there was one word that made her heart leap and her tongue flail helplessly; it was the name of their wild hunter god, whose akil staff sprouted leaves that he allowed them to pluck, the god in whose other hand was a hunter's sharp vel. As they sang, they paused, as if waiting for her to grab hold of and hoist herself on to the back of the lithe animal that was their song and hunt down the words that had been stolen from her.

They were disappointed but not disheartened that Aambal could not hold on to their songs as they did. That she was not led down a path into the dark cave of fear, at the heart of which Velan himself waited to hoist you onto his shoulders and bring you out, fearless. They saw that whatever had taken hold of her would not be fought off, it had to be persuaded to leave, with language that Aambal was unable to voice.

They did not know that whatever had taken hold of her on the battlefield of Chendur had leeched Aambal of herself, for that was what the being did. She had been unlanguaged. Though she could hear and understand, if she tried to capture meaning into words and sentences, the syllables evaded her, as slippery as the vilangkumeen in the canals of Chendur, darting quicker than thought into secret recesses, too small even for fingers.

As the days passed, the menace of the gruesome image became a little blunted by the winds of Pothigai, and Aambal was able to hold her body and mind somewhat steady. As she stopped teetering, she felt heavier, less prone to being swept up and flung here and there.

There were days on which she was able to grasp at the snatches of memory that drifted into her mind, and sometimes her hold was strong and the flimsy fragment held still and took on body. As she grew stronger, the frayed skin of her stubbornness revived and she waited for these visitings, readying to block out everything else. So, one day, when the figure that had loomed up in front of her on the battlefield stormed into her mind, she was prepared. Shutting her eyes, she focused on that moment: the first thing she recalled was the cold, a chill such as could not even be imagined in the warm south. It had spread through her, turning her limbs and her breath and blood rigid and unmoving, leaving her gasping and unsteady. When her eyes looked into the eyes of the being, it felt as if her own had been stretched and pegged there. She had felt that the being wanted all of her—limbs, senses, mind, heart—

to be focused solely on it. Mounted on a white swan, the figure rippled and undulated, slowly resolving into a being that had the appearance of both man and woman. The burgeoning breast on one side had made Aambal feel like a child looking at her mother in whose chest was life and suckle. On the other was the sinewy spread of a milk-less chest, a levelled field fallowing before a crop. As she watched, and she couldn't take her eyes off, though she tried, a mid-region became visible, where female and male halves extended, the outline faintly luminescent. They were not one, but two, merged, each sharing a half of themselves. They looked at her without stirring. One of their hands held a huge scorpion, tentacles striking out, hissing; the other hand clutched a handful of giant leeches, twisting and slithering.

She shut her eyes, trying to keep the image prisoned between her eyelids, trying to make it yield. But the beautiful twin-being, face unlined and features enchanting, was impassive: in their eyes, one unlike the other, there was no expression, neither expectation nor comfort or censure, and all Aambal saw there was her own shape, quivering in fear, unable to speak. She now shivered at the memory of that chill, the old fear stirred in the pot of her underbelly, her heart crashed against her chest, her head was aflame, but Aambal would not let go. She was still, her hands holding tight to the rock on which she sat, and soon the memory, as if riled, charged at her—a giant kangeyam, with spreading horns that scooped her up and tossed her back onto the battlefield that she had been trying to bring alive.

She was back there, in front of the fearsome being, as immobile, unthinking and mute as ever, but she saw something more this time, something was forming on their lap. It appeared a little at a time, like a picture being drawn: two tawny legs, a sturdy waist, a firm chest, two shapely hands, a long neck, thick curls tumbling down. She was looking at the enchanting face of a boy, the Beautiful One. Kandhan was on their lap, with their hands embracing him.

He was unsmiling, and the eyes with which he looked at her were not the eyes that she had known: these eyes held no expression, neither mischief nor laughter or love, and all Aambal could see there was her own shivering frame.

Though she tried again and again, Aambal could not go beyond what she had already been allowed to see of that memory, nor could she will herself to remember what had transpired on the battlefield that day or on any of the other days. She could not speak yet, and so could not ask anyone what it was she had seen. As if he had been waiting all the while for this, Ganesha came to her as she was walking with two Kani companions, the brothers Poitherutti and Raako, who treated her as if she was a young animal, rubbing her ears or stroking her spine, clucking their tongues when her feet, weighted down by her thoughts, did not move. When she saw Ganesha, Aambal's voice thrashed around in the prison of her throat and her eyes stung with the effort.

Taking the writing hand of his brother's best friend, Ganesha held it between both of his; he was unmoving. Aambal fidgeted, the urge to speak running wild in her body. He sat her down on a rock, and settling down beside her, recounted to her the events that had led to the battle at Chendur, beginning with the arrival in Pazhani of Indra, the king of the gods, who arrived with his retinue, including his daughter Devayani. And of his request to Murugan to lead an army against Surapadman and of Murugan's acceptance. He also spoke of Murugan's insistence on Aambal accompanying him as his war bard in the impending battle. As he spoke, Aambal remembered the sea-town of Chendur, her home, where her family lived and worked. Wisps of her memory collected like strands of silky cotton in its boll, and like cotton rolled between two human hands, it became firm, like a wick.

Ganesha held out something to her; her fingers trembled as they touched the metal, the cold of it passing through her fingers into her palms, her wrists, up her arms, turning her body cold as she shivered. Her eyes closed of their own accord, her head reeled and she was back there, in that time, that place, holding that cymbal, unfamiliar and yet familiar. Out of her mouth came the words 'Veerabahu's gift', and then she swooned. Ganesha held her before she collapsed, but she had slipped from this time into the timeless eddies of a trance that the magic cymbals would set off again and again. It was in the unlanguaged, ungrammared tracts of trance that Aambal would have to find what had been stolen from her, for that was where her bardic duties had taken her, through the barriers time used to grammar its flow into *here* and *elsewhere*, *now* and *elsewhen*.

3

THE BATTLE STARTS

The metal was cold, her hands were shaking a little. In her trance, Aambal was once again standing on the red sands of Chendur's beach, where they were all waiting for an arrival. She saw once more, facing each other, the two armies in formation. The battle would begin any moment now. She anticipated the stir and murmuring and the shifting from foot to foot in the rows of restless warriors before it came, as she settled into that time. Aambal too stood, like them, ears trained for the call to action. In a clear space between the armies there stood—set apart by their off-white attire—the musicians, physicians, bards and the runners, sturdy women and men, who would carry away the wounded and the dead and carry ahead messages.

Aambal felt as if she was two people, seeing the same thing, one a fragment of a moment before the other. She looked towards the end of the battlefield. Just in front of a row of ruddy hillocks, on a structure that resembled a high lookout tower, Devayani was standing with Ganesha, looking past the warriors to the sea. Aambal followed Devayani's eyes as they went to Kandhan. Images of the time Kandhan and she had first set eyes on Devayani flashed in her seeing. They had been in the temporary courtroom at the foothills of Pazhani, set up by

Devayani's father. 'Theivanai', Kandhan had given her that name when Brihaspati introduced them. As the cold of the cymbals and the seashore passed through Aambal, she remembered how Kandhan's footsteps had seemed to pass through the air that day into the bodies of those waiting there, making them billow and ripple with impatience. All their tumult had broken and sunk into the sea of silence inside him.

As musicians began to beat out ear-splitting martial rhythms on the various drums suspended from their shoulders or knotted to their waists, swelling the drum beats with the rhythmic stomping of their salangai-ankleted legs, Aambal's focus stationed itself beside them. The start of the battle would now be ritually declared. And then *She* would arrive. Aambal had heard of her and was filled with a mixture of curiosity and dread.

The previous evening, a council that included the two supreme commanders, ten commanders-in-chief, ten generals, two unit commanders, the chief physicians, the musicians and the leaders of the runners had met and decided on the battle formations the two armies would take on the morrow: mongoose for Surapadman's and snake for Murugan's. And that was how the army units stood; the deadliest warriors were positioned in strategic spots that, as in nature, were points of attack: the fangs of the snake, the claws of the mongoose. The chain of command went from unit leaders to commanders, generals and the commanders-in-chief, ending in the supreme commanders, Surapadman and Murugan, who would not enter the battlefield to fight until all ten of the commanders-in-chief were either dead or routed. Or if there were exceptional circumstances: if a warrior demanded single combat with them; if there was a warrior whose fierceness could not be met by any or all of the opposing side; if either of the bards called one of them in because their cymbals had taken them across time and they saw there a knot that could only be cut by either of the supreme commanders for the battle to move ahead.

Aambal looked around: Matri Dhumi, the commander-in-chief of Murugan's troops for day one stood at the tip of one fang of the snake army, at the other stood Veera Rakkaga, who was that day's general. Foot soldiers formed the hood, the eyes, the venom duct, while especially fierce warriors filled the venom gland—warriors as deadly as the poison that would have flowed there in a real snake. The snake army curled along the red sand, in loose curves that would side-wind or coil along the battlefield in response to the attacks that the mongoose unleashed. On the opposite side, the mongoose's snout was formed likewise by Surapadman's deadliest fighters. At the very tip of that snout stood his youngest brother, Tarakan, their commander-in-chief for the day; somewhere in the mongoose body was positioned their general, Krauncha.

The drumming paused, then resumed, accompanied by the booming of the gigantic por murasu, the battle drum, and the frenetic blowing of many kompu, small and big. From outside the battlefield, the chariots of the supreme commanders rode up close to the musicians, and they descended to stand next to each other. The drumming stopped and the piercing sound of cymbal beats flowed out over the battlefield. Aambal was one of two bards, one for each side, and it was they who would speak open the battle, wording out the ancient calls to earth, sky, sea, fire and to the space that held everything, including their own words. And to *Her*, the guardian of this and all battlefields: Mari, the Eternal Witness.

Surapadman's bard stepped forward first, as custom would have it, for they were the guests in this land. His cymbals sounded short, sharp running beats, asking for attention, more a formality than a necessity, for nothing stirred, no voices sounded. The man was tall, his hair hung in ringlets down to his shoulders, his fair, pale skin glowed in the early morning light. He was, of course, dressed in the ivory-coloured attire of bards. He raised both hands, which to Aambal looked like delicate sepals supporting the flower-like ears of the cymbals, first up to the skies, saluting the elements, then to his chest, saluting the life that filled his words, then the army that stood opposite and finally, the battlefield itself, bending down and touching the cold bell metal to its warm earth. His mouth opened and his voice rang out, 'Hail mighty Karthikeya Mahasena, Lord of Chendur, and his valiant warriors, physicians, musicians, runners, carriers and his war bard.'

Murugan smiled. Aambal's breath caught in her throat. Thennan! Like this? After so many years? When his parents moved across the Vindhyas, he had stopped visiting the kalari where Aambal, Murugan and their friends were being trained by Aasaan, Thennan's grandfather. But they still had news of him from his grandfather, and then, one summer, when Thennan's mother, Aasaan's daughter, came to the kalari, they had heard angry voices, an exchange between the father and daughter. She left the kalari in a rage, swearing she would not speak to him ever again, nor would her children or their father. Nobody knew what had transpired, not even Kuyili's grandmother—and she was one of the oldest people in the village and their chief. After that, Thennan had disappeared from their lives. And now, here he was.

Aambal looked at Murugan; he nodded. They would recognise that voice anywhere, even if not the body that held the voice. Thennan was looking at them too, his face serious, his eyes going to Murugan and Aambal and then to his king, Surapadman.

Thennan's voice broke out over the battlefield. The warriors stood straighter, their heads raised to the sky, conversing with whatever forces they believed kept them abled, in rhythm. When he finished, both armies, in a single coordinated movement, raised their weapons skywards and called out to the God of Endings, he who was innocent and butter-hearted. *Arogara*, they shouted from both sides, *arogara*.

Then it was Aambal's turn, she stepped forward, saluted Surapadman and his army, and replicated what the other bard had done: hailed the valour and might of both armies and called down the blessings of those with the authority to bless the warriors. There was no tremble in her voice, though her hand might have shook a little when she struck the first beat. She stopped, bent her head and waited while the soldiers raised their battle cries.

Then the Herald of the Battlefield, a single person chosen by both sides, the Asura mathematician Rahu, stepped forward, his voice louder than the roar of the sea and the howl of the wind, and called out the time, the day, the location and hailed the two armies' supreme commanders, as well as the commanders-in-chief and generals for that day. He went over the rules, reminded the warriors to be attentive to the rhythms of nature, to replicate the swell and ebb of the waves in their own movements, for to be unmindful of the elements around them meant their own step would weaken, and in a battle, every beat counted. He detailed the rules for foot fighters and for those on horses and in chariots, and for those who would use magic. He addressed all of them, reminding them to be attentive to each other and of the physicians, runners and the bards. Rahu then stepped back.

All the instruments sounded together and both armies, from their supreme commanders to the heralds, knelt to the ground and laid their weapons on the red sand. Thus they waited, for they could not begin until their Witness appeared. She who had little regard for time or place.

The earth trembled and dust rose. A body, blue-black, bones shining through the scanty flesh that covered it, her hair hardened into spikes by sweat, dirt and blood, charged onto the battlefield. One hand held a small battle drum, a cord wound around its middle, its ends knotted through hardy beads that struck against the drums' faces, producing a frantic staccato. The other hand held a sickle stained green and red, as if she been using it on ripened grain as well as disobedient heads; around her waist was a skirt of arms, chopped elbow down; above her waist, two dry, elongated dugs flapped against a chest that caverned inwards. As she leapt on to the battlefield, the warriors raised a cry, 'Mari, Mari, Kotravai, Kotravai'.

Surapadman raised his hands above his head and saluted the goddess. Murugan bent his head and shut his eyes, his thoughts taking him back to his childhood on Kailasa and the first time he had seen his mother in her fearsome form. That had been fun, he had sat on her hip, brandishing his akil dandam and howling and shrieking like her. The goddess raised her sickle and brandished it over the field, her red eyes roved over the rows of kneeling warriors. She roared and the sound raced out of her mouth like a wild wind, filling the two armies' flags and banners, slapping them into motion, waving and billowing madly.

Aambal shivered, and the shiver ran down to her toes and up to the top of her head; it shot through the stacks of her spine and spread through her limbs. The cymbals grew warm and of their own accord, her two hands brought the twin ears of the cymbals together in a rhythm that was staid in comparison to the feral beat of Mari's drum. Aambal recited a paean to the one known as the Keeper of All Battlefields. 'Mari,' sang her voice, unrecognisable in its thin, almost-wail, so different from her poetry-reciting voice, 'the font of life and the casket of death.' Thennan's voice sounded along, reciting words recited by all war bards, on all battlefields, in countless battles, none of which could begin without her. Their words went on, describing Mari in her many forms and all that she did and meant, and ended with the line, 'Pledge yourself to be the witness in this battle.'

The blue-black body rose into the air, spun and whirled. She cackled and called aloud in a language that could not be contained in sense. When finally she came to a rest, Mari said nothing, did nothing. But countless other battles had set the norm: now, they could begin. She had pledged herself to this battle, she would stay, watch and accompany every move of the warriors, especially those to whom she had made promises. She would maim, mangle or kill anyone who broke a rule. Murugan and Surapadman rode away to take up positions on opposite sides at the rim of the battle's demarcated arena, watching, waiting, always ready, in case they were called upon to act.

The commanders-in-chief and the generals saluted each other and gave the call to charge forward: the mongoose and the snake came to life, the snake curves trembled slightly as a snake's body would to the sun's rays coming out from behind a cloud, the mongoose's snout trembled as it would to the smell of prey.

Aambal knew that, over the coming days, deaths, woundings and defeats would be many. Those like the Sura, Gandharva, Bhuta and Asura could not die; they would instead leave the fight if defeated; if struck, some might suffer terrible wounds that would heal immediately. But something would alter in their lives, and many of these beings would choose to leave their homes and their bodies and immerse themselves in a waiting that might never end. The Asuras, of course, had the boon of being able to choose the time and means of their return to the Vast, and as the battle progressed, these choices became evident.

She wondered what events, which deaths, which encounters the scores of travelling bards who were camped on the outer section of the tents would be moved enough by to compose and tune and sing about in the future. Aambal sighed. She knew that they would sing about Surapadman, for there was none like him, and after all, he was combating Karthikeya Mahasena, Lord of Chendur, the God of Valour. Which of the manava warriors would merit a place in their songs, Aambal wondered. She measured her breath, listening for her own rhythm, set to beats that were hers, into which the beats of Life would flow to produce the rhythm that was her gati, her individual part of life's music, her fate. None knew what was to come, none knew what would result, but everyone knew that they should not, could not lose their beat.

As the two supreme commanders rode away, Aambal's eyes followed Murugan's chariot. He looked back at her, his face serious. She saw his hand close into a fist and press against his armour, as if feeling his heart. Aambal's heart swelled, he was telling her that she was in his heart. He is my heart, my life, she thought, and as always, the tears rushed into her throat and eyes, making her self-conscious. She thought about Murugan's father who had refused to come to the battlefield. Paravani had told her that before the march to Chendur when she had wanted to know who would be present at the battle. The mighty bird had sighed then and said that the soft-hearted Shambhu would have gone up the mountain, where there was little air and scant light, everything veiled by the sheets of snow that fell every moment in an endless season of cold. He would have gone into the deepest cave, iced over, its roof festooned by lengths of water frozen through many seasons, its floor glassy with ice, and he would only emerge when one of the ganas came to find him. Aambal wondered if it was possible that he was not sure whether his son would succeed. Then, catching sight of Mari, Aambal wondered if it was possible he did not want to see his wife screeching and raging, goading the warriors on to fight to their end.

Whatever it was, he stayed away, but Aambal, like all the people of Chendur, was not surprised to see in the sky overhead, even in the daytime, a cluster of six stars, their sparkle brighter than the sun's. The Krittikas, Murugan's mothers for a while. Their rays were focused on one spot: the warrior standing in a chariot drawn by twin black stallions whose names they knew to be Kalam and Neram, the dazzling vel in one hand.

As Aambal re-lived that first day in the battleground of her own trance, Ganesha followed along. When Thennan had appeared, he had thought, thus it begins. His eyes had gone to his brother and his brother's best friend, and had returned to the man who was praising the 'Lord of Chendur' in a voice that neither that lord nor his bard had ever forgotten.

    Much time had passed on the slopes of Pothigai, and Aambal's frail body uncurled from the taut coils of trance and dropped into a sleep from which she would not wake for days. And when she did, there was no saying if she would remember all that she had relived while in the endlessness of trance, where time is immobilised, unable to demarcate what was done with from what is and what will be.

4

GARJANA AND IDAYCHI

Ganesha had told Aambal that bards who had been present at the battle would narrate to her the parts that they had crafted into tales—the first of these was Akavan, who lived a night's walk away from Pothigai.

When Akavan arrived, Aambal, who was waking up very early, before the birds even, because she did not want to be distracted by their song, was sitting covered in blankets near a fire that either Poitherutti or Raako would have built for her. He stood unseen, looking at the woman whose fame had spread even more after the Battle of Chendur, because she had not only been the war bard of Karthikeya Mahasena and almost died doing her bard's duty, she had also been 'Murugan's Poet'.

Her eyes were closed. This was what she did most mornings: sit with her eyes shut and return to the image of the twin-bodied being she had seen, trying to get past the point where her mind's eye could not go. Her body would go cold, her breath would shudder and she would strain, but nothing more of that memory returned. Sometimes images from other events of the battle rushed in and out of her mind, but her attempt to try and weave the course of the battle from these strands continued to be in vain. Akavan moved towards Aambal, and the footsteps roused her from her concentration. By this time, others appeared, including Ganesha who said to her, 'Aambal, this is Akavan, the bard. He will narrate to you those parts of the tales of the battle that he has finished.'

Aambal had wondered why Ganesha could not just tell her himself, but she did not ask, and she did not care who did the telling or in what order or even that it would not be a complete narrative. This was something she was used to as a poet. She was a poet—of that she was now certain, she felt it inside her, something intangible that leapt when she looked at the world, assuring her that though she could not compose, she was a poet. It was there, despite its lightness, strong enough to make her seeing, hearing and feeling poetic. It made her feel like the ancient tahr whose hooves the sheer stone mountain slopes so dear to the God of the Kurinji mellowed for.

Akavan looked at Aambal with an expression of awe that she did not register. Like the other bards present at Chendur, he too had seen Aambal on the battlefield, how even on the verge of death she had clung to Tamizh, as if to the flanks of an animal on whose back her injured body teetered, and summoning up every last bit of determination, urged it to attack what was attacking her. He knew, as all bards did, that in such circumstances, loss of life was easier to bear than the loss of speech's rhythm, which must go in perfect step into the ears and the chest of the warrior they were meant to accompany and guard. Akavan shuddered as he recalled the last day of the battle.

He held his hands out to Aambal, one bard to another, in an ancient gesture that acknowledged the bond of rhythm. Aambal stared at Akavan for a moment before she recalled that she too had been a bard; she lifted both her hands and put them into Akavan's. He held them for a matra, his eyes on their hands as he repeated the old blessing, 'May the alphabets bless your fingers; may your tongue never lose its way; may your way be safe in Tamizh.'

Aambal bowed her head, and the words slipped into her ears and down into her chest, which heaved.

Ganesha smiled and left. Akavan sat down on the rock, facing her. 'Aambal, the Lord of the Ganas has told me to recount to you what I have recorded so far. It is not an account of the battle, for as you know, we are not chroniclers of events, but tellers of the stories of those who knock at our hearts and spur our language by their valour, strength, nobility, their humility, sorrow, loss, or by their devotion.' Aambal nodded as the images of many warriors sped through her mind, too fast for her to see them clearly or recall what they had done.

'There were many whose fight was glorious, many whose valour made the hearts of other warriors swell and leap with pride, those whom the supreme commanders celebrated, but from among them, there were some who entered my heart, and of these, I have so far only storied two: the Manava women Garjana, from the north of this land, and Idaychi, the physician warrior, from Eight Islands. They fought each other on the second day of this battle, when Banukopan was the Asura commander-in-chief.'

The look of confusion on Aambal's face reminded Akavan that she was still in the clasp of the One That Erases Everything, known to war bards everywhere, a being to be feared far more than the weapons, warriors, injuries and deaths, why, even Mari herself. He said, 'Banukopan, the eldest of the children of the glorious Asura Surapadman, the one feared by the Sun.' As he described the prince, into Aambal's mind came an image of the Asura riding into the start of the second day of the battle: glowing armour, eyes, smile—as if he was riding to a wedding feast, maybe his own. Akavan proceeded to narrate the story of the two women warriors. He had gathered the stories of their fore-life from those who knew them and melded it with what he himself had witnessed of their exploits on the battlefield.

'On the day that Garjana and Idaychi fought, the second day of the battle,' began his narration, 'the troops were arranged in a wolf and bear formation, the former being the Asuras and the latter, the Suras.' He explained that after the subtle movements required from the intricate formation of the first day—the snake and mongoose—the generals and commanders-in-chief had given ear to the fighters' suggestion of adopting something cruder, to balance. The Asuras had chosen as their commander-in-chief Idaychi, a manava of Bhuloka and the wife of Surapadman's younger brother Singamugan, and Banukopan was the general. The Suras had selected as their commander-in-chief the Manava woman known as Garjana, leader of the forces of Indra in Svarloka, and Jayantha, the son of Indra and brother to Theivanai, was their general.

Akavan paused and looked at Aambal, she showed no recognition of these names—even the flicker that had passed through her eyes when he described Banukopan did not make an appearance. He saw that he would have to recount not just slowly but also in more detail, for he could not depend on the familiarity that listeners usually had, through acquaintance or hearsay. This was like telling the tale to a child so young that she knew of nothing other than her mother and father and the words with which she asked for food. He felt a deep pity that was less for Aambal and more for what she had lost: the snatched-away fodder of memory and the starving beast of her language. He took out his little tudi and began the story in earnest, eyes moving from Aambal's face to the vast sky above them.

'Idaychi was from one of the eight islands that form a crescent between Veeramahendrapuram and Ilangkai, inhabited by the ancient healers who made them, bringing mud and stone and rubble on rafts into the middle of the choppy sea, then singing them into an unbreachable bind of land mass. These stories of their origin resonated with those who heard them, for these island dwellers still sang and spoke their cures and antidotes to heal. They were renowned in all the worlds for their ability to cultivate and use medicinal plants that only grew if tended by one of them, and for their ability to treat all manner of wounds, regardless of who was wounded and what the wound was: of the flesh, of the heart, or wounds made in dream.

Singamugan had come to the island seeking to carry across the sea some saplings of these plants, as well as one of the islanders to plant and tend to them till they sprouted and became robust. The family that had the rights to this disposition was Idaychi's. Singamugan was led there by the nomadic hunters who journeyed in the forests of these islands and on the lands across the sea, and could understand and converse in the tongues that were spoken in all these places. Unexpectedly, Singamugan fell prey to a severe affliction: as soon as Idaychi looked at him and greeted him, his heart stopped, started again, flung itself against the bars of its cage in his chest and then lay down on the floor and held its breath. He felt he would die if he did not speak, but he could die if he spoke. And so, he held his tongue and composed his face.

In the course of the days that Singamugan spent with Idaychi's family, being introduced to the ways of the many plants that they agreed to help him seed and grow in his kingdom, he began to sense that Idaychi felt the same. And she had indeed begun to feel attracted to him too, for Singamugan was intelligent, handsome and charming; he was also courteous and well-spoken, and his eyes were always filled with delight. So, when she agreed to cross the sea and travel with him to his home, it was not only the prospect of starting a nursery and training Singamugan, his gardeners and physicians in their use that made her eyes sparkle and her lips curve into sudden smiles.

The seeds were sown into the soil of Singamugan's kingdom, and many days of watering later, they began to sprout, their new tendrils and leaves translucent in the semi-shaded light of the nursery. That's when Singamugan asked her to marry him. She was eager to say yes. But before she did—perhaps her healer's sight showing her something that was at the moment not visible—she said to him, 'I must be free, too, to take another spouse, if and when I want to.' And indeed, she had. Now this is a thread that we have much interest in, for the second of her spouses was none other than Nanjil, the medicine man whom Murugan and Aambal counted among their dearest friends.

Nanjil had left home, wandered past the Vindhyas and crossed over into the northern lands. It was thus that he came to the court of Singamugan, having heard of a mysterious ailment that was afflicting the horses in the kingdom. Singamugan saw that, despite his youth, Nanjil had knowledge beyond his age, and let him try. The physician spent many days in the company of the horses in the royal stables, and with the wild horses that came out to run through the fallowing fields and had remained unafflicted. He understood that it was the doing of the Ashvini twins, the fabled wind-dwelling physicians and guardians of all four-footed creatures. Nanjil made the connection between the illness of the horses and repairs that had been done in all the stables throughout the kingdom: the wild horses were untouched because the air they breathed did not pass through the walls of the stables. Something that was due to the Ashvins had been ignored. Nanjil conveyed this to Singamugan, and suggested that all the stables in the kingdom be washed and cleaned, and a portion of their west-facing wall be broken and rebuilt, placing all the prescribed offerings to the Ashvins, inside. When the kingdom's horses lost their apathy and regained their earlier vigour, Singamugan was pleased and rewarded Nanjil. He also asked the young man to accept the role of chief animal physician in his kingdom, and Nanjil, until then too restless to stay long anywhere, accepted the role. He felt that something whispered to him, 'Stay', without saying why.

He lived just outside the palace, in a street of physicians, healers, magic-persons, medicine-makers, growers of medicinal plants, makers of medicinal implements. It was at the wedding of Ayina, the daughter of Siramutha, who made the best medicine-weighing scales in the kingdom, that Nanjil and Idaychi first set eyes on each other. Singamugan introduced his spouse to his chief animal physician, and soon, the two were discussing medicines and plants. The next morning, Nanjil was at the palace, being given a guided tour of the herbal nurseries. It was not long before the two became enamoured of each other—Idaychi as old as Nanjil's mother and Nanjil as young as the children of Idaychi with her husband, the king. It was Idaychi who began to visit Nanjil, and when she thought the time was right, she indicated to Singamugan that she would spouse Nanjil and live with him part of the time.

She divided her time between Singamugan and Nanjil. With Singamugan, she was a spirited lover, an intelligent beloved, an able administrator and queen, an engaged wife and a loving parent to their children. With Nanjil, she was like a bird in mid-air, her spirit soared and her heart stilled in a way that it rarely did, and she wanted to let Time take her where it wanted. For Nanjil, Idaychi was a thing of wonder: her powers were a gift of the island's guardian spirits who lived in the plants she used, while his own came from learning, training, experience and an instinct that was not always unfailing. When he was with Idaychi, sometimes Nanjil felt that he too could 'see' like her. The heady course of their love made him lighten up, and he was proven wrong about an old fear that had kept him single all this while: that the tumult of passion thickens the senses and leads to sluggishness in identifying and treating illness. On the contrary, he saw that his senses, satiated by love feasts with Idaychi, grew more settled and his fingers effortlessly picked up the whispers of the ailments and cures in the sickly bodies he treated.

Only months had passed in this way when Singamugan got word from Surapadman to aid him in the great battle with the son of the Goddess with the Rain-Bearing Parrot. Idaychi went with Singamugan to Veeramahendrapuram; she too would bear weapons and take part in the battle. Nanjil left the palace and travelled northwards—if something happened to his beloved spouse or to his dear friend, his king, he wanted the news to take as long as it was possible to reach him.

As the commander-in-chief, Idaychi was at the head of the Asura forces, and General Banukopan was located somewhere in the mid-section of the formation, to lead only if something happened to Idaychi.

On the Sura side, Garjana and Jayantha had taken up identical positions. Garjana was, like Idaychi, from Bhu. She came from the cold lands that lay at the feet of Himavan, lands from where the great mountain rose into the scintillating blue skies that existed nowhere else on Bhu. She belonged to a family that had spent generations in the service of battles of defence and offence by the great kings who safeguarded their lands—not only an endless basket of grain and fruit, but also a pathway between the land that ended at the sea, over which Mari stood sentinel, and those lands that lay on the other side of Himavan.

Garjana, when barely more than a child, had one day gone to the Falling Grace waterfall to collect the blue flowers that grew on its banks. It required a climb up the steep slope, for which she carried a length of cord. She also had a pouch. As she was about to loop and knot the cord to a tree branch, Garjana heard a sound and turned. She saw an elderly woman struggling to have a bath. She dropped the rope and the pouch, and went to the woman. 'Granny,' she said, 'shall I help you with your bath?' The old woman laughed and said, 'How did you know I was your granny?' Garjana was confused, was the old woman teasing her? She stopped and did not go any closer, for this could be one of the malevolent spirits that lived in forests and around water bodies. She realised that she had left behind her pouch of safeguards too. As it turned out, the old woman was indeed the spirit of Garjana's father's mother who had come to protect her granddaughter from something that would happen. She instructed Garjana on what she was to do, and then disappeared.

The young girl went back, she completed the rope loop, one end on her, under her armpits, around her waist, and the other end on a sturdy branch of a tree, to anchor her body should she slip during the climb. Midway through her ascent, she saw the blue flowers sparkling like beads, but did not reach out and pluck them. As her granny had instructed, she stopped and, turning her face away from the flowers, said, 'I have come to give, not to take. I have come to offer my life that I may live and not die as fated.' She waited. Granny had told Garjana that her parents had never drawn up her birth chart, and therefore did not know that she was destined to not live beyond her ten years.

The blue flowers rustled, and a voice said to Garjana that she was to leap into the waterfall, and that she would then die in her life on this world of mud and water, sky and fire and ether, and be born into a life where everything lived on and on. Garjana thanked the voice, as the old woman had instructed, and said that she did not want to live on and on, and that she had the protection of the Old Woman of the Waters who would fight anybody who tried to rob her of her people. In the back-and-forth that went on even as the sun climbed a little closer to the zenith of his daily glory, Garjana began to feel older, braver and much stronger than her ten-year-old body and mind could have, and in the end, the voice said, not to Garjana but addressing the 'Revered Old Woman, Mother of the Waters', that it agreed to her terms.

Garjana was to go up into the world of the Sura and acquire martial skills that would make her, in time, the commander-in-chief of an army of the Sura, led by the son of the Parents of

Creation. The voice also promised her that after that work was done, she would return to her land to be a guardian spirit that rode with her people into battle as the thrum in their hearts and the sharp in their weapons. Garjana had been carried into the heavens, and there, she learnt and fought for a length of time that in human years would be many, many, many more than she could have experienced on Bhu.

She came to the council held at Pazhani too, and met Murugan, who already admired her from the many tales he had heard of her valour. In the time that they marched from Pazhani to Chendur, Murugan rode beside Garjana, and when the army halted, instead of continuing his practice sessions with Veerabahu and the other eight brothers, Murugan sought out Garjana and duelled with her, with mace and sword, javelin and spear, with hands and with magic. They talked endlessly of warfare and of weapons and of the lands that Garjana had been born in. In the time that they were together, a deep friendship developed between them, and so, when Garjana rode into battle, nobody was surprised to see tucked into the belt of her armour the holy kadamba flower—the flower of the Lord of Pazhani.

Akavan came to the end of this introduction of his two protagonists. He drew a long breath and put his tudi down, flexed his fingers and rubbed his hands together. Lifting up the little palm-toddy container, he drew a few sips and offered the pot to Aambal. She only shook her head, her eyes filled with the hazy memory of the two women his words had just given shape to. He stood up, shook out his legs and then sat down again. Akavan hadn't sat long enough to need this flexing, and those who knew would know that what he would speak of now was difficult, and no matter how many times he repeated this part of the story, he would still need to stop and prepare before he began.

'Idaychi and Garjana fought head-on, but it was impossible to predict who would fare better: now one made the superior move, then the other, now one seemed to tire, then the other, but neither actually tired.' Akavan's voice had taken on a different timbre and Aambal unconsciously sat straighter, her hands clasped, fingers interlaced. The bard spoke of how Idaychi preferred the mace to any other weapon, and Garjana could fight with any weapon. He paused for a fraction of a moment before saying, in a voice filled with bewilderment, that Garjana may have been the most bloodthirsty warrior on the battlefield. He described how she delighted in the way that one body subdued another or drew blood that spurted with a cut, rushed out of a stab wound when a dagger was ripped out or fountained with the slice of a sword. His voice lightened when he said that Garjana had got her name, which meant 'roar' because, as a child, she would roar with delight when she walked in the forest—the darker and thicker it got, the more at home she seemed to be. Garjana the Fearless, that was the name by which she was known in the many worlds, and warriors knew of her, the stories of her valour told and retold. Idaychi, on the other hand, never engaged in battle unless expressly asked to do so, like others of the island tribes whose ability as healers was unrivalled. They were born not only with the knowledge of how to use these plants to heal wounds and restore life, but also of how to wound and take life: their attacks were deadly, quiet and as gentle as a killing could be, a vein sliced through, a nerve snapped, the heart stopped with the gentle pressure of a fingertip.

When Idaychi and Garjana came face-to-face, it was a meeting of opposites, like wind and fire, and this made them all the more deadly for each strike was met by its opposite. Garjana roared and ran, her mace flailed and waved and crashed downward with the force of many elephants. Idaychi almost skipped. So light was her movement, she was silent, and her weapon was still before it was sent on its deadly flight.

At first, the two were striking blindly, since neither knew what to expect, but as they became surer of the other's way of defence and attack, their strikes and counters became quicker and surer. They fought first with maces, then with swords and shields, then with javelins, and finally, almost at the point of exhaustion, by force of rule, as all weapons had been tried without either one being defeated, they clasped each other in the opening grip of a wrestle. One broke free, circled, kicked out, grabbed at the other, who stepped away, hopping out of reach, the other leg poised to kick. One fell, the other fell on top, they rolled with one trying to keep the other pressed down, but the other broke loose and sprung up. And so on and on they went, and those fighting in the vicinity stopped to watch. The musicians gathered around, for it was their duty to beat out the coded tunes to signal a death, and the runners also stood waiting to carry news of the outcome to the two generals, wherever they were fighting.

Akavan's hands trembled in between beats on the tudi. His face had grown sombre and his voice deeper, and Aambal sensed the change in mood and felt her heart clench. Would one of them die? Who would it be? Akavan's dramatic voice told the rest of the tale. 'How might one describe this combat, and the two combatants? A measure of Idaychi's expertise and stamina might be that she had driven Garjana to the point of exhaustion, all her moves tried and easily met by Idaychi's. The same might be said of Garjana. It had taken all of their skill to continue to meet each other attack for attack, weapon for weapon, but as with all combat, an end came to theirs too. It came quickly and with stunning impact, stilling the whole battlefield.'

Unexpectedly, Idaychi stumbled and almost fell as she took a step back to meet Garjana's speeding fist. Idaychi broke her fall by bending at the waist and thrusting one open-palmed hand onto the ground and pushing herself up to her feet quicker than anyone could blink. Akavan's voice slowed and deepened, 'Garjana's fist had continued to move, and the realisation came to both women that Idaychi was carrying another life inside of her, but it was too late for either one to stop. Neither could Garjana halt her impetus, nor could Idaychi alter her movement. Garjana's fist struck Idaychi's chest, which cracked and sent a stream of blood spewing out of her mouth, even as her own fist rammed into Garjana's throat, tearing her gullet through the muscle and tendon that cased it.

As both women's bodies fell towards the red sand of Chendur, birds wheeled overhead, calling madly, and a blue flash streaked towards Idaychi, as she fell, a blue hand cupped over the belly of the human. There was a flash of light and the cry of a baby. When Mari rose, she held in her arms the infant that she had birthed from its dying mother, and over her shoulders was slung the lifeless body of Idaychi, who may have caught a flash of her child before the breath left her. Mari flew towards Veeramahendrapuram.

Akavan's voice choked, his eyes filled with tears and he held his tudi pressed to his chest as if his heart would spill out. Aambal's face was streaked with tears, and into her eyes there came the image of Garjana, with whom she had ridden all the way from Pazhani to Chendur, with whom she had had nothing in common, except their affection for the Lord of Pazhani.

Akavan had finished. He was still, voice, hands, heart, all still. The two of them sat quietly. The sun had climbed into the sky by now, and it seemed to Aambal that it had grown dull as the story unravelled.

Eventually, Akavan left Aambal sitting on the rock. Aambal was troubled. She felt as if the gaps in the story were eddies swirling under her feet, and that she would at any moment slip and be sucked into their rush. She went to Ganesha and stood unspeaking before him, and he understood what she was asking: for the dread to be calmed, for the eddies to still, for her breath to unclench, for the tale to be lulled to rest. He gestured to her to sit down, and his mellow, unwavering voice, so different from Akavan's billowing one, described what followed the deaths of the two women. Aambal's breaths grew longer, her heartbeats slowed and the storm in her head and heart slowed and gathered into a cloud of sadness. When Ganesha came to the end of what he was saying, Aambal felt an impatience—there should be something further, a more fitting end. Ganesha smiled and said, 'The Matris, Jayantha and others gathered around the body of Garjana. They were joined by Murugan, who took off his armour and every sign of his authority and, bare-footed, bare-headed and bare-chested, carried Garjana to the charnel field where pyres were already burning. He laid her down on a pile of akil wood and himself set the body alight. The musicians played their drums and horns, the bards recited the prayers and the pyre flamed on. Murugan did not leave until every bone in Garjana's body had burst with loud pops and sputters. When he returned to his place outside the battlefield, they saw that it was Garjana's sword that he wore belted to his armour. His own lay in the pile of ash that had once been Garjana the Fearless.'

Ganesha placed his hand gently on Aambal's head and said, 'Murugan could see her racing towards her home, to the very waterfall where Fate had gone to make a deal with her. He knew that her people would know she was there through signs that she sent them, or that the oracles would divine out of dreams and visions. She would forever accompany them on fearsome journeys and in battle, and stand guard along with her ancestors at the borders of her land.'

When she slept that night, Garjana and Idaychi came into her dreams, their faces clear, their armour and the flower tokens of their clans clear, their weapons, their horses, all clear. And next to them, she saw the two men who had been the generals on the second day of the battle. She also recalled in the dream, and on waking up the following day, that the battle had lasted six days, and that she had been present on all six days as well as the seventh, but could remember nothing else.

5

KRAUNCHA, THE MOUNTAIN

Idaychi and Garjana were still on Aambal's mind the next morning, and it seemed to her that if she shook the sleep off, if she shook herself, she would wake up to the day she had witnessed their combat in Chendur. She felt as if she were floating, as if she were inside Akavan's words in another world—they said that words were alive and that one had to tend to them so they would not rot inside, especially if you were a poet, a bard, a healer, an oracle. She was a poet, and she had been a bard. Did that mean the words would rot twice as much in her and make her wholly rot too? She could not let that happen, she could not allow the healing of Pothigai to go in vain. Her helplessness made her angry, and when Aambal was angry, language stopped its careless march and waited on her. It was afraid that something she would ask of it in the moment would be lost forever. And that the god on whose tongue and in whose chest it had free passage would bar it out.

Kandhan! His name struck Aambal's chest as if with a giant mace swung by an expert warrior, shattering her rage. She held her head as a familiar pain began in her skull—the merciless battering of images that wanted to be remembered and honoured. Kandhan! It was to do with Kandhan. The space between her ears was ablaze with the funeral pyres of the battlefield, as if Kandhan's

Shaktivel was blazing back and forth, emitting sparks, as it had on the first day of the battle. Aambal stopped short, head and pain and language all forgotten now: she had just seen herself next to Kandhan; he had been taking aim with the vel, and the target was ... what was it? What had Kandhan been doing?

Aambal staggered, the sound of words that she could not make out resounded in her head, calling to her. She half-walked, half-ran to where Kandhan's anna sat looking off into the valley, the Kuru Muni next to him, but she could not speak, nor was she able, yet, to write. She stood there, trembling. Akattiyan stood up and gently eased Aambal onto the flat, warm rock, and sat himself down next to her.

Ganesha said, 'Aambal, I will speak, but I will stop when you begin to remember, for then, you must fill in the rest yourself.' Aambal nodded, and the wise God of All Beginnings paused a moment, as if waiting for the start of his narration to approach and say, 'I am here.' Akattiyan's eyes stayed on Aambal.

'On the first day, Aambal, neither Karthikeya nor Surapadman were on the battlefield for, as you know, the supreme commanders only enter the fight when all the commanders-in-chief have been killed. Tarakan, the second sibling of Surapadman, youngest of the three sons of Surasa and Kashyapa, was the Asura commander-in-chief that day. And their general was the mighty Asura Krauncha. Do you remember Krauncha?' he asked Aambal, more as a device to stir alive the flavour of the tale, which was what poets chased after. He spoke then of Krauncha, who so admired the way that mountains stood unmoving that he had himself assumed the shape of one, going to Patala where the Nagas welcomed him and offered him a place to stand next to the seven mountains that already stood there, looming and unshakeable. Krauncha rarely shed this shape or moved from his position, and his only nourishment was the waters of the seven rivers whose wellsprings were in the seven mountains next to him. In the course of time, the vast stretches where Krauncha and the other mountains stood began to be referred to as Kraunchaparva—Krauncha's Section.

Aambal was trying to recall what they looked like, Tarakan and Krauncha, when Ganesha's voice broke through, 'On the Sura side, Aambal, Matri Dhumi was the commander-in-chief and Veera Rakkaga the general for the day, but Krauncha and Tarakan and their forces wreaked such havoc that the first day of the battle was named 'Tarakan and Krauncha's Day of Glory'. Akattiyan's eyes stayed on Aambal's face—he waited with each word for some sign of recognition to appear on her face, in her eyes, and for her tongue to acknowledge that recognition with words. Ganesha smiled, he looked around at the mighty mountain and at the Kuru Muni whose might was the never-ending might of language. He sighed: language was the greatest seduction, not love, not desire, not the prize of union, for it was language that wore the gestures of love, that voiced desire and luxuriated in union.

Ganesha was lost in thought for a moment, and Aambal, impatient, touched his arm. The god continued the tale, becoming more indulgent in its evocation of the two Asuras, Tarakan and Krauncha, for the flavour of that day could only be held by them.

'Tarakasura was much feared, for his aim did not depend on the two orbs in his head. When he was ready, his sight spread everywhere, as if his eyes had multiplied thousand-fold and were flying over the battlefield. When he shot an arrow from his magical silver quiver, it split into several hundred and, with a single shot, he felled hundreds of the Suras' warriors. Krauncha crushed huge numbers of the enemy by appearing in his two-legged Asura form, then in the blink of an eye transforming into the hulking mountain. There were others among them with magical weapons and stores of magic: gifts of invisibility, shape-changing, transporting, levitating, and both armies had runners who would call someone else if a warrior was faced with an opponent they could not combat. The Sura and Asura, as well as the Gandharvas,

Bhutas and the beings of all worlds other than of Bhu, could leave their bodies at will, or not leave their bodies at all—they were immune to what on Bhu was irreversible, sometimes painful and gory: death. But if quelled by an opponent, they were duty-bound to leave the battlefield, and that was the same as mortal warriors dying, for what mattered were those present and fighting on the field.'

Ganesha paused, for his mind had gone to the end of the day, and he sighed. 'Unimaginably large numbers of the Sura warriors fell to the attacks of Tarakan and Krauncha that day. They were deadly when they fought separately, and when they came together, they became lethal: Krauncha lumbered forwards and sideways, crushing warriors under his weight, and Tarakan was like a wild wind that stormed through the enemy side, knocking them over. Krauncha shrunk and disappeared into the sea, making it froth and boil over, its steam scorching the Suras, but leaving the Asuras untouched; Tarakan shot an arrow into the sky and it streaked upwards, then curved and descended, emitting thick fumes of poison that made the Sura forces swoon. And to all this, there were two witnesses: the immobile, silent, red sea-rock hillock and Goddess Mari.' Ganesha's voice trailed off, as if he had only now remembered that Goddess Mari was his mother, as if that memory of the wild, blue-bodied goddess had swallowed up the story. Akattiyan called out 'oy', as if addressing a squirrel that had scampered past, and Ganesha smiled, his eyes sprung open and he continued his tale.

'The two Asuras cut through the Sura forces like a seasoned cutlass slices through stalks of sugarcane; the snake's movements grew swift or slowed in response to the attacks. When enemy assaults created breaks in the formation, they were quickly filled by warriors moving into the empty places, as if the wounded parts of the snake were regenerating. Veerabahu and his eight brothers—the nine, the Navaveera—left their places and, hidden by their own magic, moved towards Krauncha. When these nine were together, they became as one being, their might multiplied nine-fold. As they moved steadily across the formation, getting closer and closer to vulnerable parts of the mongoose, the Bhutas of Kailasa cast their magic lassos over the Asura troops, making them dazed, insensate. The snake body followed the rhythm of the Navaveera's movement, making minute twists and curls to disguise their passage, even as the enemy seemed oblivious.

'The nine brothers' spirits rose, thinking of how they would soon reach Tarakasura and take him captive. They imagined that he may choose to leave his body to return to the formless Vast or simply exit the battlefield. Once he was gone, Krauncha would be less potent. The brothers smiled at each other, their breathing lightened, their hearts soared. They were taken completely by surprise when, with a mocking, barely audible pop, Krauncha loomed over them, and with a swiftness that did not allow them to react, the mountain's craggy surface cracked and widened into an enormous jaw that opened, snapped up the nine men and clamped shut with a terrifying, grinding sound.

'Even Garjana the Fearless trembled, it was said afterwards, as the nine warriors who, a moment ago, had seemed invincible, disappeared into the mountain belly. The snake writhed in alarm, units broke away, soldiers ran helter-skelter, loud cries went up, the news, carried from mouth to mouth through the beats of the musicians' little drums, reached the ears of all of the Sura army. Garjana and her group fell back; it was better to stay alive and wait. She and her troop moved slowly, carefully; her companions sensed that Garjana had a plan, and she did. The disappearance of the Nine had made her doubt that she or even the Matris could stand and fight against the deadly combination of Tarakan and Krauncha. She rode towards Matri Dhumi, who gathered from the look on Garjana's face what she wanted to say, and a sign that the latter made confirmed this: the younger woman fisted both hands and held them up, tapping one against the other. Matri Dhumi nodded and gestured "go". Garjana rode off.'

Ganesha was not surprised to see that Aambal's eyes had rolled back. Her hands were still, her chest heaved, her face settled into a frozen calm.

She was in a trance, and now there was no need for Ganesha to speak, for she would herself witness it all. Indeed, unknowing, insensate, Aambal was back in that moment, on Chendur's red sands, at the juncture when she did not know exactly what was happening, but she knew that the Asura army was killing not just the warriors of the Sura, but also their morale. She knew that something momentous had happened, and by the sound of the little hunting horn made of the wood of a tree not found in the south, Aambal knew that Garjana was headed her way. Soon, her horse rode up. She looked at Aambal, into whose ears by now had come news of the internment of the Nine. Garjana touched her arm, and Aambal understood what was being asked of her—to 'see' what was to be done now with her war-bard's sight, the sight of Time, to look through what seemed imminent to what was possible.

Aambal shut her eyes and held her cymbals against her thrumming heart. The cold of the bell metal quelled the furore in her chest, the sounds around her ceased and the brightness behind her eyeballs dissolved into darkness. She waited, and from inside that black, a ray of light burst out with a hum. The sound swelled and filled her chest and rushed into her throat, crying 'Viravel, Vetrivel', for what was speeding towards her was the leaf-like shape of Mahasena Karthikaya's weapon, the mighty Shaktivel. The cymbals in her hands began to tremble, and she struck them, one against the other. The sound leapt, dashing away into the rows of Sura warriors. Combat ceased, movement halted, and in the silence, everybody, including the bard on the other side of the battle, stood listening for the words that would follow. Aambal's mouth opened and a voice that was not hers alone recited, 'What is here? What is there? What looms? What shatters? Inside the rock, fire seething, inside the vel fire churning. One fire to douse another, for only then the Nine will be as before.'

Her voice sped through the air and into Murugan's ears, urging him onto the battlefield, and even before the resonance of the words had died down, his chariot had sped towards Garjana. In his hand was the Shaktivel given to him by his mother. The two black stallions, Kalam and Neram, gifts from his aunt and uncle, their jet-black flanks rippling, nostrils flaring, their breathing rapid, whinnied, neighed and reared up, their brass-clad hooves catching the light and sparkling. Aambal saw Murugan turn his face towards the sky and shut his eyes, and knew that he was calling on his six Krittika mothers to bless him, to steady him, to remind him that he must invoke his full attention so that he could rip away the magic that hid Krauncha.

In the charioteer's seat was none other than Galabajja, he of the crystal hands, on the clear surface of whose mind would be reflected the thoughts of whoever he was aiding. Garjana rode alongside Murugan's chariot, to watch, to guide his strikes if needed, to be an added pair of eyes, and if necessary, to come between him and a weapon directed at him that could not be deflected. Aambal's chariot moved alongside that of the man who was her master at poetry, her friend for life and, here, the warrior she was sworn to guard. To the crash of her cymbals, Aambal cried aloud, 'Vetrivel, Viravel; Viravel, Vetrivel.' She began a litany of the might of Mahasena, her voice and her cymbals louder and clearer than humanly possible. The syllables of each word shoved aside the clamour of the battlefield and surged into his headgear and armour and filled his head and chest. They reached the mighty Asura Krauncha the Mountain, looming up to the skies.

Murugan stopped, as did Krauncha. The Asura's eyes blazed, flames shot out of them, sputtering, then flaring and speeding, falling on Murugan, raising cries of alarm that grew silent when the flares dissolved into the fire-glow of his armour. Murugan looked at the mountainous Asura, long and still, and Aambal wondered if he was thinking of Krauncha meditating in Patala's deeps for so long that the place was no longer what it was before he arrived. When her master's head bent in a gesture of respect, she knew she had been right. Murugan did not seem to want to attack; he would wait till Krauncha made the first move, and that would determine his own choice of weapon.

Krauncha stretched and shook himself and a landslide of giant boulders toppled off his sides, tumbling madly towards Murugan, like a river in full spate speeding downhill. Murugan snatched up his shield, its brass and copper turned to white under the sun's glare, and swung it an arc, sending the shattering boulders flying, careening into the air, plunging into the sea. Krauncha shrugged and shook, again and again, and boulders and shards of sharp rock came shooting out of him only to be repelled by the ready shield. Then, suddenly, he was gone, Krauncha the Mountain, and with him went all the rocky debris that he'd shed.

Murugan closed his eyes and waited. Aambal's cymbals crashed against each other and from her throat issued instructions, 'Eye lids close, into the eye's dark, comes the light, follow the six spots.' As if following the trail of that light, as if they had come together and formed an arrow, Murugan opened his eyes and looked out to sea: in the waters was a spot as still as a mountain. He did not have to direct Galabajja to the sea; Kalam and Nera were already rushing into the seething waves. Aambal's chariot followed, as it must. From above, twelve eyes watched the speeding chariots. The horses were all brought up short as Krauncha shot out of the waters, the waves mantling his brown rock-body in blue-white finery. Murugan shot arrow after arrow at him, but they hit the rocky sides and bent, broke, shattered or bounced back. Krauncha was shaking now, he quivered and trembled but no boulders tumbled off him, nor did fire erupt from his eyes. He was laughing, the mirth uncontrollable. Aambal heard Galabajja roar angrily. 'Kumara,' he shouted, 'Kumara, have you forgotten your lessons? Did Veerabahu teach you nothing in his training?'

Disembodied by the trance, Aamabl was now able to see, hear and sense everything that happened on Chendur's battlefied, and what she had not known then became clear to her. She not only saw the dazed look on Murugan's face, but now also knew what he was feeling and thinking. Galabajja was shouting, but Murugan heard him as if from a distance. His head was filling with a music that seemed to have been made to please him; it had the step and fall of the songs that his father had hummed to him in his childhood days on Kailasa, tapping on the udukku. His father, why had he refused to be present here at the battle? Did he think his son would lose? Why had Paravani refused to come? Did he think Murugan was not able enough? No one believed in him, did they? Did his parents? His brother? Was there no one who believed that he could do it? A crash pierced his ears, he felt as if two dark, muscled fingers had reached through his armour, and taking the flesh of his arm, pinched it sharply. His thoughts rushed together, as if they had been in a clogged canal now raked free of collected debris, and they flowed away. He heard Aambal's voice, Vetrivel, Shaktivel; Vetrivel, Viravel.

She saw Murugan close his eyes—he could see six flares of light that hovered, as if waiting for his head to clear. Aambal's voice and the cymbal beats resounded. The flares soared down towards Murugan as her voice, and the beat became louder, more urgent, and her voice recited, 'The fire that comes lights the path. The Vel of Light, Vetri, Vetri, strike now and strike quick.' Murugan's head filled with light, the white light that shines off the ice-covered rocks of Kailasa. Then the light shook itself and spread its wings into the gold and green and emerald of Paravani's wings. He heard Aambal's voice hailing him as Vetri, Victory. He had to be victorious to be

Vetri. He was Vetri, he would be victorious. Murugan reached for his vel. Arm raised, he paused, looked Krauncha in the eyes, and calling out 'Hail Krauncha', he flung the vel. It sped through the air with a hum that shook the battlefield, and made Mari, with her garlands of skulls and her dry breasts and spike-sharp hair, spin around in the air, her sickle above her head. Krauncha paused and shut his eyes to chant the words with which he would call up the magic for the moment. Aambal knew that he would not speak, for a magic as mighty as his own was stopping his tongue.

Akattiyan held Aambal's trance-bound body that now shivered uncontrollably, her head and hands mimicked the striking of cymbals, as she had struck them on the battlefield, calling out words that had shot into the Asura's chest, quelling his speech. As Murugan's vel flew towards his heart, Krauncha called out, 'Victory to Surapadman, king of Veeramahendrapuram.' The vel struck, and Krauncha's mountain-body exploded. The rocky debris disintegrated and turned to dust, then began to glow and gathered into an arch of light that stilled, stretching across the sky. As Aambal remembered, Akattiyan held her gently the whole while, not stopping her body from shaking itself back into time.

It took a long time for Aambal to wake from the stupor, and when she did, she recalled everything she had just witnessed. It did not occur to her yet that these viewings were all stopping short of their endings, and that she had to turn to Ganesha each time to fill her in, or that he seemed to draw such joy in recounting the many events of the battlefield.

He took up the tale from the point at which Aambal's vision had ended: 'Mari spun in the air, screeching and wailing, lamenting the death of that brave warrior. When she stilled, she turned towards Murugan and raised her sickle above her head, saluting the winner. The chariots carrying the Supreme Commander and his war bard rode back onto the beach, followed by Garjana the Fearless. Surapadman and Tarakan rode up to where Murugan's chariot stood, and all three descended to stand on the sand, bare-footed, their heads bent, their weapons resting in their chariots. You, Aambal, accompanied by Thennan, sang the song of life merging into the elements. Then the battle resumed; both Surapadman and Murugan rode off the battlefield. And that is enough for now. Tomorrow, there will come from Annamalai the bard Sevvi, and she will narrate to you the rest of Tarakan's story.'

6

TARAKAN

When Sevvi arrived later than she was meant to, panting and sweating, her white hair sticking to her scalp and neck, Aambal was waiting for her at the foot of the mountain, and though she could not speak, the older woman understood how impatient she was. She too had been on the battlefield and had seen what had happened to the young poet-bard. She held Aambal's hands and spoke as Akavan did, 'May the alphabets bless your fingers; may your tongue never lose its way; may your way be safe in Tamizh.' They ascended the mountain after Sevvi had rested a while in the shade, drunk the palm toddy and eaten the roasted tubers that the Kani folk had sent for her with Aambal. Seeing the state Aambal was in, Sevvi took out her tudi and accompanied by its delicate beats, even as they climbed, began to narrate the events of Tarakan's day on the battlefield following Krauncha's death.

'From the moment that Mahasena Karthikeya's vel struck Krauncha, Tarakan seemed to become even stronger. It was as if the mountainous Asura's strength had fallen into Tarakan's body, like a good magic spell enters a body to become body and enters a mind to become mind,' she began. His fury was like the combined eruption of a hundred Krauncha mountains, streaking through the battlefield, slashing, beheading, striking dead those who tried to stop him. He charged through the most complicated defence formations of the Sura army, wreaking more havoc than even the poets could have imagined. Runners picked their way through the fighters, through the sidewinding and the darting of the snake and mongoose, transporting word from one to another unit, from one general to another and then to the commanders-in chief.

Matri Dhumi, the commander-in-chief of the Sura army, no stranger to either combat or death, struggled, like a crane on dry mud struggles to find balance, to keep the morale up. She sent word to the wisest of her sisters, Matri Kalarava, as always craving her counsel in a tight spot. They held a conversation and arrived at a solution. Matri Kalarava nodded to her sister and moved in the direction from which Tarakan's roars rushed out into the darkening sky. She was a glorious sight: taller than anyone else on the battlefield, larger than most too, her head was hairless, her body rolled with the folds of flesh that fit her frame like an armour, her arms were round and soft, her thighs jiggled with the littlest movement. Her breasts were enormous and fleshly, rolling and bouncing, her neck was thick. She wore no armour over the fine loose robe that stopped mid-thigh, she wore no footwear and she used one weapon only—her sword—and never needed a shield. Each hand, with its deceptively delicate-looking flesh, was shield enough. She was on foot, for there was no horse nor elephant nor chariot that could hold her, nor did she want to ride on or in one. She wanted her body to have all the space it desired, wherever she was.

As she approached Tarakan, she blew on the little kompu dangling from her neck by a cord, a brass miniature straight-limbed version of the large curved temple horn. When he turned, Matri Kalarava saluted Tarakan with her surprisingly slender sword hefted above her head, a salute which the Asura returned with a delighted laugh. His delight swelled when she indicated that she was calling him to duel. To stand against any one of the

Matris was itself an honour; to fight Matri Kalarava was a prize for any warrior who desired a truly exceptional fight. The Matri was famed not only for her unpredictable moves, but also for the sheer joy with which she combated. And indeed, as they began duelling, Tarakan felt the heavy dread that the death of Krauncha had brought falling away from him. You might wonder why Matri Kalarava was so special among exceptional warriors, each one better than the other. She appeared to never reflect on or react to an opponent's moves in the way usual to fighters—a strike with a defence, a moving back with a moving forward. Not Matri Kalarava: her moves, her counters and strikes seemed to be set to some secret pattern, unaffected by the opponent's moves.

The Asura and the Matri engaged in a long, slow battle, and to those who stood watching, it appeared like a dance—not a step out of beat, and nothing disturbed the arcs, curves and loops of their weapons. They neither roared nor shouted or grunted, and the silence flowed like music along with the graceful dance of their combat. As the fight progressed, their moves became more complex, slower, more nuanced—a test as much of rhythm, movement and agility as it was of expertise at the sword. Tarakan's eye and hand were as one; the hand did not follow the eye, sight and strike now moved together. The sight that allowed him to see as wide as a thousand eyes was now concentrated in one spot, and sometimes it seemed as if Matri Kalarava's body barely managed to move out of the way of Tarakan's sword. For the first time since the day began, he was panting a little, straining to keep in step with the heavy warrior whose steps were feather-light and as unpredictable as a leaf in a strong wind.

Warriors stood around them, hundreds of them, their faces and bodies animated, clapping, calling out their appreciation, as if enjoying a performance. The duel went on and on. Then, suddenly, Matri Kalarava emitted a loud roar and leapt into the air. As she descended, she spoke the name of her opponent, 'Taraka,' she called, 'Taraka.' He smiled and stepped out of her path; his body relaxed, as if something that had bound it into tautness was now loosened, his expression changed from alertness to stillness, and the stillness fell over all those who stood watching; they did not know what was occurring, but the feeling that something was about to happen filled the hearts of all. Here, Sevvi paused.

She stopped climbing and sat down on a rock in the shade of an old tree, panting with the climb and the exertion of the tale, though Aambal had taken her bundle and water bag before they began the ascent. Sevvi wiped her face, closed her eyes and drew long breaths, then took a few sips of water and resumed the narration.

'The sun was nearing the west; the skies had begun to purple. The waves were roaring in expectation of the moon's rising. The hum that surrounded Veeramahendrapuram was so loud that it reached Chendur. Matri Kalarava now spoke, "Brave Taraka, you whose might honours me with this fight, I bow to you, to your expertise, but the time is come to end this." Tarakan raised his sword and answered her without speaking, bowing his head. To those who stood there, it was apparent that something had changed for Tarakan; he looked as if he knew something no one else did. She took several running steps back, and then, charging forward, leapt into the air, her body rippling, its flesh-folds rising, undulating and settling one over the other. Her sword swung, its hiss as loud as a hundred snakes sounding the alarm. Tarakan, who should have stepped out of the way of the sword, instead charged into its path, and a collective gasp and many loud cries of protest went up from the warriors. A wide smile spread across Tarakan's face, which shone with the purpling gold of the setting sun. Matri Kalarava's sword struck his neck, slicing through. His head shot into the air, accompanied by the deafening cries of the watchers. The head curved into the ruddy sky and his body crashed to the ground. A fine drizzle fell from the clouds, sea birds shrieked, scores of vultures rose into the air, calling raucously as the waves seethed and broke against the red shores. On Veeramahendrapuram, the bells for the evening prayers rang loud and clear.

'As Tarakan's head began its descent, Mari leapt high into the air, and she gathered the beautiful head, with its still-smiling face and its curly hair, and gestured. Tarakan's body rose up and joined its head. She rose and flew over the leaping waves, their crash ululating, in the direction of Veeramahendrapuram.'

Aambal felt as if Matri Kalarava's sword had lopped off her writing hand. She was sobbing loudly, her hands were clenched and her eyes were fixed on the sky, as if Tarakan's head had appeared there. Sevvi did not comfort her, for she knew that Aambal had to plunge again and again into that place that was neither here nor there, neither now nor then, the only place that could manifest and return what she had lost. Aambal was unaware of Sevvi's eyes watching her and of the expressions that passed over her face, but she sensed that the older woman was holding back from sympathising and she was glad when the narration resumed.

'Surapadman transported to Veeramahendrapuram in a blink of his beautiful eyes, now darkening with sorrow, and he was there to receive the body of his brother as Mari descended. Tarakan had chosen the means of his return to the Vast: at the hands of one of the deadliest of the twelve mighty Matris. He had not specified which, wanting to be surprised, and he had indeed received the one he himself would have chosen—the gregarious Matri Kalarava. Before the battle, Tarakan had asked a boon from the Goddess of the Battlefield, "I wish my end in the battle to be at the hands of one of the Matris, and I want a promise that my head will not touch the ground till my brother lays me down on Veeramahendrapuram for the final return." Mari not only promised Tarakan that it would be as he asked but also promised that she would be between the heads of his siblings and their offspring and the battlefield of Chendur, that if their heads must rest on mud, it would be the mud of Veeramahendrapuram.

'Mari handed over the body of Tarakan into the arms of Suran, who received it in silence. He laid his brother down on the mud of his home, each grain of which trembled. Tarakan's wife, the beautiful Manava woman Nila, knelt down and pressed her face to the still cave of her husband's heart. Her body shook as she sobbed; the waves joined her weeping. Then she sat up, wiped her tears and, with both hands, took off the tadangkai, the battle anklet, from her spouse's lifeless ankle and tugged it over her left foot, pulled it up to her shin, pressing it to fit tight. She would go into the battle the next day, and thus was forbidden to speak the words of prayer that would send Tarakan onwards. She gestured to Suran, who picked up his brother's body, and addressed the waters around his beloved island home with the ancient words to start this last journey. He stepped into the sea and stood a moment with Tarakan's body pressed to his heart, then he laid it down on the white-rimmed waves that came rushing to hold aloft the body of one whose glory would never fade. They carried him away, till he disappeared to join the ripples of another sea-like place: the Vast.'

Aambal sat looking unseeingly into the distance, sobbing. Sevvi sat unspeaking and still. After some time, they resumed their climb and arrived at the top of kindly Pothigai. Ganesha welcomed Sevvi, patting her on the back and smiling. He said, 'Aambal, come, and I will tell you what happened after that,' and when all of them had settled down, he began, 'There were severe losses on both sides. From among the Sura, the younger of the three mighty daughters of Yama, the Keeper of Time, had been struck down by Tarakasura, as had five of the brothers of the band of twelve Gandharvas, known as the Dancers. They left the battlefield. They could not die as humans did, but they would now turn their faces away from Fate and let Time carry on without them until something inside them changed and they once again became time-worthy. Of the manava, several thousand died, their bodies bleeding and torn, their bones broken, their limbs ripped away. The charnel ground was filled with flaming pyres, and the air filled with the stench of burning human and animal flesh. The evening wind echoed with the sound of popping bones and the cries of the vultures who circled over the cooking bodies.'

Aambal, Sevvi and Akattiyan were quiet. Ganesha said, 'Aambal, the bards who witnessed the Great Battle of Chendur have begun to compose their hero songs about the warriors that took their fancy. You have heard two of them, and in a few days, a group of twelve bards will come to Pothigai, accompanied by musicians. Their songs will bridge you into the last day of the battle. They will be the brace to support the fabric of your trance. But tomorrow, I will describe to you each day of the battle, the formations, the commanders-in-chief, the generals, the deaths, woundings and other significant details.'

Aambal felt strange: as if she was standing close to something that belonged to her, and which, like the mist on the mountain, seemed to be still, as if waiting for her to reach forward and grab it, but floated away even as her hands began to stir. She felt as if parts of her were coming towards her from the mist at the same time that other parts were coming loose from her and drifting away.

THE KNOTS IN AAMBAL'S MEMORY

The following morning, Ganesha kept his word. As he spoke of the events of the six days, Aambal's memory began to thicken, like the knobs that come before shoots, gathering sap and strength to thrust out towards the light.

Ganesha walked to a flat clearing, cut a stout stick, shaved off the wood to a pointed end and drew two boxes. In one he wrote 'Asura' and in the other, 'Sura'. He drew columns and rows and labelled them: formation, commander-in-chief, general, the number of animals, horses and elephants killed and wounded, the number of warriors wounded or dead and those who left the battlefield or went away to continue a fight on the following days, the numbers of wounded or killed runners, physicians, musicians and bards, the number of chariots crushed and weapons shattered, and lastly, those, if any, killed by Mari, had they done something that warranted divine punishment.

On the first day, the formations of the Asura and Sura sides were the mongoose and snake, the commanders-in-chief were Tarakan and Matri Dhumi, the generals were Krauncha and Veera Rakkaga. Ganesha enumerated the numbers. As Aambal listened, her head began to hurt, so many animals wounded, so many dead, so many warriors, of them so many manava, wounded and dead. She did not care about weapons and chariots. She was curious to know if Mari killed anyone and, if she did, why. Her mind turned deaf to the count, but stayed alert to the other details.

On the second day, the formations were wolf and bear, the commanders-in-chief were Idaychi and Garjana, the generals Banukopan and Jayantha. Many animals perished on this day as well, and Aambal tried to keep her mind from dwelling on that—vague images of an elephant in death throes assailed her, but she shut her eyes and shook it out of her head. Ganesha went on with the count of woundings and deaths, and Aambal stubbornly stayed unreceptive to these numbers.

Day three was shield and spear, the commanders-in-chief were Iraivi, the daughter of Indrajith, king of Ilangkai, and Iyanan, the hunter from Annamalai. The generals were Yazhini, sister to Idaychi, and Thisan, the potter from Keezhadi. It was on this day that Mari killed a warrior, the only one she killed: it was the woman named Izhayini. In a fit of anger, she had cut down one of the runners who stumbled in her haste to fetch a physician for a wounded elephant, causing Izhayini to lose her aim.

Aambal did not recall the event.

Ganesha moved on to the fourth day, and it was much the same, large numbers of two-legged beings wounded and killed, smaller numbers of animals likewise. But on this day, someone left the battlefield, and that was a curious tale. It was the Gandharva who fell in love at first sight with the manava woman Mathai, and to her disgust and fury, refused to fight her. He left the battlefield to the disapproval of his unit, and waited beyond it, following Mathai with his eyes. He said to her that he would wait for her till the battle ended, and when she snapped at him that she might die, for she was no coward who would stay away from deadly combat, he said that his love would be an amulet that would steer fate's javelin away from her life.

On the fifth day, the formation was cloud and eagle, the commanders-in-chief were Singamugan and Matri Dhirghajihva …

Aambal's head was spinning, no longer making sense of Ganesha's voice. This was not like the accounts of the bards, who built their narratives with the finesse of embroidery around the achievements of heroes, all of them noble women and men whose feats already possessed the grandeur that the bards drew out and spelt out. The story of the armies attacking each other in large numbers of their many formations was devoid of grandeur. Its heroism was bloody, because hundreds and thousands of warriors moved as one, in large blocks determined to kill, maim and defeat the foe, folks who, on other days, could have been friends, acquaintances, lovers. The gore and terror were so large that they spilt out of the narration and pervaded the air.

The bards had sung only of those warriors who took their fancy. What of the stories that the bards would not compose, maybe not now and maybe never? Aambal wanted to know the story of every one of the warriors who had been on Chendur's battlefield, but she knew that that was beyond the bards to compose and beyond anyone to hear out. Besides, Garjana the Fearless and Idaychi— who would not want to sing of them?

Aambal's thoughts were like indigo in a vat, bubbling and gathering, but not yet ink. As the fire burnt down, the boil slowed and stopped, her chest's heave settled as well, and her mind turned to the variety of stories and how and who made and sang them. She recalled the travelling gypsies' stories of daily events, a little squabble between a woman's two spouses, a childbirth, the moon, a first love bite, a rabbit. And the hunters' love songs, full of detail about wooing and mating and sly, humorous digs at 'noble' forms of love. Then there were the stories that the priests made up about the gods they worshipped, and stories that women, in confinement after a childbirth, made up. Stories were endless, as were storytellers and the subjects of their stories.

She wondered what Kandhan had felt on the evening of the fifth day, the day before he would fight, and Ganesh's voice answered: 'Murugan was restless. The days had passed rapidly, with losses and deaths on both sides. He had hoped that, as the battle proceeded, he might get some insights into the secret—the secret of himself, secret even to him until he found it. Over the five days, sometimes, among the many sounds that the wind gathered up and dispersed, he heard his own name, its syllables sounding one after another, ma-ha-se-na. And he did what he had done a thousand times before. He tried permutations of the four sounds ha-ma-na-se ma-na-ha-se na-ma-ha-se se-ma-ha-na and so on and on.

'He missed Paravani. This was the first time that the wise, kind bird was not beside him. When the battle deliberations were to happen at the foothills of Pazhani, Paravani had refused to fly him down to the town. He had said, "I will not come with you now, nor for the battle." And he had not budged. Murugan had tried everything, persuasion, threats; he had even tried to make him feel guilty, but nothing worked.

'Finally, resigned, Murugan had asked him why he was being so stubborn: "You said to me when we went on our first ride together that you would do whatever I asked you to. And until now, you have never refused. Why now, at the most important part of my life?"

'Paravani's reply had been firm though not clear. "I cannot be your vehicle, for this game of guessing requires that you ride the twin horses that have been waiting for you, Kalam and Neram, to face the valiant King Surapadman on his horses, Svasti and Kshema."

'Nothing Murugan had said succeeded in making Paravani say anything more, or change his mind, but as he walked away, his shoulders sagging, Paravani had called out to him, "You will see."'

⊙⊱⊙

Aambal could see clearly what was being recounted, but her own memory, the details of what she had seen, heard and felt in Chendur seemed ephemeral, out of reach. As was language; she could hear it and comprehend it, but if she so much as tried to shape a word herself, the very syllables evaporated. If she tried to force memory to stand still and gather, it hurt so much. It seemed to Aambal that her head was preventing the thoughts and images from crystallising, afraid of what they might bring. Sometimes, the pain became a sliver as sharp as the tip of a duelling sword, and it slashed away her seeing and hearing and scooped out her bones and flesh and blood. Then, into the empty bag of her, at times there rushed the image of the one that had done this to her. These snatches were never the same and never showed her the end of the encounter.

But one day, as she sat in the sun, her head covered with a paste of the medicine leaf that the Kani called agachha, a swarm of birds flew overhead, the sound of their calls dropping from the high sky into the unwary poet's ears and bursting into that image: the familiar being, the fearsome double-bodied one, with scorpions and leeches in their hands. Their eyes were blank, they were still and beautiful, and there was someone seated, so beautiful, it seemed nothing could be more beautiful—a beautiful little boy, his ebony face serious, riotous curls tumbling down his shoulders and chest, in his hand a staff of akil, its fragrance hanging heavy in the air. Unexpectedly, he started laughing and began to tap the dandam, not on the ground, but in the air and the air was solid, like ground, and the taps resounded, the sound became solid waves that hung above their heads, moving to and fro in the same place. Aambal felt as if she was floating, dipping and rising on the crest of a gentle tide. Four eyes, from two heads, watched, their faces serene. Kandhan was looking straight at her, his lips opened as if he was about to say something to her, and a voice came out, shrill words she had heard before, *do not slip and do not let the slip fall on him*. Aambal's head throbbed so hard, she was swaying with the force of it. She clapped her palms sharply against her temples. The images dissolved into the evening sky.

Later, Aambal sat still, her eyes shut, trying to summon the image back, to somehow coax herself back into the seeing, but to no avail. Aambal was desperate, unable to even speak, let alone compose. Her body was racked and battered with blinding pain because, for so long, language had run through her, delighting in the rooms of her head, in the vast fields of her heart, waiting every day for her to work, that now head and heart were rebellious, as desperate as her.

The Kani worried for her, and were happy when they went down the mountain to bring up the band of twelve bards, including Akavan and Sevvi, who would hold up the trance into which Aambal would enter to see the last day of the battle—the day she had been robbed of language. Neither Sevvi nor Akavan would be enough. So now they were twelve bards, and as many accompanying musicians.

8

BANUKOPAN

First, two of the bards, Chekinda of Ilangkai and Natramanar of Madurai, each would recount a story of two Asura commanders-in-chief, Banukopan and Singamugan, who fought on the second and fifth days of the battle. After that, the entire band of twelve, along with accompanying musicians, would start their narration of the sixth day.

Chekinda started with, 'On the second day, when the troops were arrayed and the commanders-in-chiefs and the generals rode out, the sky grew dark and stayed dark because the sun had retreated behind the ramparts of clouds.'

On this day, the Asura general was Banukopan—He Who Had Become Enraged at the Sun—Surapadman's eldest son who, when he was but a baby in his cradle, had snatched the sun from the sky and tied the flaming orb to his cradle. 'And I will tell you why,' Chekinda said. They say that this event occurred on the day that Banukopan's mother, Padmakomalai, gave birth to him. She went for her bath and his nurses put the baby in his cradle and positioned it so the sun's fiery rays would filter through a creeper-covered trellis and fall gently on the child. The sun—who knows what got into him—decided to play a prank and moved ahead in the sky so that his rays fell untempered onto the sleeping child. The startled women quickly moved the cradle, only to find that the sun's rays followed them. Banukopan, who had just quietened down after he was taken from his mother's breast and laid in the cradle, woke up and began to cry. The women moved the cradle again, and the sun moved with them. The child was by now bawling so loudly that Padmakomalai called out in alarm from her bath. One of the women picked up the child, and cradled him against her. But the sun wasn't done yet. He slid right into the room and mimicked every move the nurse made. She went to the right, he followed, she went left, he was there, she sat down, his rays bent, she hid behind a curtain, he shone through it. The infant abruptly stopped crying, opened his mouth and emitted a roar so thunderous that the sun shot right back into the skies. The child shot after him, the women calling out in alarm. The dark arc of his flight ended where the sun stood quivering. Before anyone could do anything, and before Padmakomalai returned from her bath, the baby was back in his crib, laughing and kicking his heels. At his feet, knotted to the cradle, was the sun. It was one of the nurses who gave him the name 'Banukopan', and that name stuck.

When he heard of the death of his aunt Idaychi, at the hands of Garjana, a transformation came over Banukopan. His head was filled with the images of his uncle Singamugan and their children, and with the face of Idaychi's other spouse, the gentle healer Nanjil. His chest felt as if a raging poison had splashed there, its deadly fumes burning everything. Nanjil could save him, he could make an antidote, but Nanjil would remember nothing when he heard that his beloved Idaychi had died. Who was to tell him?

Banukopan had been in single combat with Jayantha, the Sura's general for the day, son of Indra and brother of Theivanai, when news of the killing was brought to him by a runner. Rage coursed through his body, he turned and charged like a maddened bull, knocking Jayantha off his feet; the latter barely had time to shove his shield upwards to fend off the sword descending on him. As he rolled out of the way, Banukopan turned away from him with a loud scornful laugh.

He took from his belt a small length of coiled and knotted rope. With a flick of his arm, it uncoiled, came alive like a flying snake, hissed and sparked and snaked through the air. Enemy troops in its path fell down in a swoon, for this was a mayapasam, a rope of delusion, though it left untouched the Nine, the Matris, the Gandharvas and the Bhutas. Jayantha's warriors were dropping mid-fight as the magic cord sped past them. Banukopan had to be stopped. Once he was defeated, his weapon, magic or not, would become powerless.

Jayantha sent for Veerabahu, who sped towards them and saw that Banukopan had erupted in flames, burning anyone who came within its range. So great was his fury that his body had turned into a blazing sun. Banukopan saw Veerabahu approaching—chariot flying through the air, magic horses neighing with an unearthly sound, face set and eyes fiery. He charged forward to meet Veerabahu head-on. There was nothing playful or boyish about their combat. There was no laughing from Banukopan this time. The air trembled with the sounds they made as they struck, moved back, moved sideways, paused and gathered aim again, and the sparks from their weapons swirled around them like haloes. It was Veerabahu who roared and shouted, not only with the exertion of defending himself from Banukopan's unrelenting attack, but also in admiration of the lethal accuracy of the Asura prince's strikes and parries. If anyone tired, it was Veerabahu.

As they fought, the images of Idaychi, Singamugan and Nanjil flowed through Banukopan's mind, dampening the flaming rage that had been driving him on. He felt like a child that had wandered away and lost sight of a guardian. An endless stream of tears ran from his eyes, and where he had once been sun-fiery, he was now like a cloud, his tears a deluge that confused all those who were watching. Veerabahu, who should have been jubilant that his foe was tiring, was filled with sadness. He did not temper his strikes though. Banukopan's parries were no less effective, but he wished that he could summon back his fury. A part of him knew that he ought not to be feeling like this, but so heavy was the burden of his aunt's separation from her two lovers that Banukopan wished he could cut out his heart to stop this sadness.

He looked at Veerabahu, ran backwards till there was a good ten feet between them, then bounded forward with a mighty roar. Raising his sword, he leapt into the air, ready to slash. Veerabahu stepped aside and, in the matter of a matra, snatched the dagger from its scabbard at his waist and flung it upward. It sped through the air and met the muscled chest of Banukopan, ripping it open, piercing the mighty heart, now filled with more sorrow than it could bear, and stopped its beating.

Mari materialised before the body could fall, and sat down on the sand with the young Asura's body on her lap, wailing loudly. She blew sharp, shrill notes from her hunter's horn. Surapadman's chariot, followed by Murugan's, arrived there from the edge of the battlefield. Another one descended onto Chendur's red beach from the sky, bearing Padmakomalai, who had refused to fight saying, 'I who make homes for people will not take a life.' Surapadman knelt down and took the body of his eldest child in his arms, weeping, and kissed him on the forehead. He spoke softly to him, and sat a moment clasping the body, from which the warmth had not yet left, to his own burning chest. Padmakomalai did not weep as she lifted her son's body in her arms. Saluting Mari, she walked towards the sea whose waves, as if dredged by an undertow of sorrow, were pulling away from the shores of Chendur. She spoke to the boy she had given birth to in words that none could hear, for nobody approached her. She stood for a time, the man-body of her baby held to her chest. Then she dropped him into the sea, calling on the salt to bless him. The sea rushed in, the body rose up on a bed of waves, melted and disappeared. Mari blew on her horn repeatedly as Surapadman and Padmakomalai rose into the sky in their chariot towards Veeramahendrapuram, where another body waited, a mortal body that had to be cremated. Veerabahu walked back towards his tent, deep in thought, his head hanging.

'A pall fell on the battlefield, for Banukopan had been like the light of the early morning sun—warm, stirring laughter and speech, quick-witted and without rancour, and much beloved of the warriors who felt he was their comrade, whether they were on the same side as he or not,' said Chekinda, his voice falling into the still pool of silence that surrounded them as he drew to the close of his narration. Even Pothigai's winds had fallen silent. Aambal looked at neither him nor anyone else, but at something in the far distance.

The narration continued, after a break, with Madurai Natramanar.

'The battle saw remarkable feats of courage and weaponry; some of the deaths and defeats were heart-wrenching, others went unnoticed. There were losses and gains on both sides. Mari ran everywhere, sometimes beating on her little drum, sometimes blowing staccato notes on her horn, at other times thumping her chest. She snatched up corpses as if they were slender bales of grass and flung them up into the air where they disappeared, blending with the elements, or fell, with a hard thud, onto the charnel field, where they would be burnt. Vultures swooped down and pecked away at fleshy bodies, a thigh, a buttock; they gouged out eyes, ripped open chests and set their beaks to tasty hearts that might have been still attempting to beat.'

Aambal was restless, she felt as if she wanted to get up and run away from this narration, away from Pothigai's slope and plunge into the battlefield to challenge the foe that had ambushed her and robbed her of her only treasure, language. She wanted, like the warriors whose stories she had been listening to, to thump her chest, to roar, to brandish swords, to curve her arm back and fling a spear, aim a mace at her enemy. She wanted back what was hers.

Natramanar could see that Aambal was in that state where language entered through the ears and into the heart, assailed the mind and reining it to the heart's plough, drew it along. He and the other bards exchanged knowing looks. She was ready. Soon, soon she would break through the barricade of time. They breathed deep before they started the next section, one that they were all too aware would move them to tears.

9

SINGAMUGAN

The narration bards' heavy mood added a pensive note to their voices. On the fifth day, Surapadman's younger brother Singamugan was the chosen commander-in-chief for the Asura side, and Matri Dhirghajihva of the Sura side. These two were the last of the designated commanders-in-chief, and when either one of them left the battlefield, the two supreme commanders would take their places at the heads of their respective forces. On this day, the two armies were in the shapes of eagle and cloud.

 Singamugan, born to Surasa when she and Kashyapa had taken on lion forms, looked lion-like, his hair leaping in a mane around his face, his valour was a lion's fearless courage, his roar a fierce roar, and he possessed all the nobility of the great beast. When in the throes of battle, he sent shivers down the spine of whoever saw him. Many were the tales told of his bravery and also of the generosity of his spirit that not only lauded his rivals' moves, but also encouraged them to push themselves further. In the tales, as in life, Singamugan was a valorous warrior and a man of great affection and goodwill. On the day that he appeared on the battlefield, he had cremated the body of one he had loved from the moment he set eyes on her, she who had borne him children and given him a happiness that he had not thought possible, flowering in the smallest of things. When he entered the battlefield, Mari appeared. She laid both her hands on his head, then his chest and blessed him.

Instead of Natramanar's voice, Aambal was hearing the narration in another voice. It sounded over the bard's voice and filled her head, continuing the narration, 'Mari ignored the Sura forces, and Murugan felt a familiar pang, which he dismissed, looking to the sky instead and his eyes were filled with a glow that came from between the clouds. He knew his six mothers were there. Once again, their constant, unwavering love gave him comfort and strength. They are my mothers, and I their son, he thought, and they will never set my interests aside to tend to something else.'

Aambal could not know that this was her own voice, the one that had been unable to sound, the one that failed whenever she tried to grasp at language and snatch syllables for the words that she desired to speak. She did not realise that, finally, a floodgate had opened, and from the trough of her dammed-up memory, words were rushing into her mind.

The bard continued his narration, 'The eagle and cloud moved in suit: units met other units in combat, duels were fought, the group of musicians, runners and physicians, common to both sides, ran around busily. As always, in a battle of this kind, there are many fights and fighters that deserve a telling, but not here, for it is Singamugan we follow, and it is his deeds on this penultimate day of the battle that will be the most sung and celebrated of those who fought on the red beach of Chendur. For he did not die, nor was he defeated in combat.' Natramanar paused for effect. 'Singamugan raced through the battlefield in a chariot driven by the Gandharva Malayakeerthi whose home was in the high mountains, the Malaya.'

The best of the Sura warriors came up and engaged Singamugan in combat, but he neither lost nor fell, or even tired. Every time he combated someone, he seemed to become more energetic: his eyes glowed, his heart slowed to an even beat, he smiled and any thoughts that rose in his head dispersed like mist at the arrival of the sun in his chariot of dawn. As opponents faced him with their chosen weapons, Singamugan never refused a duel, nor asked for a weapon of his choice—whatever the opponent proposed, he accepted. It seemed that Singamugan and warfare had a pact, so perfect was his every move. All through this time, Mari never left his side, cheering him on, delighting in every move he made, clapping her hands, blowing on her hunting horn.

The Sura warriors were losing their spirit and their numbers were falling rapidly. Matri Dhirghajihva called for a quick gathering of all the leaders, and it was decided that they would request a concerted attack on Singamugan, which was allowed by the rules. If a warrior was too quick, too able, too tough to be beaten by a single opponent, then they could come in groups of twos or threes or even five at a time to attack. When this was communicated to Singamugan, he laughed uproariously and said, 'If you must come together, come ten thousand of you at once, or not at all.' Thus it was that a group of ten thousand—in which were units of chariots, foot soldiers, swordsmen, archers, mace-fighters, generals and the commander-in-chief herself—moved as one towards Singamugan.

Their quarry did not move, he waited, his laughter rising into the air and falling back onto the battlefield. When they were gathered around him and had positioned themselves, Singamugan raised his sword and began to turn on the spot he stood, his mouth tossing out words, like flowers to an invisible deity. By the time he had turned full circle, his body had become gigantic, looming over the land and sea, spreading out across the sky. He had a thousand heads, in which a thousand mouths opened and bellowed with a force that made the line of red hills quake and splinter. His hands covered the sun; he opened his mouth and breathed and all the air went rushing in, making everyone else's mouths fall open in alarm. Then he blew out, sending the bodies of the opponent warriors flying. He turned again, and the battlefield shook. His thousand hands flung weapons at the enemy, striking thousands of them together.

The Matris, all twelve of them, approached Singamugan from all sides, encircling him: Bhiti, Bhini, Dhirghajihva, Meshavahini, Dhumi, Chitrasena, Kalarava, Urdhvavenidhara, Megharava, Dhuma, Keshamushtika, Truti. He looked at them and hailed them by their names. They put down their weapons and challenged Singamugan to wrestle them. Singamugan shrunk back into his old body-shape and stepped forward. The Matris are amongst the fiercest warriors in all the worlds, and even the likes of Veerabahu would think twice before wrestling one of them. But Singamugan delighted in meeting head-on what was considered unvanquishable. He swung his two brawny arms round and round, humming a little.

Singamugan divested himself of sword and dagger, and removed his armour. He stepped forward, and the Matris did likewise and stood in a ring, greeted by lusty cheers from the warriors.

With palms pressed together and a bent head, he said, 'O valiant Matris, you into whose care Mother Parvathy placed the Lord of Chendur when he was two years old and known as Kumara, the Boy, I am fortunate that you have sought me out and invited me to wrestle you. Combat with you is a test that any warrior would welcome and not many have received the honour of an invitation like this. I will wrestle all of you, but on one condition. I know that I will beat all of you, each of you will face defeat. And I want a promise from you that you will overlook the condition that requires an opponent defeated to quit the battle.'

The Matris looked affronted, angered, disbelieving and then quizzical.

One of them said, 'That is a condition that no warrior will accept. It would be a dishonourable action. And we cannot accept it.'

Singamugan said, 'Then I will refuse to fight.'

The Matris did not know what to say to Singamugan, indeed, they did not know what to say at all.

So it was Singamugan who spoke again, 'There is a way this can be done honourably. I can ask of you a penalty that your defeat will require you to pay, and I will promise that the forfeit will not be easy.'

Matri Truti grunted, 'No defeat. Have you ever heard tell of any one of us being defeated?'

But Matri Urdhvavenidhara stepped forward and said, 'We accept your condition.'

Singamugan fought the Matris, one after another. Each of them was tried to her utmost, and it seemed as if the same scene was being repeated again and again: one of them grasping him by the arms, and attempting to get him to stand still, while he spun round and round and broke the hold. Singamugan disarmed them with his charm and his irrepressible goodwill as much as by his skill— he cheered, called out praise, sometimes even steered them away if one or the other seemed as if she might make a hasty move. The warriors around them clapped and cheered for all the wrestlers, but clearly, Singamugan was their favourite.

The Matris' eyes shone with twin emotions. On the one hand was admiration for the adept Asura, and on the other, the humiliation of not being close to beating him.

Singamugan was like a seasoned ebony tree that had come to life and grown hands and legs. The wrestling was tough: the women were sharp, their strength enormous and their moves so quick that he found himself constantly tested. Sometimes he panted with the exertion of trying to move his feet or to swing his arms or to get free of the vice of one of their practised holds. On the rare occasion when the tempo eased up a little, Singamugan felt as if he could see past the wrestling, or perhaps through it, and what he saw made his steps slow a little. It took the edge off his moves, and the Matris slowed as well. Then the moment passed in a snap, and their bodies sprang back into the frenetic rhythm. One by one, Singamugan toppled them, and as each of the Matris stood before him, vanquished, he asked of them something that they granted him.

When he had defeated eleven of them and reached the twelfth, Matri Meshavahini, she said to him, 'I will not wrestle with you, but I will tell you a story about what is to be in a time after this. It is about what the future holds for three people on this battlefield, all of them connected to the Lord of Chendur. What my telling and your hearing manifests will determine the end of the story of our duel.' Before she could finish her sentence, Singamugan's voice broke out, the syllables rising and falling in the excited rise and fall of his breath, 'Ah, a story as weapon.' Those who stood around noticed the knowing smile that appeared on his face, a smile that also appeared on the face of the man known as the God of the Oracles, far away, on the edge of the battlefield. Singamugan's eyes had travelled from the faces of the twelve to the young man they had helped raise when he had been at his most wilful. Singamugan laughed and slapped his chest and said to all the Matris, 'Whatever else happens, my fame will forever be swelled by descriptions of this fight with all of you.'

Natramanar took a swig of toddy before continuing, 'And now I will tell you the story that the mighty Matri Meshavahini told Singamugan. It was about a man who cultivated lands to the north of Pazhani, a farmer whose name meant He of the Enchanting Fields: Maruthan. There is a secret in that story which was not revealed, and thus cannot be told of, but which Time will reveal.'

Maruthan had fields that he ploughed, planted, cropped and fallowed, season after season. It was said that he had come here a long time ago, leaving his home and his fields near the holy hill of Annamalai after his wife of a few months began to turn on him because he could not satisfy her need for admiration and wealth. She wanted him to give up farming and seek employ at the court because that would give her status. She didn't approve of his giving alms or of his general modesty. Maruthan's heart was sore, and when he could bear it no longer, he left home and wife, siblings and parents, and went to the home of his cousin Yaazhini who had married into a farming family living in the foothills of Murugan's home.

She was a soothsayer, and as soon as she saw him, bedraggled, bearded, his eyes hollow, she looked up. There she saw two crows in the kondrai, and heard the rustle of cricket legs in the grass, and knew that he was living out what was written in his stars, and that, like all fates, his too could change. She welcomed him, and he lived with her and her family, but the sadness never left him. His hands grew pale, for no mud or green sap stained them. He found himself quite unable to plough or sow or reap anymore.

The smile did not return to his lips, and Yaazhini felt deep sorrow for the loss of Maruthan's spirit. She took him up Pazhani Hill, and when Maruthan stood in front of Murugan, he wept like a child, and the god once called the Child God got up from his throne and held Maruthan's head, looking into the weeping face. When he said something in the young man's ear, Maruthan heaved a deep sigh. With a few words, Murugan had dislodged the thorn that had pierced his heart so deep he thought he would never be free of it. Maruthan assented with a nod, his tears stopped and he knelt before the kindness of those words. Murugan gave Maruthan a plot of fertile land, where the man would build a hut and cultivate crops. Yaazhini was waiting; she knew something was approaching and that it would return to Maruthan his loving, happy spirit.

And so it happened: one day, as he was driving birds away from his field, a voice called out his name with a hilly twang, and turning, saw in front of him a short, sturdy woman dressed in the white clothes of bards and healers. Her back was straight, her head high, the features on her dusky face were those of the women of the south: high forehead, big eyes, a shapely nose, wide nostrils, black curling hair. 'Are you Maruthan?' she was asking. It turned out that she was the niece of his neighbours and a travelling bard. She needed indigo to make inks, which her aunt told her was growing on Maruthan's land. Maruthan did have indigo on his land and he did lead her to it. But with the indigo, the woman also took his heart. He felt a hollow in his chest where his heart had been, and at a loss, went looking for Yaazhini. She saw in an instant that the time had come for Maruthan's life to be altered, but could not speak of it to him. Instead, she said, 'Let's give her some more indigo, I have some here.'

They went to find the 'indigo woman', as Yaazhini called her. When they reached the house, the woman was outside, standing over vats of leaves boiling in a vat. Her hands were blue and there were blues stains on her clothes. Maruthan felt as if he was the vat on the fire, on the boil. He walked up and said to her, 'I have lost my heart to you. Will you marry me?' Yaazhini felt as if she was standing on the top of Pazhani Hill, and the God of Oracles and Soothsayers was breathing into her ears once again the secret words that kept soothsaying ears and eyes from taking in too much of the world, giving them the ability to search, to listen for what was hidden, what had not happened yet and what had gone before, and the language in which to speak of it.

Maruthan and the indigo woman, whose name was Panimalar, were married in a few weeks. He was a changed man thenceforth—his hands once more glowed with what fed his spirit, the rich, fecund mud and the green sap that flowed in the crops he grew, and his spirit became fertile and sprouted shoots that spread and bore fruit. Panimalar was to him as the mud to his crop, and to her, he was as the rain to mud.

Natramanar stopped here and looked at his listeners, as much for dramatic effect as for all of them to take stock of the situation, to see how close or how far away Aambal was from the anticipated state. Then he continued.

'At this point, Matri Meshavahini stopped and said, "That is the story as far as I will tell it." She neither asked nor said anything more.

Singamugan's eyes, which had a faraway look as the Matri neared the closing of the story, were wide and unblinking. They were settled on the faraway chariot of Chendur's Lord. There was a stillness in the air, an expectant holding of breath, for a story that has no end unsettles the listener. All faces were turned to Singamugan, who burst into jubilant laughter. His eyes followed the lines of soldiers, going back to the commanders-in-chief, and then stopping at Aambal in her white clothes, her cymbals sparkling.

At this point in the narrative, Aambal started and her body began to tremble. Her eyes were staring right at Natramanar, who continued his story.

'Singamugan smiled and said, "Each of us is a story in portion and Time is the go-between that persuades Fate to make the match for us with who are the other parts of our story, and we, the other of theirs. Fate is a language that Time makes to fill its loneliness, for Time is always alone. I have been allowed to see something that is yet hidden, but certain."

'The Matris were nodding and smiling. He said no more and the bards do not know what he had seen. To ourselves, as we narrate this, we ask, "Did he think of his dead wife and his friend? Was it of his newborn child that he was thinking?"

'Singamugan stopped and let his hands drop, He bowed his head and said, "It is time. Now that I know the start of another's story, let me mark the end of ours." So saying, he saluted the twelve sisters, looked around the battlefield, pausing at Murugan and Surapadman, and finally, he turned in the direction of Veeramahendrapuram, and his body slumped, falling towards the ruddy sand.

'Mari had already dropped down, and now stood with Singamugan's body in her arms. The drums beat furiously, horns blew and the musicians began their dirges. Surapadman's chariot came racing. He descended, removed his crown, weapons and armour. The late afternoon light hit his body and he seemed translucent, made of light. Kneeling, he took the body from Mari's arms. His eyes were dry, but the hand that he put against Singamugan's chest trembled. He recited aloud the prayer for the dead, known to all in the south. Mari wailed, shaking her little drum, her other hand beating her chest. Murugan's chariot reached the spot, and he descended to take a place in the circle around Singamugan.'

With this, the bard paused. But Aambal did not register the pause, for she was there, in the midst of the battle on the field. She heard the blood-curdling shouts, saw the frenzied duelling, swords that sliced off an arm, or plunged into the pot of blood inside a ribcage that shattered with a sound she did not know the right word for. She heard the terror-stricken shouts of the thousands of manava fighters to whom the magic and the illusions of the asuras, devas, gandharvas and others was far more confusing and fearsome than was the might of a mace, the sharpness of a sword or spear, or the tight manacling of arms in a wrestle. She saw the vultures as they descended onto the field looking for carrion, she recalled the wailing of parents, spouses, children, lovers, friends, siblings and masters who had lost their own in the battling. She felt in her nostrils the strange sting of the blood of those like her, dwellers on this earth, who would bleed and die when wounded.

The bards now began moving in a circle, their anklet-clad feet stomping and their tudis and cymbals clamouring. But Aambal's ears heard them only faintly, for the voice of Surapadman filled her head. She was one of the many standing close to him at the edge of the sea as he faced Veeramahendrapuram, cradling the body of his younger brother. His voice was low, his words glowing and resonant, and through the daze of Aambal's here-there state, it pierced like the sun through dawn mist. 'All relationships are but reflections of the bond one has with one's siblings. My life would have been inadequate without this brave and gentle Asura, who is like a giant wave.'

Aambal's lips quivered and her clenched fists tightened as, behind her shut eyes, Surapadman bent and kissed Singamugan's forehead, then lifted his face and looked towards the sea. Mari seemed to be extremely agitated, her drum beats and her movements got more and more frenzied. She was brandishing her sickle and spinning on her feet, and the crowd moved back in alarm. The sea began to churn violently, emitting an eardrum-splitting hum. As the waves crashed into each other, giant plumes of spray shot into the sky. Mari suddenly became motionless. Tossing the drum and sickle onto the sand, she snatched up Singamugan's body and ascended to the skies until she was right above the churning. She dropped the body into the swirl, which closed up and stilled, enclosing the brave Asura's body in its foam-bejewelled casket.

Aambal's eyes opened. She heard the bards' words, 'The great Asura bent down and kissed Singamugan's forehead, then he lifted his face and looked towards the seas as if waiting for something. Mari seemed to be extremely agitated ...' Hadn't they already finished this part, Aambal wondered, even as realisation set in that she had seen the scene before they recounted it. Her heart rose in a swift flight, then sank as if weighted by stones. She was afraid. What more was going to happen to her? To her body and mind?

Did this mean something was changing? Would her memory come back? Would she be able to compose poetry? What if this made her worse? What if she went back to how she had been?

As the bards finished their narration, they saw how Aambal was less at the mercy of the trances, and how she had held her place in the threshold between the Pothigai of now and the Chendur of then. They understood what this meant: she was getting closer to the door. She was at the door. Nobody spoke to her or, in any way, engaged her. Aambal went to sleep that evening, feeling that something was waiting for her and that she would need all her strength. She willed herself to empty her mind and to sleep. Her friends Chakki and Poitherutti rubbed her head, and Aambal's restless hands continued to strike cymbals that she no longer held.

10

SURAPADMAN AND MAHASENA

Aambal slept a dreamless sleep and woke the next morning long before the sun did. She sat on the hidden ledge where they had brought her every day when she was first able to walk, for here the winds came in off the agachha, the magic plant that could transform all ailments, including those of the heart and mind, and the sun came in filtered through the vetiver that had grown to tree height. The previous evening, she had remembered the events before the bards recounted them. She had not felt helpless, as if she was a bag of cattle feed, flung from hand to hand to be loaded onto carts. She had felt as if she could pull back, pull out of the trance. Her tongue had grown warm as Surapadman was speaking the benediction for Singamugan, and she had felt it tingle, as if there was a word stirring there.

Aambal was impatient for the narration to start, to slip into another trance. She did not dwell on whether she would feel words come alive under her tongue again or whether she would be able to make poetry again. But she did know that this was the last segment of the bards' recounting, and so her last attempt, at least for the time, to go back in time and reclaim what was hers.

Everything about that day's narration was different: the bards were all standing, none seated, all of them carried a tudi strung around their waist and a pair of cymbals, and the musicians held aloft giant kombu, their curved stems opening like flowers into the air. Aambal noticed none of this. When Ganesha and Akattiyan appeared and sat down, the Kani sat in a ring around all of them, with Chakki, Poitherutti and Raako sitting behind Aambal, close to her.

As the narration got underway and the voices of the bards soared, inside Aambal too there was a soaring. To those looking at her face, it would have seemed that she was, like all of them, in the grip of excitement, but to the bards it was clear that Aambal was caught by that twined feeling of delight and dread that only the anticipation of language could produce. All their lives they had seen poets with that look on their faces, leaning into the hefty gales of language, and then the stilling as language passed through their bodies, minds and hearts, upturning, fertilising, furrowing and planting. And when they recited, the words came stout-bodied, thought-lean and moist with heart-damp.

Aambal could feel something stirring inside her belly, swimming about with a vigour that sent it crashing into her stomach wall, making her want to hunch and clutch it close. She swayed with its force, and no one steadied her. Aambal knew that a change was coming, and she was not alarmed, nor did she feel any certainty.

To the Kani, who had never had to study their language, the loss of Aambal's language was frightening, and they waited, hoping that whatever was happening now would cure the affliction.

Meantime, the bards took up their instruments, drew breath and started the narration of the concluding events of the battle, passing from single voices to refrains in chorus with practiced ease. 'The days passed, the sands of Chendur turned darker with gore, the sky loomed, not wanting to miss a single movement. The air trembled with the sounds of weapons and of the vultures that hovered, their wings beating. The last day of the Great Battle of Chendur was come, and with it came the expectation of an ending.'

'Today,' the warriors determined, 'we must shine.'

'Today,' the charioteers determined, 'we must show our expertise.'

'Today,' the musicians determined, 'we must invent a special beat on our instrument.'

It was the day of endings, the day that Surapadman and Mahasena would face each other. Did those two mightiest of warriors wake up thinking of the other? Did each determine that he must win?

In a leisurely, ambling pace, the bards described the morning scene, 'In the east, Ushas appeared, to fling her mantle of light over Night, to take him captive, as she did every day, as he knew she would, but on that day, he struck out, trying to dodge the daily cloaking, to avoid huddling against her, his head against her heart, all her secrets resounding in her ear. Night was rebellious, he wanted to see, he wanted to be free of the mantle, and it seemed as if Dawn had allowed him to linger behind the clouds, for on that morning they were unusually dark.'

Next, the bards described what everybody was doing. The warriors had woken before dawn to wash, exercise and to eat before the battle. Surapadman offered prayers and went to Ganesha to offer obeisance, and as the Asura king was leaving, the god, who was also sometimes called the Gateway to Time, embraced him and blessed him, saying, 'May the wait bear fruit.' They narrated how Surapadman then went to see his mother, and how the two sat for a little while, neither of them speaking, and how she blessed him and he returned to his tent. Their voices too became light when they said he ate nothing because he wanted to be light that day for there was much he must bear. They broke into a chorus, singing, 'What awaited the king? Was it the weight of pressing disappointment or the weight of triumph?' Then pausing, giving their listeners time for the descriptions to settle inside them. 'On the last day,' the bards reminded their audience, 'the supreme commanders were also the commanders-in-chief, and the two generals were Ajamugi, Surapadman's youngest sibling, with Veerabahu, eldest of the Nine.'

Aambal's breathing grew laboured, and Chakki prised open her clenched fingers and placed in her palms the cymbals that had been there all through the battle on Chendur's red ground. Aambal's hands moved and the beat of her cymbals joined that of the bards. She was facing them, but did not see them, focused on trying to recall the battle: how had the battlefield looked, where had she been, what had she been doing before the battle began? What of Thennan? And Kandhan? What of the Asura king?

The bards began describing Surapadman and Murugan, both in full armour, resplendent, as were their steeds—milk-white Kshema and Svasti and pitch-black Kalam and Neram. They sang of how Murugan's chest leapt under his armour, making the garland of coral kadamba ripple, as did the garland of dark-blue lotus buds on the expanse of Surapadman's. They said that, beside each warrior was his bard, driven by a swift-armed charioteer, and then spoke the names of the bards—Thennan and Aambal.

Aambal's head was flooded with images of that moment. She remembered how their charioteers were fully armoured and armed, in case they needed to deflect weapons that accidentally flew towards the two bards, or in the unlikely event that someone attacked them. On the other hand, the charioteers of the two supreme commanders, like those of all warriors, were not armed.

The bards described how Murugan and Surapadman appeared on the battlefield to the cheering of thousands of warriors. 'He rode on to the battlefield,' the bards sang, 'the glorious king of Veeramahendrapuram, the mightiest of Asuras, Surapadman, resplendent like the white curl of foam that rides a wave, like the glow of a well-burning flame, like the lightning that rides unseen in clouds. And all eyes were riveted.'

Behind her lids, Aambal saw the Asura, his frame clad in armour, his head uncovered, with no crown or wreath on it, his hair braided and coiled from left to right and right to left at the back of his head. His eyes were long and dark, his beard thick, his moustache twirled into two smooth crescents, and Aambal felt again the stirring that she had felt then, a warmth that sprouted in her chest and belly and suffused her body. Aambal recalled the thrill she had felt when his eyes turned to her as he greeted 'Karthikeya's war bard, the poet Aambal of Chendur'. She remembered the timbre of Surapadman's voice, the way each syllable had left his throat and ambled towards her, kissing her ears and entering softly, lingering.

She shook her head free, and heard the bards speaking Murugan's name, 'Lord of Pazhani, and king in all the lands where Tamizh lives. When he rode on to the field, Lord Surapadman, supreme commander of a force that had the might of all the armies in all the worlds combined, held up both arms and hailed the younger man, the god of a language that he too adored, "Karthikeya," he said, "Karthikeya Mahasena, lord of the hosts of Svarloka, Senani, I salute you, your might, your valour, your equanimity and your generosity as a warrior."'

The bards sang on, 'Mahasena Karthikeya, Lord of Chendur, raised his left arm and the mighty vel, the Shaktivel, given by Mother Parvathy, and hailed the Asura in words that rang with admiration. Like two stars, like two suns were they, and the whole battlefield was aglow, for when two suns come together, their light will shine on all the worlds.'

Aambal recalled the glow—it had enveloped her too, and it had caught the four horses, white and black. That light had seemed to be alive, and spread like the wings of a giant bird into the sky and in all the directions.

The bards continued to sing, 'The battle lasted one whole day and took many lives. It burnt the veil that hid the secret of the birth of Karthikeya.' Aambal was still thinking of the two men, splendid, one older, the other younger, both handsome, both fish-eyed, curly haired, broad-chested, both breathtakingly beautiful. But the one made her heart swell with joy, and want to grab his hand and give it a sharp pinch, the other seemed to have taken her heart in his tawny, slender fingers and, raising it to his moustachioed lips, given it a sharp nip. It made her gut clench with a feeling that she was not used to, a heavy feeling that filled her breasts with its weight, making her shoulders stoop, slipping around her waist a secret band that made her want to angle her hips more snugly into that welcome hold. Even now she could feel the damp, the sweat in her underarms, on her forehead, upper lip, and a rare moistness sprouting from the unattended cave between her legs.

The bards could see that Aambal wasn't hearing their words, she had halted somewhere. Their eyes went from her to Ganesha, who smiled and gestured for them to continue. One of them tapped out a quick, sharp rhythm on her tudi, which was picked up by the shrill notes of a kombu and a bell-metal gong. Their voices soared to evoke the soaring emotions of the scene, and Aambal's attention snapped back to the bards once again. Accompanied by a tapping of their salangai-clad legs, they sang, 'No knowing the final combat's end, a day? Two? Many more? No knowing when one or the other, Suran or Murugan, would be defeated, for only then could there be an end. Would Murugan see through the veil, would he see the secret of his own name and being? Would Surapadman return home? Would the Asura then take over the task of creation? What would become of Brahma? What would become of creation? What would become of Murugan?'

The instruments of the bards sounded a staccato beat before slowing to a pause. Thereafter they followed the rhythm of their own slowed breath as they resumed narration.

The bards described the Suras' net and the Asuras' shark formations, how the net moved in two halves, sideways and forward, and the shark moved backwards, its jaws opening wide, its teeth ready, with parts of the net stretching away from the main body and moving closer, while parts of the shark, its fins, its head, its belly likewise moving away, but able in an instance to join the mother body again. They recounted how soldiers broke from the formation, like drops of water from the net, like drops of water from the shark, and engaged each other, straining to cause breaches in the body. How whole units rushed towards an enemy unit, roaring, their spears and javelins speeding ahead of them as they charged forward. Their words spoke of the way the waves ran onto the shore, scooping up the bloodied sand and bringing it back washed. Of how Murugan and Surapadman and their forces cut and slashed, pierced and shot their way through the body of the opposing army. The shark panted, shuddered, convulsed and spewed blood; the net was ripped, its loose ends hanging threadbare, it had sprung leaks and could not close.

These images played in Aambal's mind's eye, given life by the well-worded narration of the bards and like on the previous day, she did not notice that she was, in fact, recalling the event, remembering how it had happened, not imagining it through the words of the bards. Even before they began describing the deadly feats of Dharani the Sura and the Asura Lalata, she saw Dharani spinning round and round till her body became a column of fire and she spun towards the enemies. She saw, too, how Lalata bored down deep into the earth and came up under Dharani, sending her plunging downwards. She saw, too, the man who had once been the querulous sage Dhritiman on the side of the Suras, like an elephant in rut, stampeding through the enemy ranks, slaughtering scores of fighters, and how Ajamugi met him head-on, the two striking, and defending on and on, until the delicate Ajamugi cut the brawny man down with her sword.

Aambal was now entirely inside her own memory, and everywhere, the battle raged. The two Supreme Commanders were in the thick of the fighting. Murugan's vel sped outwards and returned to his hand, as swift as thought, hissing like the pent-up hot breath of fire inside the earth. Surapadman's Maya, the keen sword that his mother gave him, slashed with a whisper, its glow like a hundred thousand fireflies, now bright, now muted. They would only fight each other when the battle was at its most ferocious, and after they had each fought with all units of their own armies, moving from one to another part of the anatomy of their battle formation.

Into the drama that was unfolding behind her eyelids, the voices of the bards came flowing, 'Like the shark that flips, twists, races ahead of the flowing net, which tightens, closes shut and sometimes flows with the shape of the waves, the warriors and units moved continuously, their shape-shifting almost unnoticeable.' After a while, their drums beat a quick sharp medley, indicating a break, the percussive code also hinting that something spectacular was coming. In the silence that followed, Aambal's body slumped into its own cushion of flesh and bone, she held her eyes shut tight with her palms. Her head hung down, chin resting on the drum of her thin chest, which had expanded like a por murasu when the bards were speaking.

The musicians and bards went off towards where the Kani were cooking, to drink the potent palm toddy that was mixed with hot water and spiced with pepper, and to eat little nuggets of well-cooked rabbit meat, which would sit lightly in their bellies and not weigh down their voices.

11

THE SECRET

When they came back, Aambal, Ganesha and Akattiyan had not moved at all. All three sat silent, pensive. The bards were clearly on the edge of some emotion that was palpable in the slight shifting of feet, the rough breaths, the slight shiver of the hands that tapped their tudis and cymbals, and the way their eyes narrowed and squinted into the brilliant sky. They looked at Ganesha and began, their eyes then shifting to Aambal—she was one of them. It was she that they were singing for, it was to her that they were offering an antidote. 'The sun,' they started, 'had moved closer to the west, the battle was at a high tide. Surapadman indicated to his bard Thennan that he should play the beat on his cymbals that signalled he was ready for combat with the commander-in-chief of the other side. Murugan heard the beat and signalled to his bard Aambal to reply with the same.'

As their chariots moved forward, the battle slowed. Thousands of warriors shifted subtly till a space was clear in the centre of the two armies, as if the net was in mid-air, and the shark was some distance away. The sudden stilling of the chaos of the battlefield was remarkable. Everybody knew that the battle had come to its real purpose: to play the game the Great Asura had devised for the Lord of Chendur, Mahasena. They were all waiting for the revelation. Nobody asked if it was worth all this loss, death, chaos and bloodshed just so the secret could be revealed. Some said that it was the secret of creation itself that was to be revealed. The wise knew that, while everyone on that battlefield would see and understand the secret, it would be lost from memory to those among them who could not bear such knowledge.

Murugan's face was drenched with sweat, his eyes seemed to be emitting sparks, his chest heaved. The force of what was expected of him seemed to weigh on the young god, but that had not got in the way of his fight. Surapadman was the picture of composure. His handsome face glowed in the light of the evening sun, he smiled widely and laughed often. He called out words of praise for Murugan and cheered him on, his lithe body seemingly weightless, the way he leapt high and came down twisting, or ran backwards and came racing forward.

Even as the bards spoke, Aambal had slipped into the battle, her body swaying slightly, her eyes glazed, her ears ringing with the deep voice of the Asura king, in whose voice Murugan's name sounded even more valorous. Karthikeya, Mahasena, Senani, Muruga, Kumara, Chendura—Surapadman addressed Murugan by his many names, while Murugan did not address the older man at all.

Aambal found it took all of her concentration to stay attuned to the moves of the two warriors, to know beforehand what Surapadman was about to do, and looking at Thennan, she sensed that he was feeling the same. It was their beats on the cymbal, the gait of their singing that would sound the alarm for the warrior whose bard they each were, alerting them to the dangers imminent in their opponent's moves, guiding their moves. Aambal knew she must keep all five senses alert, as well as that sixth, which had no name and could not be trained, but which she knew would come to her aid if she called at the right moment. Aambal was like a wound-up top readying to spin. If she so much as turned her attention to the ground she was standing on, she might flop down, like a top spun by nervous hands.

Thennan and she summoned up lyrics that on other occasions might have taken them days to conceive and set down, beat-perfect, harmonious. To Aambal, Thennan was a comrade, not enemy, he was a fellow bard and she drew strength from his presence.

Through the haze of her trance, the voices of the bards on the Pothigai mountain wafted in, softened by Pothigai's kindly winds. She could hear them saying 'Suran was aiming his mace at Kumara' at the same time that her eyes followed the curve of Suran's arm raising the mighty-headed mace into the air, and even as she recited 'Like lightning, now the Great Asura lifts, now he strikes, the Lord of Pazhani needs his shield', Murugan was reaching for his shield. The words, the shield and the mace all moved together. The brass shield thrust upwards into the crash of the mace, one inscribed with the kadamba and the other with the blue lotus emblem. The impact shook the two warriors and the ground they stood on, and the crash sent the clouds scrambling. Mari darted this way and that on the sand, then rose into the air as if to get a better view. When the combatants made good moves, she roared and thumped her scrawny chest, making her breasts shudder. She clapped her hands and raised her voice and praised both the warriors. The sky was darkening, but the battlefield was bright with the sparks that flew.

The battle went on and on. Aambal was tired. She seemed to be slipping in and out of her trance, sometimes she heard the bards' voices on Pothigai mountain, at other times, she heard her own and Thennan's voices at the battlefield. She felt as if the ground was rising up—was it the stony flanks of Pothigai or the red sands of Chendur? Aambal could not tell. But she could see Thennan now, he didn't look tired. Aambal's head spun, she was having difficulty keeping track. Her limbs were heavy, she felt that she could not hold up their weight. Her belly and throat hurt, her guts were on fire, her tongue was thrashing about like a fish without water. Her head hurt most of all. She was not trained for this. For what? For a life without words? For a battle with words? Where was she now? On the top of Pothigai, with its healing winds? Or Chendur, by the sea?

Wherever she was, she could not speak. She wanted to speak, she had to speak. She had to. She was Murugan's war bard. Aambal of Chendur, War Bard to Mahasena Karthikeya, that was her title. But she was also a poet, Murugan's Poet. Bards like Thennan were trained to stand and move and continuously strike beats on their cymbals or tudis. They were taught to assume a position for long standing, they were taught how to move without taking a step. Their hands and arms were tied with weights and flexed and stretched so that their shoulders and arms became firm and their wrists became strong and flexible. They learnt how to draw breath and hold it in, so their lungs became capable of keeping the voice strong. Thennan's slender frame was strong: he had muscled, hardy legs, and his wrists and hands were powerful.

It seemed to Aambal that her own hands shook violently, her cymbals slipped a little, and the sound that came from them was minute, audible only to her ears. She felt that, instead of rushing into her ears, it pushed and flopped against her ribs, making her chest shudder. She shook her head to free it from the descending cloud of self-pity, and remembered that she, too, was sturdy. She had well-toned legs, for she came from stock that had for generations walked all over the land for work, for community and for worship. And on Pazhani-Pothigai, she had been walking endlessly once her dizziness had passed. And her hands were no less muscled—from hours and hours of wielding the stylus and from cutting, washing, straightening and threading palm leaves. From knotting her wrists to the slender trunk of the jasmine or the neem and pulling. She took care of her hands, her wrists, her legs, her back: she swam, she climbed, she ran, she walked. And her hearing was sharp, acute, as was her sense of rhythm, fall and gait. She guarded her breath, she trained it to slow when she wanted to ambush a particular word, just as her breath knew when she wanted to stealthily track an elusive image. She was strong. Her stamina would not fail her—it never had in the endless nights and days when she climbed all over Pazhani Hill, unable to finish a line or a verse well enough that she could be sure that Kandhan would like it.

Kandhan! This was Kandhan, her best friend, the little boy that she had held by the hand and pulled along with her to places that she knew but not he. This was the boy she had protected from the good-natured ridicule of their classmates, the boy that she had sat down and taught things to. This was Murugan, whom she was apprenticed to, without whom she would not have learnt her way with Tamizh. Without whom her words would despair and die. Who loved her more than he loved anyone else. Who would be lost without her because he had no other friend like her. Aambal was filled with paralysing doubts, rooted to her despair. Would she ever be able to speak again? Would words ever be her companions? Would she be a poet again? Would Kandhan be her friend, and master, then? Would she be able to keep herself alert enough to catch all of Surapadman's subtle moves? Or would she fail at that? Would Kandhan be in danger because of her?

As if he had heard Aambal's thoughts and was mocking them, Surapadman shouted, darted into the sea and disappeared. Her eyes lunged after him, the words formed in her mind, but her tongue stayed curled up on the floor of her mouth. She heard Murugan's roar, and only then did her eyes go to the vel that was already speeding towards Surapadman. Murugan's arm had flung the vel in the instant the Asura's leap began, and Aambal's eyes had followed after. It should have been the other way around. Her attention had been dulled by the heavy thoughts of her own weakness, but Murugan had been attentive. Through the curtains of Aambal's mind and senses, the sound of the bards' narration came, loud and resonant, 'Would he have been quicker, Aambal, had you been alert? Would he have been swifter, Aambal, had you kept your gait?' Tears streamed down Aambal's cheeks, her face was burning so much, it was like a blue aambal caught under a moon's lustful glare. Her hands shivered violently, and one of the bards knelt down next to her, steadied her hands by holding them in one each of his and guided her into the beat they were following, and slowly, she slid into it and out of her trance.

The bards continued the narration, 'The vel curved through the air and struck the waves, which churned madly, and curled upwards, as if a giant mouth was sucking it all up from the sky. In an instant, the sea was dry—not a drop of water remained, as if the waves had been a dream, its billows and heaving gone. Where the water had been, there stood a giant mango tree, upside down, its roots convulsing, like creatures rearing their head to sip from the clouds, its trunk stretched downwards to open into thick branches, like a dome of green and brown and yellow, from which came the sound of birds, hundreds and hundreds of them. The tree hung there, mid-air, and Mari grew tall, taller than the tree and stood over it, roaring and calling out her blessings to the Great Asura.'

The voices of the bards swelled as they took up a refrain, 'What is Murugan doing? What is Mahasena thinking? Where is Senani? Where is his bard, Aambal of Chendur? Where is the bard's voice that should pierce the warrior's chest, and turn him to attack?'

The bards' tudis sounded in a feverish, martial beat. All eyes were on Aambal, whose own eyes were swimming in a pool of endless water. Like fish dodging a spear, they darted fear-stricken, her teeth chattered as her mouth tried to form words that refused to be gathered and held. Her hands went back and forth, snapping one disk of the cymbal to the other. The bards were silent, the winds were still, the beats of the drums crashed into everything and echoed.

Ganesha's voice leapt into the air, as soft as always, as gentle, but in the absence of other voices, it was sword-sharp, chiruthai-swift, battering-ram forceful. 'Aambal,' it said, 'Aambal, where is Kandhan? He can't hear you.' A shudder went through Aambal's body, as if she was the shark and the net had caught her, tightened and cut off air, as if she was thrashing about in deathly agony. Where was Kandhan? Why couldn't he hear her? Was she speaking? He should, he must. She should speak, she must speak, for only language could reach through everything else, only to language would Kandhan never be deaf. The words of the oracle came into her head. *Do not slip and do not let the slip fall on him.* The cymbals in her hands continued the beat, unbroken, unshaking, sure. She shut her eyes, and let the beat fill her head. As she struck the cymbals, words pushed through her chest, they rose to her throat and she called aloud, 'Kandha, Kandha, Kandha.'

Aambal's voice rang out on Pothigai's slope, filling everything. The gate of the sky crashed open, battered by a stick of akil that was the thickness of an ancient tree grown over many generations. The gentle, healing winds of Pothigai turned into a gale under the fan of giant peacock wings. A swelling wave of sound rose up from the mountain to meet the lightning and thunder that was hailing downwards, the Kani, the bards, and Akattiyan called, 'Muruga, Muruga.' To them, he was Murugan, Karthikeyan, Kumara, Skanda, Mahasena, Senani, but to her, he was Kandhan, her best friend Kandhan, the boy who loved everybody and everything, but who loved her specially, because she was his best friend, too. 'Kandha, Kandha,' she called, the word rushing out of her mouth. In the silence that fell over the mountain scene, Aambal's voice spoke as her hands tapped out an accompanying beat. She continued to call his name aloud, though she felt she was only breathing. In later times, when the bards put to words all that they saw and lived through there on Pothigai's holy heights, they would say, 'Blessed was Aambal, war bard to Karthikeya Mahasena, wellbooned was she, friend to Kurinji's God, Lord of Tamizh, for he was the breath in her body.'

Back on the battlefield, Aambal shuddered. She had to speak, she must speak, where were her words? Where was the dam that she had built drop by drop, syllable by syllable of her language, Murugan's language? She could feel her ribs stretch and groan, her breath leave her body, and then she gasped. Something had come to life in her mouth and it was striking outwards, its wings flailing. Her body quivered, like an arrow quivers under the sure fingers of a seasoned warrior in anticipation of the target it knows it will strike. Aambal was an arrow now, drawn back, and impelled forward into speech by the memory of the language made by a god whose longing filled every syllable of it. She spoke, 'The Great Asura is and is not, you are and are not. Chendur's Lord, take heed, count the steps and step in or out.'

In Pothigai, her eyes were shut and she felt the coils of her memory stir and sidewind away into the moment when she had first uttered those words on the battlefield. She felt as if Kandhan was holding her hand and pulling her along, much like she had done to him when he needed to be pushed into doing something. Her eyes cleared and she saw Kandhan standing there, looming over the trees, his head touching clouds that formed a halo of ink-black streaked with silver lightning. He leant down and placed his hand on Aambal's chest, on the thin ribs that shielded her heart. He spoke her name, 'Aambal. Aambal, my friend. Come.' It felt to Aambal that the skies and wind and the mud and the thing that held everything all streamed into her, and she herself flowed through Kandhan's hands into his heart—a dark and vast beach, its sand red, the sea of his breath beating against the red shores. She felt as if she was home, as if this was where she had always been, as if this place had pined for her. She sighed, and Pothigai's winds snatched it up and rushed around the great mountain, tossing it back, bigger, louder and sadder.

On the battlefield, Aambal heard that sigh. It came riding on the flanks of the giant waves that repeated themselves every day, back, forth, ebb, surge, ebb, flow. The air was warm, the wind salty, the cymbals in her hands cool. She struck them loud and clear, facing Kandhan, Mahasena. As her voice broke over the silent battlefield, Mari also fell silent, hovering over the mango tree, every leaf of which seemed to be leaping with light. 'The Great Asura is and is not, you are and are not. Chendur's Lord, take heed, count the steps and step in or out.'

Aambal took in the expressions passing over Murugan's face: confusion, uncertainty, concentration, determination, sadness. What was going through his head? What was he thinking? And then she felt it all swirling around inside her, the dark clouds of his dread, the rocky waves of his regret, sharp slivers of his excitement … she *knew* what he was feeling. She felt what he was feeling as if they were her feelings. As if an echo, the words of the oracle rang in her hearing, 'Do not let—' But where was she? Was she *here* in Pothigai or was she *there* on Chendur's beach, there in Pothigai, here in Chendur, or neither? Was she on Velan's Hill? Aambal could not say, and the terror that gripped her was a measure of the timelessness of the ancient one's words: 'Do not slip, and do not let the slip fall on him.' The words were not an instruction, they were a warning. She must be alert, she must catch the attack before it was made. She must defend herself with a counter. The attack must not reach, it must not pierce through the armour that covered the spread of her chest, nor could she allow her chest to be invaded by dread or distraction.

But why was she wearing armour? She only ever wore soft white cloth over her frame. She had come into the battlefield wearing white, its lightness meant to keep her back, chest, arms and shoulders unencumbered. When had she put on armour? Why? It was not hers, this chest, or rather, it was not only hers, for inside it there was also the beating of Murugan's heart, the rise and fall of breath running through it was not hers, it was his. But she was breathing it, she was there, and he was there, right there, exactly where she was. Her breath was flowing in and out of Murugan's body. She was herself and she was he, too. Her thoughts were hers. And his thoughts were hers, too. She knew that the moment had come, and he knew this was it—the moment of his testing. The dramatic force of the scene was incomparable: the inverted tree, the dried-up sea, the Asura who was and wasn't and he who was and wasn't. Murugan's eyes closed, the beat of the cymbals filled his head. Aambal felt the beat flow through her hands all through Murugan's body, like excited carp in the fields at Chendur, lightning fast.

Aambal said, 'You are and you aren't.'

As the words left her mouth, they came back to her, repeated in Murugan's voice.

I am and I am not.

Aambal said, 'The Asura is and he isn't.'

Murugan repeated: *Surapadman is not the tree. He is the great Asura emperor who rules over Veeramahendrapuram.*

'You are and you are not you.'

I am and I am not. I am Mahasena—the supreme commander of these forces. But I am not Mahasena, the supreme commander.

'What is he,' Aambal sang, 'what is mighty Surapadman? What are you, valorous Mahasena?'

What am I? What is Mahasena? he asked.

'What is the secret?' she sang.

What is the secret? he repeated.

The tree hung there mid-air, a giant riddle. Mari hovered overhead. Twin voices continued to utter the same lines, on and on.

'She is and she isn't your mother.'

She is and isn't my mother.

Murugan's head began to spin. He felt a rush of bitter bile in his throat, after all this, after all this, was he going to fail? Aambal's head felt as if something had taken hold of it and was twisting, dunking it in water till she couldn't breathe. She wanted to breathe. She must breathe. She must shake this off.

What could she do?

What could he do? He had to understand, to see. Where were the clues? Where was his brother? He knew. He had all the answers. Where was Theivanai, who could hear the gati of all things? She knew. She had heard it resounding inside him. Where were they all? He felt again all the things he had felt when he left Kailasa: he was alone.

Aambal felt alone. So alone. Where were the others? Thennan? The musicians? The healers? Where was her charioteer? He was her bodyguard too, wasn't he? Couldn't he see she was cold? She shook her head. Kandhan! He was here, he'd been here all this while. Why hadn't he spoken? She had been calling him for so long. Bah! Thinks he's a child. She would show him. Her fingers reached out and pinched, her voice continued, 'What is the secret?'

Aambal's voice cut through Murugan's thoughts. This, he knew. From the time they met, Aambal had pinched him when he did something she thought was stupid, and the bite of the pinch forced attentiveness: it reminded him that when he was among others, he could not play the fool. To Aambal, it was a matter of pride that he got it right, whatever it was. The sting of that memory now made him blind and deaf to everything but her voice, as it grew louder, sharper, more piercing, not the voice of a poet, but of a war bard, his war bard, Aambal, War Bard to Karthikeya Mahasena. Her voice swelled with the voices of all the bards that had sung to the warriors they guarded. Her words would lead him, direct him. She would not leave his side, of that he was sure, and Tamizh would never leave her—of that too he was certain. He waited.

Aambal was drenched in sweat flowing down her body, streaming over her eyelids and filling her eyes, but she sang, 'From the waves, more waves; to the waves, more waves. To Chendur by the sea and to Veeramahendrapuram. It is and it is not.'

The beat of her cymbals was now louder than the drumming of the bards, louder than the hiss of the mountain winds, the sea winds. The cymbals had come to life, with Aambal's desperation giving them a voice to outsound everything else. It was these cymbals that had been her constant strength, they had been measuring rod and flagpole, and so had the cymbals in Thennan's hand, its sound different from hers, but it had been beating along with hers. Thennan had stopped singing when Surapadman ran into the sea and became the suspended tree, but his own cymbals were echoing the beat of the one in Aambal's hands, and his voice joined hers, repeating words in the refrain of the beat cycle. 'Waves, waves, waves,' he repeated. 'Wave upon wave upon wave,' sang Aambal. The cymbal struck, one-two-three-four-one-two-three-four; one-two; one-two; one-two-three-four-one-two-three-four; one-two. The rhythm took hold of Aambal, the breath in her lungs lurched, her words crashed together and shattered, and the fragments came out of her mouth as something between moan and a growl.

Suddenly, it was as if the rhythm came to life, took hold of Thennan's hands and changed the beat and the tempo that he was following, the beat that Aambal was following. His became a quick, sharp rap of three, three, three, and from his mouth there issued words, 'On the hill, in the sea, the two cannot be two; it is time for the child-god to see his own face.' Aambal saw Murugan's head swerve back to the sea and to the giant mango tree, its roots writhing upwards. The beat of Thennan's cymbals continued, it got louder and he was repeating, 'In the sea, in the sea, look into the sea.'

Aambal's head felt like it was being kicked by wild horses raring to snap the ropes that had dared to bind them. It was difficult to breathe, and difficult to follow Thennan's beat. She looked up and tried to send her eyes towards the sea that Thennan was singing about, towards the 'child-god' that he was urging forward into the waves.

She was turned towards Thennan, but saw nothing, neither Murugan nor Thennan nor the sea or the Asura tree, for her eyes were filled with the form in front of her: mounted on a white swan, both woman and man, with chest and bosom, brandishing in one hand a large scorpion, its pincers snapping, and in their other, clutching a handful of twisting and slithering giant leeches. Aambal's eyes would not turn away. They were beautiful, their face was unlined, their features enchanting, their twin eyes showed no expectation, no comfort, no censure—all Aambal saw there was her own shape quivering in fear. Her tormented gaze began to make out a shape seated on their lap: the Beautiful One.

Why wasn't he smiling? Why wasn't he calling out to her? Why wasn't he saving her? Why was he not breaking free? It struck her then that she had to save him, she had to save Kandhan from the impassive being that had hold of him—they could not take him away. They must not. She must save him, she must prise him free. The thoughts charged through her mind, words spilt out of her mouth with neither sequence nor sense, the unhinged syllables became only sound, sound to the beat of cymbals.

Aambal's head rang with the voice of the oracle. She felt the press of the gnarled, ebony-stained hand. It seemed as if that hand was pressing her eyes shut, so Aambal closed them. The gnarled hand was at her back again, pressing down, down into Aambal's cold back, and a warmth spread through her body, her eyes, her throat. She felt her chest shudder as her heart warmed up, her hands moved and she raised her cymbals to her chest. The ancient oracle's voice was now a wordless grunt that grew deeper and louder, and Aambal felt her throat repeat the grunt, over and over, like an animal about to attack. She had to stop it, she must. But what was *it*? What was she? What was stopping? Where was Kandhan? She was slipping, the cymbals were slippery. She clutched it hard, pressing it deeper into her chest. And it seemed as if a beat sounded from inside her. Then it sounded outside her, it was everywhere, on the mountain, on the red beach, in the sea, inside Mahasena. And it was inside the great, beautiful and terrifying being, which she understood to be the Great Word-eating Being, Death, the one that bards and healers alike always set aside a place for when they imagined their work.

The beats were calling her to step closer and closer to the magnificent being, to become like them, serene, composed, beautiful, with a body of magnificent black. She wanted to let the cymbals slip, she wanted to slip into the arms of Death, to be seated next to her best friend, her master, the God of Tamizh, to become light and float away. She would no longer dismay at not being able to remember something, or feel the agony of being ignored by her playmates, the ones who always waited for her: words, language, poetry. She was tired, so tired, she was tired with the weight of what she had been. What did it matter? That was gone, she did not want to go chasing after it. She did not want to move.

Even as her body's weight seemed to pull her downwards, there was a voice in her head that asked, 'Everything? Kandhan? Tamizh? Poetry?' Kandhan, poetry, Tamizh. No, not those, she thought, her limp body stiffening, rising. She wasn't going to let go. She would fight even harder, for her friend, their friendship, their language and poetry. Her belly clenched, her feet stirred, but before she could step closer, the little boy seated on the lap of Death reached across and rapped her hand with the akil dandam, then tapped her heart and throat. A smouldering warmth, like the heat of the sun-soaked rocks on Pazhani, spread all through her.

A warmth burnt through Murugan's chest, it spread in waves to his arms all the way down to his fingers; it slipped down past his ribs, into his gut, loins, down his legs, to the tips of his toes. He shut his eyes and in his head the words resounded: *From the waves, more waves; to the waves, more waves. To Chendur by the sea; to Veeramahendrapuram, waves, waves, waves.*

He heard the waters surging back, its waves once again endlessly heaving from one to the other side, like the chest of an immeasurably large creature spanning both shores. His own chest heaved as if the sea was rushing in. He felt his ribs dissolving, his body heaving, rocking, ebbing and flowing. He was sea waves. The sea was his hands and legs, it was his hair, it was the vel. He was waves. His heart stopped beating. He did not have a heart. He did not have a body, he was … and he was not … his eyes flew open.

The upside-down tree hung there, over the waves of the sea, the sky leant down, the sea rose up, thousands of birds soared, swift-winged and raucous, out of its green. The air trembled with the call of birds, clouds drew closer to each other, and then suddenly, Surapadman was in front of him, the tree was gone: the mighty Asura spread everywhere, piercing through the stacks of the worlds, downwards and upwards. In his left hand, Maya flamed as if it was on fire. Nothing else was visible, no one else but the two of them. Murugan's vel now throbbed and grew fiery. Its heat moved through his hand, into his body, then outwards. Murugan felt himself flowing, surging, billowing, wave upon wave, he was and wasn't waves. He was and wasn't himself. The vel was burning, his hands were burning. Sparks darted and flared off the vel, his hand was glowing, he was glowing.

Murugan looked at Surapadman, who shone as if a fire burnt inside him. On his face was a question. He raised an eyebrow and laughed, and the laugh moved through Murugan's head like an expertly wielded broom, clearing everything in its path. The sounds that came from Aambal's throat rushed into his head, grunting and growling in his chest. Something stirred and rose, like the thousand hoods of a snake, its thousand fangs drawn, and from its thousand mouths, it hissed. In that hissing he could hear half of his own name Maha— Maha— Aambal's cymbals, accompanied by Thennan's crashed in an unforgiving beat. Murugan lifted his hand and raised the vel, which caught the light of the sky. He took aim, drawing his hand back, and hurled the vel towards Surapadman, who stood still, smiling. Murugan's eyes stayed on the vel, following its path towards the mighty Asura.

As the vel neared the Asura, Murugan felt something stirring inside his head, like a memory. He blinked, and Suran's chest was transparent, and inside it, Murugan saw his own hand, with its bracelets of aquamarine and pearls, reaching out towards the flying vel. He shuddered, his own chest began to hurt, as if it was caving in on itself. He stretched and his chest rent as if it were flimsy cloth, and light burst through, filling the sky and the red earth of Chendur. Ah! So this is what he was!

A sound filled the air, a word, a name—the name that was his, the name he had to go through all this to recall. Murugan felt himself break away from the hold of his body. He was back in the forest with his six Krittika mothers, and they were teaching him, answering his questions: What took life? *Mrtyu*. What gave life? *Ojas*. They had explained to him how ojas made everything grow and live, and mrtyu took that life away, but that there was something inside everything, moving and unmoving, everywhere in the universes, that is never destroyed—it is called the rasa, the sap. He remembered distilling the sap from plants to make the rejuvenating rasayana, carrier of rasa, which strengthened the rasa of those who partook of it and brightened their ojas. He remembered the other rasa, the supreme rasa that the wise ones imagined all creation to be made of. They imagined it as a being who nourished all creation, about whom they said, 'raso vai saha', it is truly rasa. That rasa had a name, it was in everything, it was everything ...

I am everywhere, I am in everything—there is nothing that I'm not in. There is nothing that is not I.

Delight rippled through Murugan, and through every being present on the battlefield, and it ran through all the worlds. Like the ripples of the sea. Murugan felt the joy flow though him and multiply endlessly—it was so vast, his joy was vast, he was vast, so vast. He was the Vast! He was endless rippling waves of delight from which and in which everything was. The Vast which was in everything. He was in everything, for he was everything, he was life, he was what flowed as the Supreme Sap in all things. He was what stayed unchanged. It was he whom they hailed, saying 'raso vai saha', for he was supreme, he was the Supreme Rasa. He was Maha-Rasa. He raised his head to the skies and called out over and over, 'Maharasa, Maharasa, Maharasa.'

Suran's laughter ran out of his belly and exploded from his mouth. He had won, he had won, the boy had done it! 'Vetri, Vetri,' Suran called. Murugan called out again and again, this time accompanied by Suran, 'Maharasa, Maharasa.' The warriors assembled there picked up the chant, 'Maharasa, Maharasa, Maharasa, Maharasa, Maharasa, Maharasa.'

Something burst inside her head, like the blue kurinji buds that thrust up through the mud and burst into flower. Death was looking at her, their mouth opened and they spoke, but Aambal did not hear what they said. Their eyes dissolved, their heads and their chest dissolved, their lap turned liquid and the beautiful little boy turned into a man in whose hand was a vel, its glow rivalling the sheen of the mid-day sun, in whose other hand was a stick from which endless green leaves sprouted and winged outwards. A hum filled the air, it fell all over her, her body thrummed and trembled with the hum. As Aambal watched, she saw the dissolving being's body take the shape of the many worlds. She saw that the man's head rose upward, higher than Kailasa and his feet stood lower than Patala. She saw the man bend his face to her, and she heard herself calling out 'Kandha' even as he too began to dissolve into rippling waves; everything dissolved to the rhythms of the hum. She herself was a ripple, billowing and surging, her heart became a tide of waves, curling upwards then crashing down. Her voice swelled into waves of sound, it rose in her throat and surged out towards the shore of language, it crashed and sounded out resonant, full of meaning, 'Maharasa, Maharasa, Maha Rasa,' it called out, and as she fell into a swoon, the last thing she heard was Kandhan's voice: 'Maharasa'.

12

IN THE AFTERMATH

Inside the watch tower, the fog that entered Ganesha's head on Chendur beach shifted, and the lost image became clear: a majestic red-and-black rooster, soaring into the air as no rooster could. He smiled.

Surapadman handed Murugan his vel with the words, 'Mahasena, Maharasa, the Supreme Rasa, I am glad that we were here, in these bodies, in this land, where the manava, who have neither immortality nor death-at-will, live each day searching for meaning. Here's your vel. I now take leave of you and of this shape and return home. Before I leave, I give you this.' So saying, he took one of his ears, one eye, a fistful of his own hair and flung it all into the air, and it turned into a red-and-black rooster that spread its wings, squawked and flew down to land in front of Murugan. Surapadman laughed and said, 'Muruga, here is Seval. He will be your companion, and he will carry my spirit, since you had wished at some time that I were your friend, Kumara. Seval will be your herald, he will go before you, heralding victory, and you will be known as Vetrivelan, and wherever they speak of your victory, there they will speak of me too, repeating the truth that I am you, I cannot be anything but you, for you are Maharasa.'

Aambal's cymbals sounded and she called out, in a loud and clear voice, 'Rooster red, rooster black, Velan's herald,' and fell down in a swoon. Thennan rushed to her side, breaking her fall. He squatted with her in his arms, rubbing her forehead to halt the passage of whatever she had seen in her trance from going deeper into her head. Then, Matri Dhumi took Aambal from him and carried her towards the physicians' tent, with Thennan running beside them.

Ganesha and Devayani had walked on to the battlefield by now. Mari's blue body had stilled, and she now stood beside the two Supreme Commanders, her hands raised in blessing. Surapadman, his handsome face itself again, turned towards Mari. He laid his head at Mari's feet, then embraced Murugan, and stood a moment, unspeaking, before ascending to the skies. The ululations of the dark waves sounded a lament for one who was beloved of them. When he was over Veeramahendrapuram, Surapadman exploded in a burst of light, the sound of the explosion ran through the battlefield, making every warrior's hair stand on end and the tears flow from every eye. The red sands heaved and trembled as if they had dissolved into water.

Murugan stood looking out at the sea. 'Aambal,' he said, and walked away, towards the tents. He blinked to get the image of Suran out of his eyes. His ears were ringing with the sound of Aambal's heaving breath. A giant, curling wave of despair rushed at him, but before it could crash against him, a shrill sound filled the air and Seval rose up, his red-and-black wings open, his crimson comb swaying. He was blowing on a little horn, its pip-pip-pippiri insistent, sharp. He called out, 'Hail Mutthukumarasami, who is like the bead that crowns Creation.' Murugan's steps did not slow, he did not turn his head, so Seval flew close to his ear and snapped, 'You'll fall if you go rushing blindly like that. And you'll scare everyone else. Slow down, you're Chenduran, the Lord of Chendur.' Murugan didn't stop or turn, but his steps did slow, he straightened his back and unclenched his hands. He drew a long breath and let it go slowly. Seval flapped around Murugan's ear and said, 'Good. That poor Aambal will be waking now, and she doesn't need to see you looking like you're going to her death bed.' Murugan stopped now and looked at Seval. He smiled and walked towards the physicians' tents.

༄

The next morning, after the battle was over, the field had been cleared and they were gathered to offer prayers and thanks to the elements and to Mari, who had been their witness. After this, those of the Asuras who remained would return to Veeramahendrapuram, accompanied by Surasa and Ajamugi. In their presence, Surapadman's daughter, the youngest of his children, Iraivi, who had been kept out of the battle for just such an eventuality, would be crowned the ruler. Those who had come to join the two armies from other worlds would wend their way homewards, perhaps making stops to offer prayers for those they had killed and defeated or for a sibling, friend or partner they had lost to the battle.

Seval had organised everything. He flew overhead, blowing on the little horn, a sound that could not be ignored. Murugan, Surasa and Ajamugi stood at the edge of the sea, all around them, the warriors were sombre. Aambal and Thennan, with the accompaniment of their cymbals and a muted chorus of the other instruments, sang the song sung after all battles. They ended by praising the two sides and eulogising the battle's last moments when Supreme Commanders Surapadman and Mahasena had brought an end to the six days of battle. They thanked and blessed, as bards are required to, the earth that had allowed the warriors to stand and fight, the sea that had borne witness, they thanked the Lord of Obstacles and Mari. As their voices died down, Seval let out a crowing that caused them both to start. He was glaring. 'How did you forget me, you two bards? Clearly you need a lesson in battlefield etiquette.' With that, Seval snorted and flew on to the helm of Murugan's chariot, hovering over the two black horses, and as the amused crowd watched, an image of him, red and black, appeared on the flag that flew from the chariot. He turned to Murugan and said, 'What are we waiting for? Let's get on with the day.' Murugan smiled, a little embarrassed at the laughter that broke out. Seval was not going to be easy, he thought, not like Paravani. He sighed. He had missed Paravani, but the wise bird had been right. He could not have been the vehicle for Murugan in this battle.

Murugan went to meet Aambal, who was walking in his direction. He knew that she would need to rest, and it would be a long one, for there was a road she must traverse before she could return to her life. Time had snatched Aambal and taken her into the otherwise-forbidden cave of his heart. What she had seen there had retreated into its lair for the moment, waiting for a time after she had successfully completed all of her duties as this battle's bard. And then it would return and it would not let her go. She would have to fight her way through, for Time, like Death, did not suffer trespass, even if they themselves had initiated that fracturing of boundaries.

Aambal smiled. She looked towards her grandparents, parents, brother and sister, but she was distracted. What about Thennan? Would he disappear once more? And be gone for ten years before she saw him again? Seval was watching her, his eyes narrowed in concentration. He rose up into the air, circling, scanning the milling crowd. Seval called out to someone, and when he flew back to where Murugan and Aambal were, Thennan was with him.

Thennan saluted Murugan and said, 'My Lord, I take your leave now.'

'Where are you going?' Murugan asked. 'Now that the king is gone?'

Seval said, 'He should come to Pazhani. There's much work for him. So many poems and songs to tune.'

'Yes,' replied Murugan, as if remembering something, 'you should, Thennan. Come to Pazhani.'

'I have to go back to Veeramahendrapuram for the crowning of the young princess. I also need to go home for some time. After all that is done, I will come up to Pazhani.' He looked at Aambal, and asked, 'Aambal, you live in Pazhani too?'

She felt her ears tingle with the sound of his voice, her chest was warm. She straightened up—that always worked—and said, 'Yes, I live there. I too will return to Pazhani later. I will go home now.'

Murugan told Thennan and Aambal that he would send word for them. He turned to Seval, and said, 'Okay, let's go.' Then he held Aambal's hands for a moment, his own trembling, and lifted her writing hand to his chest, pressing his lips onto the cold, clammy skin. He could feel the waves of his heart roaring, the tide of tears rushing. Aambal smiled at him and he smiled back. He let go of her hands and said, 'Go now. I will see you soon at home, in Pazhani.' She turned and walked towards her tent, and her brother and sister came running, calling, 'Aambu, Aambu.' The elders waited by the tent, their eyes wet with tears, their faces blossoming with happiness.

Ganesha and Theivanai were waiting for Murugan. The giant rooster winged ahead, the sharp notes from his horn flying forth and assailing all ears. Ganesha turned to Theivanai and said, 'Theivanai, here comes Maharasa.' He smiled. She too smiled and repeated, 'Maha-Rasa, Ma-ha-ra-sa.'

the poet's victory

1

A SOJOURN IN MAYILAI

Ganesha and Murugan's parents sent a message with an invitation to all on the battlefield to their seaside home in the old town of Mayilai, one of their favourite dwellings on Bhu. Many accepted, including Theivanai, and on the day after the battle ended, a large group began the journey that way. Ganesha travelled with them a little way and then took his leave of them, saying, 'Pothigai waits. I have work to do there, it will come looking for me.' Murugan embraced his brother who uncharacteristically held on, kissing him over and over on the forehead before letting go.

Murugan, Theivanai and the others travelled on to fabled Mayilai, nestled like a bright jewel in the protective arms of the sea. This was the city where everything was available, where everything was better than anywhere else. A visit to Mayilai, the proverb went, could turn one's head, make one forget the way home. Head for Mayilai, they told finicky folk who fussed over the quality and variety of goods sold in smaller towns, you'll find ten when you look for one, and when you need ten, you'll want a hundred. The streets were a delight to the eyes, the buildings that rose upward past the tree tops and spread outward like embroidery around the magnificent dwelling of Kapali and Amba, as Shambhu and Parvathy were called here. Their home was the heart of this ancient town, close to the seashore from where boats went out from and returned to after fishing and trading, crossing the waters to the islands of Ilangkai, Veeramahendrapuram and beyond.

Mayilai was dear to their parents, Ganesha had said to Theivanai, and like most things that they held dear, this was also part of their love story. Here, their mother had come once long ago, following a quarrel with their father. Firmly putting him out of her mind, she decided to concentrate on herself alone. She wandered through the streets, entering shops that caught her eye, and walked along the beaches, singing songs she had heard on the street. She sat down with other women in the open courtyards of the big trade houses, waiting for the auctions of cloth, jewellery and spices left over from a season's cycle of trade. She walked with the women to the markets, happily taking part in picking out vegetables, fish, meat, spices and oils, and accompanied them as they went in and out of stores, looking for a colour of fabric they had caught a glimpse of somewhere. She ate with them at least once a day, and accompanied them on their weekly outings when they went in bullock carts past the town, along the beaches to secluded seashore villages, where the fisherfolk worshipped the sea with feasts of rice and fish and offered up ornaments fashioned from shells and fish bones. She abandoned the rough white kora selai she wove for herself up in Kailai, bought fine silks and soft cottons and put on ornaments of gold and precious gems, and she learned to cook like Mayilai's women, who were delighted to have the Mother of the Worlds in their midst.

'Mother,' Ganesha had said, 'was irrigating herself. It was here that she experienced the joy of being alone. Of being separate from Father.' Murugan, who knew the story, had laughed, adding, 'And to their relief they found that though they were so close that they were like one, they could separate and be happy on their own, too.'

Ganesha then told the rest of the story. After days passed and Parvathy neither returned nor sent for him, Shambhu became restless. He was desperate, he thought of all kinds of things he could do, but she'd been clear, she had said, 'Don't follow me.' And he knew her anger well enough to not disregard this. His dejection allowed him to do nothing else, and with all the time that he spent thinking about how to get her to relent, it wasn't long before an idea struck. She had said nothing about him appearing in her dreams. And so he began to do that. As soon as she fell into sleep, he would appear, on his cloud-like bull, his ruddy locks tumbling down his bare chest, the udukkai knotted to his waist, knocking against his hip, his eyes dark and moist with tears. She would wake up, and her thoughts would go to him and to their home on high Kailasa.

But she was determined to not succumb. This was a trick, she knew it. She asked her friends to procure for her a charm to ward off night-time spirits, and the women, to whom she was one of them, and so they treated her like they treated each other, not only got her a charm but also came in groups in the evenings and sat up with her, singing songs about the divine couple that lives in all things. Parvathy laughed to herself, a trick for a trick, she thought. But she waited for the next trick. She knew there would be one.

Shambhu called on the birds and trees and sand and wind and all things in the town to whisper his many names. The bees that swarmed around the garlands hung up outside the flower stalls buzzed 'Sham-bhu-Sham-bhu'. As she passed by, storekeepers called out 'Shiva Shiva', and did not know why. Parvathy was prepared, and didn't let all this drama distract her.

As he observed this, Shambhu thought that he had to surprise her, and so, decided to lie low for the moment. One day, as she sat listening to the distant roar of the waves of the sea, she saw ahead of her an army of ants marching up and down, in and out, and before she knew it, they had built a linga rising out of a yoni, the symbol that the wise ones had created to represent her and him, always attached, in union, him inside her. Even as she admired it, the wind suddenly picked up pace, the roar of the sea grew louder, and the waves leapt over the distance of the shore and rushed towards the sand structure, moments away from washing over it. Without thinking, Parvathy leapt up and embraced it, and the sea washed over her, then retreated. And she felt the sand turn to flesh as the man-half of the structure took on body, and her body, which had missed his, allowed him in. This spot was where their Mayilai home was built, and where the two waited now to welcome their son and his retinue.

Theivanai, Murugan, the Matris, the Bhutas of Kailasa, Gandharvas, Rakshasas and all others who had accepted the invitation travelled slowly, resting at spots along the way to let their bodies discard the frenetic rhythm of the battle and become like the swaying trees that let down their guard and let the winds go on their way without challenge. It was Seval who decided that Murugan should put on his armour when they neared the big town, 'The people of Mayilai would like to see you in your martial grandeur.' It was also Seval who had decided that Murugan and Theivanai should ride together in the grand chariot from which Murugan's new standard flew, a yellow background against which the black-and-crimson of a martial-looking rooster stood out. In fact, it seemed to be alive, its hackles and wings tossed about by the wind. Seval sometimes perched on the helm of Murugan's chariot or flew ahead, chatting with Matri Dhumi, who rode in front of the train of battle-weary warriors making their way to the rest and luxury that Mayilai promised, before taking the homewards road. Whenever Murugan and Theivanai's voices drifted into his ears, Seval smiled.

Theivanai was glad to go to Mayilai—she had enjoyed Ganesha's company during the battle, and was glad that he was accompanying them a little ways. She was curious about Murugan, with whom she had hardly spent any time. During the journey, more than once, she thought back to how amused and pleased she had been when he caught sight of her at the war council and his steps slowed. It was clear he was drawn to her—that was not unusual—it was the fact that he slowed and paid attention that she liked. This must be the effect he has on everyone, she thought, he is, after all, the handsomest man in all creation. And the most intelligent, she added. She looked forward to seeing Murugan and Ganesha's parents in Mayilai where, it was said, they grew lighter, more jovial, and they did things separately, differently.

While Mother Parvathy wore bright clothing and jewellery, and spent her days with Mayilai's woman, the butter-hearted Shambhu took to the roads, going hither and thither with bands of renunciates who had journeyed to Mayilai from all over the land. He cast off the animal skin from around his waist and wore a swathe of mud-coloured cloth, took up a skull and unbound his luxuriant jata from on top of his head. When the ascetics came to the gate of Shambhu's dwelling, called his name and beat on a parai or tudi or twanged an ektara, he dropped whatever he was doing and ran out to meet them, trident in one hand, skull begging bowl in the other. And then they were off, the wild bunch, matted jata swinging, bald heads shining, music playing, voices singing, letting their feet decide where they were to go. They crossed streets, fields, forests and went up the hills and into the valleys, and as they passed, women and men left their work and came out to stand and stare. Their hearts leapt and some of them left their homes and their people and followed the untethered footsteps of these nomads, whose hearts were so on the boil that they could not stand still.

⁂

When the guests finally arrived, Mayilai was festive and jubilant with the grand welcome Murugan's parents had arranged. The streets were lined with townspeople—dancers, musicians, men and women carrying lamps. Garlands hung from poles and posts lining the roads, minstrels stood in groups singing songs of the battle, the beats of ten types of parai and of the tavil resounded, interweaving with the melody of nadaswarams that played mallari and joining the drumbeats. As they neared the palace, the parents came out to welcome their son and his companions. Theivanai was delighted to see the cloud of chattering parrots that flew around the goddess. Seval had told her that, here in the south, when parrots flew overhead, people stopped and bent their heads and asked for the benediction of the messengers of Mari, Goddess of Rain, and of her companion, the gentle wild one.

Mayilai immediately gladdened Murugan: the bustle and rush, the sounds of variously inflected Tamizh, of carts laden with goods rolling down the streets, the shouts of the cart drivers as they yelled to bystanders to move, the colour of the grains, vegetables, fish, fruit, meats, the glass ornaments, flowers and the endless variety of goods that lined both sides. This was exactly what he needed after the rigour of the battle, the losses and deaths. And because his parents were so different here, the associations of Kailasa did not cloud his thoughts, and Murugan too was lighter.

He was delighted by the way his father ran off with the mendicants, and by how the women teased his mother about this.

'Your handsome husband's gone wandering, has he?' one asked.

'Are you sure he'll come back home?' asked another.

'What if he finds someone he likes better than you?' someone else asked.

Another one cackled and said, 'And you as dark as a seed, burnt by the sun.'

And his mother laughed and said to them, 'If he goes, let him go, I'll come and live with you.'

They laughed, and so did Murugan and Theivanai.

The two of them spent virtually all their time in Mayilai together, and when Theivani left, Murugan felt like the days had been too few. They went on outings and visits that Seval arranged every day. In Mayilai, Murugan had no dearth of jewellery, clothes, footwear, and the flower-sellers vied with each other to bring him garlands of the just-about-to-open red kadamba that he so loved, of the sharp-needle malligai, of kuvalayam and handfuls of delicate thumpai. They looked at him and beamed with pride as he walked down the streets of their town, or rode by in his chariot, wearing the intricate garlands and arm bands they had made, his long hair, oiled, perfumed and braided with their flowers, and they called out to him, 'Vela, Vela, Singaravela.' They said to each other, 'Singaravelan, the beautiful dandy, those are my flowers over his heart.'

Theivanai wanted to see everything, she wanted to buy bangles and beads and yards of cloth, she followed the smells that came wafting in the wind. Sometimes it would be the hill honey that hunters brought down from the distant hills north of Mayilai, or grain being threshed somewhere, or newly plucked chillies being fried in fresh oil. She bought flowers and wore them in her hair and around her neck and wrists, and Murugan, who needed no persuasion to wear more flowers, added whatever she held out to the garlands of kadamba that were always on his chest and in his hair. She asked where the weavers lived and where the children were taught, where the scribes lived and where the maroon kungumam was made.

In her company, Murugan forgot all about the battle, about the secret and about all those who had died or left their bodies and returned to the Vast. He forgot that he was the Vast and that everything was he, and that everybody lived in him and he in them. He became what he was happiest being: a companion. Like with Aambal, with Theivanai, he felt the thrill of receiving affection that was weighted and deliberate: Aambal had chosen to be his friend, she chose to accompany him and to save his life. Theivanai had chosen to accompany him, to spend time with him. He delighted in his attraction to her and in hers to him, and how it flowed into everything they did together: how they spoke to each other, how they walked with each other, how they waited for the nights to pass so that they could wake up and meet to begin another day. He forgot that he was Love and Language, and instead became a vessel in which love and language awaited the catalyst that would blend them into one.

Murugan was waiting to speak to her about what he was feeling. We don't know what she was thinking, but it was clear from the way she looked at him and the way she laughed and flirted and fought with him that she had allowed him to get so very close to her. That was what Seval said to Nandi, the wise bull who was his favourite friend, perhaps because Nandi did not speak at all, and he could run on without interruption.

On many a day that he spent with Theivanai, the secret of her birth came back to Murugan. It was Matri Dhumi who had told him the story. An infant Theivanai had appeared out of nowhere in the inner courtyard of Indra and Indrani's palace, her presence announced by a disembodied voice that said, 'This is a blessing given to Sachi Indrani, queen of the Suras.' At that time, Indra and Indrani's first child had just been born, and Indrani was afflicted by a terrible sadness that would not pass. She neither ate nor slept, and could not bear to look on other people. When news of this other baby's arrival was taken to the king and queen, he was filled with a sense of helplessness. Indrani looked at the baby and turned her head away.

In the cradle, their infant son, Jayantha kicked his hands and legs and gurgled, as if he was calling to be taken out of his mother's joyless room, and his nursemaids, knowing this, complied and did so for a little while. Airavata, the white elephant, scholarly, musical, kind, gentle and enormously patient, said to the king that he would be glad to care for the girl child who had come from nowhere. Thus, Theivanai, then Devayani, grew up in the care of the elephant. Airavata also persuaded the king to allow Jayantha to be brought out of the queen's chambers to spend more time with Devayani. Many moons passed before Indrani regained herself, and resumed her life, eagerly leaving the confines of her room. The two children were walking and talking by then, and Indrani's heart filled with all the affection that had lain there, like the snow that ices over on the topmost caves of Kailasa and melts in the overwintering. She hugged the two, and as she held Devayani close, she understood that this child had come to her as a boon from the universe, for it was because she had been a companion that the boy Jayantha had been able to shake off the breath of the creature that had taken his mother in its claws.

In Mayilai, Murugan heard the rest—or rather, the before—of this story from Seval, who had it from Nandi. Before she had come to Indrani's court, Theivanai had appeared in the home of Vishnu and Lakshmi in a little basket, wrapped in soft cloths. There was a flash of light and a voice spoke in the air to announce that, because Lakshmi has been longing for a child, a girl child, here were two little girls for her. Lakshmi was beside herself with joy, and gathered up both children in her arms and kissed their faces, her own glowing. What a turn of fate! She was forbidden to have children, since she was the Goddess of Fortune and Success and needed to keep her head, and apparently, children made that impossible. The voice continued, 'But beware, let them not become distractions, for the order of the worlds depends on you.'

The two girls were named, one by Lakshmi and one by Vishnu, the former was called Amruta and the second, Pushpa. Vishnu and Lakshmi loved the little girls and spent as much time as they could with them. Lakshmi longed to nurse them at her breast, and as if her breasts couldn't bear her sadness, they became full with milk, and as she sat by the window, under the stars, or by the glow of the sun, there was a look on her face that made Vishnu stop and sigh. She woke several times during the nights to watch the sleeping faces of her daughters, and Vishnu stirred on his side and smiled at her. He was afraid for her, for himself, but he could not tell her that he feared she was becoming distracted. He tried to ask her what she would she do if the girls had to go away, but Lakshmi snapped at him.

Then it happened—a curse on the couple. As it has been before and as it will be after, this fatal curse came from a discontented man, the sage Durvasa, the Angry One. He came visiting Vishnu, and at the door, called out in his cranky voice that had never uttered a word in love, nor knew the embrace of a lover, or tasted the salt of sweat on a beloved's lips. When the sage came, Vishnu and Lakshmi were on their bed, embracing and making love, the twin girls asleep in their cradles. Lakshmi was amorous, and Vishnu nuzzled at her neck, her shoulder blades and as his face moved downwards, Lakshmi's breasts swelled and the milk spilt, his lips opened and he drank deep of the sweet, warm flow and she sighed with pleasure. The sigh resounded and rang through the worlds, filling all growing things with quickening delight.

The sage's anger surged when he heard it. He had sensed that something was happening that was distracting Vishnu and Lakshmi from the sound of his voice calling their names, and the sigh confirmed that they were lost in amorous play, they did not know he was there. He was furious. Happiness! Pleasure! Delight! Those blights that covered the eyes with cataract and blinded people to duty. These two, the Lord Who Sleeps on Time and the Goddess of Good Fortune, they were deaf to him, and he, a sage of such merit. They had a duty to do, and if they didn't do it, they must be cursed. He held out the palm of one hand and poured into it water from his water pot, and flinging that water into the air, began his curse, 'May they lose that which is most dear to them.' As the words were leaving the dour sage's mouth, Ganesha materialised there and held him by the arm in a vice-like grip, full of an anger that he rarely felt, and he whispered to the sage, 'Only to find them later and to bring them back to the family.' The sage was afraid. Here was the gentle Lord of Obstacles who never got angry, and he was furious now. He acquiesced and was about to scamper away when Ganesha said, 'No, no, don't leave just yet, let's tell them what you've done.'

Durvasa stood facing the couple and their nephew: he was afraid, not of Vishnu, who was calmer than he felt, but of Lakshmi, whose face was clouded and whose hands were clenched.

She said to him, 'You whose anger is the cause of so much distress wherever you go, may it turn on you and burn up your merit. May the disdain you have for women and their happiness cause you to be born again and again into lives that are cold, without love and may your anger make you reviled and rejected. As for the two little girls you've caused to be lost to us, they were never ours, they were made from my longing and Vishnu's, and they will merge back into the Vast, but they will come back to us. For they will be reborn.'

Thus it was that the two little girls disappeared, and then they reappeared. One of those two girls was Theivanai, who appeared as a little baby in a golden basket wrapped in silk cloth in the court of Indra and Indrani soon after the birth of Jayantha. As for the other one, we don't know where she is just yet.

Airavata cared for the child with all the warmth and love that a mother would. He educated her, ensured that she grew up to be intelligent, kind and curious, and named her 'Devayani', the Path of Deva. She was, like her name, shining and splendorous. As she grew, Airavata doted on her, taught her music and recitation, and sent her to teachers across the worlds to learn all their languages. She could, he realised, understand the speech of animals, especially the four-footed, and she had an uncanny sense of rhythm: she could hear the beat inside of things and beings. She could sit beside a tree and its thrum would tell her that a part of its trunk would one day become a drum, a seat for the Poet's Assembly on Bhu, a swing for a garden, a cradle and whatnot.

Unexpectedly, Murugan had a glimpse of Theivanai's felicity with sound, its implicit rhythm and beat cycles. One day, Father Shambhu sent word for Murugan and Theiva. He sat them down and read to them a passage from a compendium that a scholar was putting together. It spoke of the metre called Manasa-sahasa: the valour of Mind-Heart. This metre did not specify a sound pattern in its grammar or commentaries, but for it to fall into that sound pattern, what was required was the insertion of 'a pause so minute that perhaps it sounded only in the mind'. The author's lumbering prose was not only difficult to understand but also robbed the actual process of its liveliness, the burst of spontaneous 'seeing' that such a metre, when sounded, would bring to the listener.

Kandhan knew that Father was itching to be off with the drunken mendicants who were camped outside, waiting for him to be free, but he had to finish the editing because he had promised to, and the writing was driving him to despair. Mother, Nandi and several others had already declined to undertake this thankless task. Perhaps each of them was also a little envious, mildly resentful even, of how Father could just abandon everything and be off when his friends came calling.

When Murugan and Theivanai entered the room, Shambhu was smiling benignly. Murugan grinned. Ah, he thought, he looks as innocent as a baby.

'Children,' Father said, with a wide smile and fake casualness, 'I have a riddle for you.'

Theivanai knew something was afoot, though not quite what, but she cheerfully joined in.

When Shambhu explained the riddle and said, 'It is heard but unsounded,' she immediately replied, 'Rhythm cycles.'

Shiva clapped in appreciation, and then read out the passage. He was pleased to see that Theivanai frowned hard at the clumsy part, as if it hurt.

She said, 'I can sense the meaning of what he is saying, but I am not getting it from the words. He's describing a metre that has an unsounded beat. I get that, but the sequence isn't clear—does the gap come first in thought or in the fingers?'

Shiva picked up his udukkai and beat it out, while speaking the beats, and Theiva's tongue clicked in wonder. She said, 'I see! Like that. It is not so much a matter of thinking, but of not thinking about it—the regular beats are thought of, but this one is a negation of thought. I see, but how to describe it?'

Shiva held out the udukkai to Theivanai. Kandhan's eyebrows shot up, but Theiva was unaware of the significance of this moment. Father was handing her his udukkai: he never ever gave it to anyone. Theiva took it from him and momentarily held it in both hands, she could hear the impending sound, and she tapped away to approval from Father.

'That's exactly it,' he said. When she stopped, he took the udukkai back and looped it into the band of his waist cloth, and said, 'My child, you appear to understand this so clearly, better than I. My dear wife and son and Nandi didn't get it at all. I think this passage deserves to be edited by you.' He thrust the palm leaf bundle into her hands, turned on his heels and was out of the room, grabbing up the skull begging bowl on the way out.

Seval appeared at the door as Shiva was making his dash, and said loudly, 'Neatly done, my Lord,' with the little sneer in his voice that nobody resented.

Every day there was something new that had been planned for Theivanai, and Murugan was so happy in her company that he lost track of the days. It was a season such as Murugan had never lived in—in many ways, it reminded him of his early childhood in the forest, hidden away from everyone, the unrestrained joy of his spirit running wild in six stout, glowing little boy bodies, his joy accentuated by the joy that flung itself at him from everything else. With Theiva, Murugan was unguarded in a way that he rarely was. Even with Aambal, there was the slight reserve, necessary now that he was her master and she his apprentice. He felt sometimes as if he was floating in the river of his childhood, unthinking. He didn't have to worry about what he said or asked for—it was as if, in Theiva's presence, everything was just right. The days were light, effervescent, and Murugan wished they would just go on and on.

Then, one morning, something happened that fell into their mood, and like a well-aimed pebble, created ripples. It also brought an end to their sojourn, sending them both back to their respective homes. The day began, as did many other days. They walked down towards the sea, their steps almost skipping along, when Theiva said, 'I want sea-blue glass bangles.' They turned to the northwest, where the glass-makers lived, the spot where the wind was least likely to disturb their fires. The streets were ordered in grids that fell away from the enormous workshop that ran the breadth of the entire colony. Suddenly, Theivanai stopped and grabbed his hand, steering him away to their left. She led him down a couple of streets and then stopped outside a house where people were gathered, many of them elderly women. She looked at Murugan and said, 'Go in! They need your help.' Murugan looked at her quizzically, but knew her well enough by now to understand that she was not joking. As he moved through the crowd, he was quickly recognised and a buzz went up. 'Singaravelan,' they whispered. 'Singaravelan and the daughter of the king of the gods.' An elderly man stepped up to him and greeted him with folded hands. He said, 'Vela, your mother had said that she would send someone in her place, but we didn't expect it to be you. Help my granddaughter, please.'

Murugan couldn't help smiling. Of course this was no accident, nothing Theivanai did was accidental. And nothing she had initiated had been uninteresting. The old man told him that his granddaughter was in labour and Mother Parvathy had promised to bring midwives from the neighbouring town as Mayilai's midwives were on their annual renewal pilgrimage. But a messenger had come with a message from her to say that she was sending someone else instead of the midwives. 'Help us,' the old man appealed to Murugan, and Murugan assented. Also, his interest was piqued—his mother never failed a promise. He turned back to look for Theiva, and she was standing with a group of the younger women of the household. She smiled, making Murugan's steps quicker. He wanted to do this task, do it well, do it with a flourish!

The young woman was enclosed in a circle of people, her tawny face aglow with her exertions, eyes wide with alarm, breath quick and sharp. A midwife was fanning her uncovered belly with a bundle of tender, translucent neem leaves. It was distended and rippling with the movements of the babies inside pushing to come out. Murugan stopped short in his tracks. Three? Three babies? He was delighted. If he had stayed as he was at birth—six of him—or if not six, at least three, instead of one, how different his life would have been. So what was keeping the babies inside, he wondered. Murugan turned to Theivanai, who nodded towards the bed. He had to help the woman give birth?

The women were abuzz now, the older ones' eyes shone with reverence for the son of the parents of all things, some of the younger women's eyes were leaping to his broad chest, his strong arms, his lips. The woman on the bed looked at him. She said, 'Velan has come. It's time.' She held out her hand and all eyes turned to Murugan. He did not know what he would do, but sat down next to the bed, facing the young woman. She reached over and took his free hand, the other one held the akil dandam. His fingers curled around her hand, and he began to understand what was happening.

This young woman had held on to the birth till he arrived. So she knew he would come there, which meant his mother knew that the girl wanted him there. Ha! This meant the girl had had a bet with someone that she could make him come and deliver her babies! He handed the dandam to one of the women, retrieved his other hand from the mother-to-be's clasp, and placed both on her belly.

He smiled at her and asked, 'Why?'

'I was angry,' she said, 'when I heard them say that you were not like your father, who they call Ammai-Appan, Mother-Father, and that, unlike him, you could never be gentle enough to deliver babies. They said that the maker of Tamizh was too caught up with language to care about mundane things.'

Was that true, Murugan wondered, was he detached and forgetful of the things that made the mundane world? Was this world less interesting to him than the world of language? The thought made him sad. He turned to Theivanai, who shook her head. With her left hand she made a gesture, the pointing finger turned up, then down, and then she clasped both hands together. She was saying to him, 'This is that, you love both.' He felt as if he was standing on Pazhani Hill, cool winds blowing, the valleys around the hill lit up by a full moon, the stretch of black sky speckled with stars, of which six were always brighter than the rest. His chest heaved and settled his tumultuous heart.

He called for water, took off his headgear, the jewels on his fingers and hands, and after washing and drying both hands, leant over the pregnant woman. With his eyes closed, Murugan invoked his brother, the One That Guards All Effort. His mind was full of the memory of Chiruthai, who had been delivered by his father, high up in Kailasa, on a cold, cold day when snow was falling and the wind was a giant hissing creature thrusting its claws into every pore of the body. He smiled and said to the woman, 'You have won your bet. Make me a promise before your three children come into the world.' She nodded vigorously, and he whispered something to her that no one else heard.

When he put one hand on her belly, the three twisting little bodies stilled. 'Breathe slowly, and push.' As she began to push, the elder women moved quickly, holding up a white cloth, shielding the birthing. Murugan's other hand, oiled and gentle, entered the cave of her, and into it swam the first head. He tugged gently, and out came the first child, a girl with a bald head and a tinkling laugh. One of the women stepped in and cut the cord that bound the girl to her mother and to her siblings, then the other two births happened quickly, a boy and then another girl. The mother lay there, beaming and spent. Murugan wiped her clean and folded a soft white cloth between her legs and looped its end into her waistband. He took her hands and kissed them and then her forehead, and took leave as the babies were being placed next to her. Someone was helping her up, so she could nurse them at her breasts, which were leaping with pride that the King of Pazhani, the God of Tamizh, had not only delivered her babies, helping her win her bet, but he had also demanded a gift.

Later, when Theivanai questioned him, Murugan told her that he had asked that the three children be sent to Aasaan at Pazhani to be tutored in Tamizh. He said, 'When Aambal is no more, one of them will be her.' He looked pensive, and Theivanai said, 'That's a long time away.'

She took Murugan's hand as they were walking back. 'You look thoughtful. What are you thinking of?' He did not answer her, and later, he was restless. He could not drop off to sleep as gently and effortlessly as he usually did. So he stepped out and wandered the streets till he came to the sea. There, as Murugan sat watching the stars and the waves, his mind went back to the sea at Chendur, and all that had passed. But that was not what was keeping him awake—he soon had to return to the thing that was bothering him. What was it about today? Why had Mother left town? Why had

Theivanai walked him towards that house? What was that look he had seen in her eyes? When he held the babies, looking into eyes that were seeing the world for the first time, had she seen his thoughts? Had she known that he was thinking of his own birth, of how he had always had to leave one home for another till he built himself one? And what that had made him resolve?

He heard the calls of owls echoing in the beach groves. His thoughts turned once again to his exile from Kailasa. No, nothing about this day had made him change an old resolve: he would never have children.

Murugan did not fear that he would neglect the world for love of language and poetry, nor did he believe that he might neglect his own children for that love. But who would have thought that his parents, who parented all of creation, would neglect theirs? Murugan sat on the beach for a long time, but did not call to his six mothers who were looking down at him. He wanted to be alone, as he was back in his cave of silence. Also, he was settling his heart, for he knew that his carefree sojourn in his parents' home was at an end. He had to go home now, and settle it and himself down. He had work to do, and he also had to mark another stage in his and Theivanai's relationship. Finally, he fell asleep, lightened: he had made his peace with the decision to never father children of his own. And he decided to ask Theivanai if she would marry him.

The next morning, Murugan asked Theiva if they could go for a walk in the kadamba grove. The air around them filled with the cries of birds and animals who, sensing that Murugan wanted to be alone, did not approach them. Theivanai felt the stilling that came over the forest as everything, including the wind, fell silent, and she thought, ah, they're going quiet so that I don't lose any of what he's going to say. As they walked, Murugan stumbled, but Theivanai's left foot pressed into the ground and she grabbed his waist. For a few moments, they were frozen like that, Murugan mid-fall, Theivanai bent over him, one arm around his back, the other ringed around the front at his waist. As he looked at her, against the green of trees and the blue of the distant sky, the two sparkling eyes in her face seemed like two silver-winged birds, ready to soar. He did not want to move. This was a feeling that he had not felt since he was a child: that someone was strong enough to still him, to make him let go of his wilfulness. He exhaled, and it seemed to crack open the spell that had bound them. She pulled him upright. 'You almost fell,' she said seriously. Murugan said nothing, his back was still tingling with the strength it had felt in Theivanai's arms. She had pulled him up effortlessly.

They sat down and Murugan looked at her, suddenly feeling as if he had nothing to say, as if she knew what he was going to say. 'Muruga,' her voice broke in, 'were you not going to tell me something?' He felt his body growing warm, he couldn't hide anything from her. This was how it was when he first saw her. He wanted to slow his footsteps and let his breathing calm so he could match her breath, to let her look at him and to hear her voice in his ears. And so he spoke—of the competition for the fruit of wisdom, of the feeling that the world was crashing around him, the revulsion he felt towards his parents, towards all parents, the despair, the shame. He spoke at length, and he held nothing back. It was like a weight had fallen from his heart and an old skip returned to its beat.

He felt the rightness of it: he who was the God of Language giving word to his experience, languaging an unarticulated part of his life. At the end of his narration, he said, 'I will never have children of my own. I may believe now that I could never be the kind of parent that my parents were to me, but I cannot be sure that there will be no times when I am distracted by the life of my language, the growing needs of poetry and poets, of music and lyric.' He did not know what to do now that he had revealed himself to her. He sat still, his eyes turning, as they always did, towards the six stars that were now invisible, but present in the northern sky. They were proof of how well a child could be raised, he thought and smiled. Maybe he took after them? But no! He would not take that chance. Or perhaps it was that he already had a child, one he had carried and birthed, not once, but twice? The spirited, demanding child that had grown into a full-bodied adult, but was still a child to him: his beloved Tamizh.

Theivanai placed her hand over his and said nothing. They sat like that for a while. Then, Murugan turned to her and asked, 'Will you marry me?' She smiled, but was silent for a little while, and then told him that she would like some time to think about it and that she would also like to return to her parents' home soon.

Murugan had grown so used to Theivanai that he felt as if a part of him would be missing when she left. He did not want her to leave. He wanted to take her to the forest where he had been born, and where he had been undilutedly happy, where he had first understood how life was an inseparable mix of activity and rest. But she would leave. Murugan had not thought that asking her to marry him would happen so spontaneously, it had followed the moment of their closeness. Had he been too hasty? Had she thought that he wanted to marry her because she was comforting? Had he been clumsy in his proposal? He had, after all, said nothing about falling in love with her. About how each day spent in her presence had been a celebration for him. About how she always brought everything alive, about how, for the first time, he was encountering someone whose delight in everything matched his. It made him feel as if he were back in his forest, and there were six of him, touching, tasting, smelling, joying, and there was six of Theiva doing the same. He had never felt this resonance with another.

A few days later, Theivanai left for home. Murugan felt as if someone had blindfolded him and, as they do in the child's game, sent him spinning. He couldn't stop turning round and round. He longed for the one place that would always steady him, to be free of the box that Mayilai had shrunk to, and go to Pazhani Hill, which tricked one into thinking it was a smaller and easier climb than it actually was, and he could walk and walk and still feel as if it stretched on and on. He set off for home.

2

AAMBAL RECOVERS

While all this was happening, Ganesha was on Pothigai and Aambal was struggling to heal. In the trances induced by the bards' recitation, she began to regain memory, but when she tried to grasp language, it continued to run from her. Even after her final trance, in which she came back face-to-face with Death and saw that Murugan was the child seated on Death's lap and that he was the Maha Rasa, Maharasa, and despite having spoken the name aloud, she remained mute.

The Kani took her up the mountain, as close to the sun as they could get, and made her strip and lie down on the sun-warmed rocks. They sang to her, held her hands, rubbed her forehead and embraced her when she shivered. Slowly, Aambal's insides began to warm, and then the faint memories of the syllables also stirred and stretched out towards the sun, and she started to imitate the Kani's speech. Every sound she uttered fanned the tiny flames that had begun to spark inside her belly. Weeks later, in the warmth of that fire, she spoke her first word. That word, spoken in consciousness, burst out of her shell of dread, stretched and winged through her throat and flew out of her mouth. The word spread its wings, soared up and filled the air: Aambal. She had spoken her own name, in its fullness, as hers, as the name her father had given her, in the knowledge that this child of his would grow into the qualities that the blue aambal had.

Immediately, she looked around for the one who had spoken it the most, the one with whom she could be everything that the aambal was: sturdy, stubborn, brooding. She wanted to see herself in his eyes and hear him call her name. She wanted to pinch him hard for not being by her side when she wanted him there. 'Kandhan?' she asked. They smiled at her and said 'Velan', and stretched their arms high into the air, pointing to the heavens and the nether worlds and to all the things that were around them. But that didn't help Aambal. She did not want to know where else he was, she wanted to know why he wasn't next to her. But when she looked at the grass waving in the wind, the way the sun fell onto the wiry hair of her companions and onto her head, face, shoulders, her belly, her hands and feet, and she laughed, then wept. Kandhan was here, she thought, he was everywhere. She could feel his eyes on her, his hands taking hold of her hair and pulling, his hand at her back as she squeezed into the crack of the cave on the sacred mountain, where the kurinji lay waiting to bloom, and as she stood on the mountain where everything had called out to her, naming her 'Kandhan's poet'. She wanted to compose poems, to recite them aloud, and befriend again the words that had once come trekking out of their mountain crags to find her, to look for a way to coax them into her mind, into her stylus and inkwell, onto her palm leaf.

On the mountain top, there was barely any difference between the language of humans and of nature, and as the days passed, Aambal's memory shook itself and unfurled, it spread its fronds and became greener, stronger. The last time she had been here, the Kuru Muni had told her that she had finally acquired the last of the poetic attitudes, and now she began to remember each of the other nine, and what Aasaan had said to her on these occasions. Her memory took her back to how she had felt when she understood that these attitudes didn't come, you laboured and found out what was stopping you from having that attitude, then through sheer determination and Aasaan's guidance, you gave up the thing that got in the way. The last of the poetic attitudes was the one that she and other poets had the most trouble with, the one called 'The Self-Possession of the Looming Ashoka Tree': to not be overwhelmed by poetic thoughts that fell like torrents of rain on the Ashoka, but like it, to stand, bent downwards, as the cascade poured and flowed towards the ground, which swallowed up the water and sent it back upwards through the tree's roots in just the quantity that was needed. Akattiyan recognised that Aambal had reached the state where she was like the Ashoka, perpetually standing, attention tilted towards the ground of language, to let thoughts and ideas sink into that ground-bed and seep inwards.

On Pothigai, as language and grammar returned to her, and she began to compose poems again, Aambal began to feel restless. She longed to be back in Pazhani, to go to Madurai and to stand in the Assembly, reciting. She knew that she had a lot of work to do, she would have to complete the recitations that she had missed, and so she turned her attention to composing poems, and as their numbers grew, so did her excitement, especially when Akattiyan listened to her and sometimes corrected something here and there, saying, 'Only a little. He is your Aasaan, Murugan. His ear hears things I cannot.' She recited her poems aloud to groups of the Kani who came to sit with her, and they would laugh and say, in their way, that she was fine now.

She wondered when Murugan would send for her. And who would come to take her back. Would he come? Where was he? Had he already returned to Pazhani? Or was he in Mayilai? What about the daughter of the king of the gods? Had she gone back to Svarloka? Had Murugan gone with her? Was that why it was taking so long? But he would come, he would come and take her home. She had almost completely forgotten the frightening visions of the battle, and of a Murugan who stretched beyond visibility, and that he and she had shouted out his name—Maharasa. She was just happy that Murugan was safe, happy that she hadn't failed in her war-bard duty to protect the warrior at all costs.

Aambal was also glad that Thennan had been unharmed, and as she thought of him, she heard, once more, their voices, joined together. She was reciting and he picking up the refrain, and then, for the first time, she recalled the darkness that had come into her eyes as she fell towards the ground, and Thennan's arms around her body. His fingers had rubbed her forehead, easing the excruciating pain downwards, away from her head, as fellow bards, musicians and healers had done through time when one of them was invaded by a vision that could either return alone to where it came from or take the bard with it. Aambal smiled as she remembered the coolness of his fingers and the fragrance of him, vetiver mixed with sweat. She was happy that Thennan was coming to Pazhani.

It was Paravani who came to fetch her from Pothigai. When she heard the familiar swishing sound of the giant birdwings, Aambal ran to the ledge of rock, the lookout place cleared of overhanging branches, and laughed and clapped her hands. The sun fell all over Paravani's body and his brilliant colours became invisible, as if the gold of the sun had licked them all off and then set the feathers on fire. For a moment, Aambal staggered, the old fear rising in her throat at the disappearance of colour, but Paravani called out, 'Aambal, Aambal my dear', and she ran to him, all thoughts other than the comfort of an old ally leaving her head.

'Where is Kandhan?' Aambal asked.

Paravani said, 'He's back, now,' and added with a laugh, 'And someone else is due too.'

'Who?' Aambal asked, though she knew it was Thennan. Kandhan had said he would send for both of them when he was back in Pazhani. She didn't want to admit to thinking of Thennan, but she didn't want to lie either, so she asked, 'Is it our friend

Thennan?' and felt herself go warm at the memory of his arms and the smell of his body.

She looked into Paravani's smiling face, to bring herself back to the tasks at hand. There were heavy farewells to be said, to Ganesha and Akattiyan and to her many friends, the inhabitants of Pothigai to whom she owed her language now, in addition to her life. Aambal quietly packed the palm leaves that held her new poems, feeling a shiver of joy at the thought of reading them to Kandhan and at the Assembly. She knew they were good, these poems had something new, something more. Kandhan would be happy—he always said, 'Start from the last triumph, go forward, grow.' She had grown, her verse had grown. Her language bag was fuller, and all the ten poetic attitudes that she had earned through labour, sacrifice, longing and dreaming had come together, they were no longer ordered in a line, formal. On the holy mountain, her silence had bade them come closer, to sit beside her and comfort her, and to offer her little gifts, and she understood that what she was feeling was her own mastery, and the ten attitudes fell over her like a mantle.

3

PAZHANI AGAIN

Thennan had thought of Aambal often in his home far away from Chendur and Pazhani. He remembered the terror surging in her voice before it shrunk and stilled and she collapsed. How her body had convulsed violently in his arms such that his own frame had shuddered, until her body went stiff, as if dead. He also remembered screaming her name aloud, repeatedly, till Matri Dhumi reached them. He couldn't recall if he actually had screamed 'Aambal, Aambal, don't die', but he remembered the panic, as if one of the giants from the battlefield had held him till his body stilled.

He was impatient to see Aambal again. Had she recovered? Did she have her mind back? He also thought about what would change if Aambal did not recover: Murugan would not need him in Pazhani, for he had wanted them to work together, with Aambal writing poems that he would tune and put to song. A messenger brought word from Murugan for him to set out for Pazhani, and Thennan began his journey.

As he travelled, Thennan's fears about Aambal began to dissipate. He remembered her as a child, her sturdy body and how her unbending will had made her fearless and stubborn. Suddenly, he was filled with a longing to be with his two best friends once more, and to once more adventure with them, this time in language and music. He was eager to get to the verses that Aambal would write, and to search for tunes for them and sing them to the best ears in all the universes—Murugan, the God of Sound and Song. Then, for a moment, his heart wrenched and he wished that the great Asura, his patron King Surapadman, was still alive. He would have delighted in this venture, and it would have been two sets of the keenest ears listening to him sing.

Thennan began his journey at midnight. He stood at the crossroads, waiting to get a ride on one of the grain-laden bullock carts or the carts of performers, healers, hunters and gypsies, heading towards the towns and temple festivals. The hunters and gypsies were favourite performers at the these festivals, especially in the temples of the Lord Who Drank Fresh Toddy and of his son, the God Who Was the Mud of the Kurinji. Scholars and commentators came in from the study centres to listen to them and to talk with them. They saw that the roots of the language were in the songs and stories of these performers. It was as if the God of Tamizh had given them the first mouthful of that inebriating honey, for what came out of their mouths was as perfect as what the poets and scholars laboured over.

Such pleasant company met, Thennan felt as if buds were springing open and honey-drunk bees were surging against his insides. Song lines and verses burst from him, and his companions happily took up a refrain or a chorus, and sometimes accompanied him with sharp beats on a parai or tudi or by shaking bands into which salangai beads were stitched. Sometimes, someone jumped off the bullock cart and danced in tune. Thennan's excitement grew as they moved along, and his head filled with other images of Aambal from Chendur: her eyes widening when she first saw him on the battlefield, her ease with bardic duties, of how when they sang together, her smile swelled the refrains.

But then Thennan quietened down. The early morning sun, darting through the tree branches, leaping on the waves of the streams and playing hide-and-seek on the ground had made him light-headed. As it got hotter, the moisture in his belly, on his lips and in his eyes dried up, as did the eager stream of words that had danced out of his mouth. And he asked himself what he was doing. Why was his mind filled with Aambal's face? Was this possible? What about—he shook his head vigorously, shaking off that thought. Not now. There would be time for all that. Right now, he just wanted ... what did he want? The face of a little girl came into his head: a girl he had once called 'bossy' and tried to run away from, a girl who had pushed his head under water to rid him of his fear of swimming. It made him smile. But almost immediately another face pushed Aambal's aside and stood there glowering at him: a little boy with a head of curls, whose hand held a dandam, poised to strike, and that was enough to jolt Thennan out of his reverie.

⊙⊱⊙

It had been many months since Murugan left Pazhani. The hill of old rock, its bushes and shrubs, its little animals and birds that called and darted about, and its streams that gushed and tumbled, were all beginning to get impatient for the return of the young man who had transformed himself and them when he said, 'You are my home.' Paravani, too, missed Murugan. He had not accompanied Murugan to the war, pointing out, 'Your twin horses, Kalam and Neram have been given to you for a reason. Like Suran's Svasti and Kshema, they will carry you into and out of the great battle.'

At that moment, Murugan had not seen what he meant, and Paravani could not tell him what he knew. But now, after he had recognised that he was Maharasa, the Supreme Rasa, he chuckled at the symbolic flourish of the four horses, his two black and Suran's white ones. Kalam, neram, svasti and kshema were terms regularly used when working with the rasa, the sap of life in all things. Murugan's amusement increased as he thought of it. Those who worked with rasa spent all their intelligence, insight and efforts in trying to invoke the 'maha', the supreme rasa into material, in order to transmute its qualities, to turn a thing into its most perfect aspect. These efforts were conducted in Time, 'kalam', but depended on the contextual time, 'neram'. When someone set out to invoke the maha rasa, others wished 'svasti', so be it, and together also prayed for well-being, 'kshema'. The four horses had brought an extra playfulness to the drama of Suran's game.

Pazhani town was abuzz with excitement: houses were cleaned and streamers of coconut fronds and flower buds were strung along the eaves, the verandas were covered with fresh coats of cow dung mixed with camphor. In the palace on top of the hill, everything was astir. Paravani would have to go to Pothigai to bring Aambal as soon as Murugan reached home, and he was running here and there, reminding everybody of the many things that were left to do, including living quarters for Thennan. So much work to be done, Paravani thought, so much work to be done. He jumped out of his skin at a loud, most unpleasant sound, and looked up to see a large rooster winging downwards. His red, black and tan feathers brilliant, the plumage on his crown heraldic, the talons on his claws sharp and shiny. As the bird landed, he was already talking briskly, 'Paravani, here you are. There's so much work to do. I told the young man I would have to be here to make sure that everything went well.' Paravani smiled. So Seval had come home. He had heard about him from the soldiers and Matris who had come to Pazhani instead of travelling to Mayilai. 'Well,' Seval was saying, with an impatient toss of his head, 'haven't you seen a bird before that wasn't a peacock? Come now, stop staring and show me around.'

Paravani had heard worrying things, that Seval was loud, temperamental and shrewd. But this let's-talk-as-we-work attitude greatly appealed to Paravani. He could now go off without having to worry about the boy. Paravani had cared for Murugan as a child and never left his side until the battle at Chendur. As they talked, and Seval got the layout of Murugan's home, Paravani warmed to the flamboyant bird. They may be vastly different in temperament, but they had one thing in common, their love for the God of Pazhani. This regard only increased when Seval sat down and filled Paravani in about things he thought the latter should know: Theivanai and Murugan's closeness, the incident of the birthing, Murugan's proposal and Theivanai's rejection. 'Mutthu was shocked,' Seval said, 'he couldn't understand why she said no, but she explained to him that she needed more time to make up her mind.' He saw the look on Paravani's face and snapped, 'That's what I call him. It's short for Mutthukumarasami. He's like the mutthu that sits right at the top of the crown, the most precious of all. Don't look so shocked, I'm not going to call him such a long name with no one else in hearing.' Paravani felt a pang, he had never been separated from Murugan for so long. Seval said, 'Mutthu speaks of you often.' Paravani's attention returned to Seval, and he smiled, thinking, 'Ah, the brashness is displayed. The sensitive is kept in check.'

Murugan returned to Pazhani before either Thennan or Aambal arrived. Inside the palace, Seval seemed to have redone everything. As he walked along, Murugan recognised new arrangements, new curtains, new furniture and he could not help but admire Seval's taste. To his surprise, Seval steered him towards the room that Murugan had kept aside for visitors. 'This is your room now. This one gets more sunlight everywhere, both morning and evening. And it has more room, you will need more room soon.' Murugan looked around and saw that all his things had been brought from Kailasa. He stepped out to the balcony and stood looking out at the town when Seval's voice broke in, impatience making it sharp, 'Mutthu, stop dreaming. Come and see your clothes. And then you have to go down and meet Aasaan.' Murugan saw that Seval had arranged his clothes in order of ornateness.

He asked the bird, 'Are you going to keep calling me Mutthu?'

Seval said with a sniff, 'I'm not calling you "my lord" or "my god". And I like Mutthu better than Murugan. You are a little bead of immeasurable value. Mutthukumarasami, that I will call you in public, but it'll be "Mutthu" otherwise.'

Murugan smiled. Seval was indeed a force to reckon with.

As we saw, when the three friends headed for Pazhani, they each had someone on their mind. Aambal and Thennan did not dwell long on images of each other, thinking instead of the work that was waiting for them and of once again being the triad they had once been. But Murugan had no desire to set aside the image of Theivanai: he was in love and it was all he could think of. He spoke of her to Paravani and Seval, and after Aambal arrived, to her, and then as the days went by, to Thennan as well. Soon, all of Pazhani knew that their lord was besotted with the lovely daughter of the king of the Suras.

On the day that Aambal reached Pazhani, Murugan was waiting outdoors, watching the sky for Paravani. As soon as she got off, he exclaimed, in what seemed to her an unduly loud voice, 'Aambal, how beautiful you look,' making Aambal feel like climbing back on and disappearing into the sky. But already Murugan had hugged her tightly. Then he dropped his arms and said, 'Aambal, I missed you,' and taking her hands in his, added, 'Welcome back home.' Footsteps approached, and Aambal recognised their fall. She did not turn. Murugan, who was looking at her, said, 'And you can welcome our friend Thennan.'

Aambal turned and faced Thennan, who became a bit flustered but smiled, his eyes widening when they fell on Aambal. Murugan was right, how beautiful she looked, her tawny skin was burnt deeper, her frame was sturdier and more filled out than he remembered. Her head was still covered in the white shawl she had thrown on for the journey from Pothigai to Pazhani. She was in white, as he was, as were all bards, musicians, songsters, oracles, poets and scholars who journeyed seeking palaces, patrons and performances, who wore white to stave off the heat of the sun, and of the visions that burnt through them into language, grammars, medicine and rhythm.

'How are you, Aambal?' he asked, his trained voice keeping equilibrium.

Aambal could see Murugan's lips twitch, but ignored it, answering, 'I am happy to be back home. And you?'

Thennan began to answer, but Murugan broke in and said, with a guffaw, 'He's happy that you're finally here.'

At which point, Seval, whose face showed displeasure, said, 'He wants songs to tune and you're the poet, Aambal.'

Murugan continued to grin, happy because the three of them were together, and soon, work would begin, and because Tamizh would resound around him, and because he was in love with Theivanai, and because he was home at last. He stood looking at his two friends; she should fall in love with Thennan, and Thennan had always been a little in love with Aambal. It would be good to have company in this business of love. He wanted company in his pining. But these two were so proper. Especially Aambal, he thought, her love for Tamizh and her ambition to be in the Assembly would make her see everything else as a distraction. And Thennan was in no position to ... but so what? It was not unheard of. Murugan liked the idea: his two friends in love with each other and he in love with Theiva.

He jumped out of his skin as a pip-pip-pip sounded next to his ear. Seval had the little horn at his lips and was blowing, a frown on his face. Bah, this bird! 'Time to take Aambal home, my lord.'

Murugan thought, oh that's how it is, is it? Every time you disapprove of something, you're going to 'my lord' me!

Thennan looked like he wanted to say something, and Murugan asked, 'What is it, Thennan?'

When Thennan said, 'I too could stay in the town and come up the hill every day.'

Murugan giggled and asked, 'Why, would you prefer to stay near Aambal?' He was pleased to see Aambal's face grow a shade darker. She did not look up.

Thennan said, 'No, it's just that ...'

'Aambal,' Murugan continued, his face innocent, 'maybe Thennan can stay with you, in your house?'

Seval snorted and said, 'No, he cannot, my Lord of Pazhani. Not only would that be inappropriate, because Aambal needs to concentrate, but that house is too small for two people. Thennan will stay here, on the hill.' To himself, he muttered, 'The slyness of him. That poor Aambal. Look how he's plotting to make them fall in love.' Then he caught himself and thought, 'But she feels it. And so does he. Mutthu isn't doing it—in his presence everything that is, will blossom'. He had selected a room for Thennan away from the bustle of visitors and guards and the hall for performances. Its window looked out at the sky and down at the valleys that stretched below. Seval had wanted to ensure that there was no way that Thennan and Aambal would see each other when Thennan was in his room and Aambal was climbing up the hill. 'Let them meet at work.'

Pothigai had healed Aambal, and the images of Death had faded almost fully from her mind. The nights had once more become restful, but now the thought of being alone in her cottage, when the skies darkened, filled her with dread. What if the nightmares returned? So she lingered, finding one reason or another not to go down into the town and to her house, even though the evening was darkening. Paravani's heart melted. He had seen her from the time she was a child, like the little boy he had guarded and mentored, and all these years later, it was that little girl he saw now. Poor child, he thought, she had to see things she ought not to have, and now she is afraid and will not admit it.

'My Lord,' he said to Murugan, 'I have work down in the town, and I will go with Aambal. If I am unable to get it done, I might stay at Aambal's and come back tomorrow.' Murugan's head shot up. He had not thought of whether Aambal was afraid to be alone, so immersed was he in the joy of having her back. He felt a little bad, and instinctively, his eyes went to Seval, and he saw the bird had raised an eyebrow.

Aambal sighed, thankful for Paravani's offer. He sat with her until she fell asleep, and then went outdoors to perch on the kondrai tree in the backyard, visible from the window in Aambal's room. As she slept that night, Paravani called out softly when she stirred in her sleep. In the morning, she woke feeling as if she had crossed a treacherous bridge and would not need return to it. Paravani thought of how this was the first part of the many transformations that Aambal would undergo. One day, she would be like the little boy he had brought to Pazhani all those years ago, who had said, 'I want my own home and I want to be free of every rule.'

Meanwhile, up on the holy hill, where the Lord of Poets lived, his bard, come newly from the plains, could not sleep. The cool hill breezes and the proximity of the bright stars stirred inside him feelings he had not prepared himself to deal with. Aambal's face appeared to him when he shut his eyes, leaning close to his own. He felt as if the warm exhalation from his nostrils was Aambal's breath caressing his lips. Aambal had thick lips, like so many women of the south, dark, so inviting when she smiled, and she was smiling at him. She was also silent. When she was reciting, it was impossible to move past the veil of words and admire her face. The veil stopped you, and demanded that you retreat. And here she was now, leaning over him, smiling and unspeaking. Unguarded. He half rose from his bed, and then could not fall back into sleep. Thennan walked outside for some time, then lay down again and must have barely dozed off when Seval's early morning alarms sounded.

On the morning of their first day of work together, Aambal was clear-eyed and her thoughts and words sharp and able. Thennan's eyes were swollen and his voice was a little thin as he sat down with his two friends. Thus, they began to work together, the three of them, on her verses in praise of Murugan, and it seemed as if it had always been like this. The days when only two of them, Murugan and Aambal, sat with her work felt like it belonged to another time. And indeed it was—that was before the battle. They worked separately and together, with Murugan moulding the writing and the singing, sometimes with delicacy, and sometimes with the rough impatience of one who can read and hear better versions.

Sometimes, the impatience came from his thoughts about *how long* Theiva had been silent and had refused to make a decision. There was a time when Murugan had not worried, because it had seemed to him that her feelings for him were the same as his for her, but now he was uncertain. What if she said no? What if she was bored with him?

Murugan's mind seemed always to spin around Theiva. He was thinking and talking about her more and more each day. Sometimes, he walked down the secret paths on the hill to find the cave in which he had slept before waking to a new life, a new version of himself. At other times, he got up from his reading sessions with Aambal and went to his room. Or, as Thennan was singing one of Aambal's verses, his brow furrowed and he muttered under his breath. Sometimes he told Seval of his impatience—he said he was at his wits' end and he was going to go to Theivanai and demand an answer. To Paravani, Murugan said nothing, but it was when he was in the skies with Paravani that he could speak of sadness, to say, 'My heart is ailing. Nothing is the same.' Paravani's wings wrapped around Murugan and he said to him, 'Boy, it is as it should be. What you are feeling is the pain of absence. The wound of longing. It, too, must be felt.' Murugan put his face on the kindly bird's neck and shut his damp eyes. Only this bird could handle Murugan's sadness and his tears, for the other one, the god reserved all his bad behaviour. Seval was often seen skulking in some corner, hopping up and down exclaiming, 'That Mutthu!'

The hill was happy. Bustle had returned now that Murugan was back. Visitors came streaming in, and the twelve Matris were in Pazhani. They did not stay in the palace or in the town, but sought out hidden caves on the hillside and spent their days and nights there. People sometimes sighted them, sitting silently on the rocks under the early morning sun and did not approach them, some out of fear, most out of respect for they knew that the women wanted seclusion. But the hunters, who wended their way up the hill's secret turns to bring hill flowers, tubers, honey and the wild kadamba for Murugan, walked close and sometimes stopped and sat beside them. They did not speak, neither did the Matris, but there was an unspoken bond between them. To the hunters, the women were the teachers of their god, the Kurinji Kizhavan, the Hero of the Kurinji, and to the women, the hunters were dear to the boy they had mentored, and they knew that he sought out their company whenever he was out roving in the wild.

The Matris had been affected by the deaths and the defeats that they had caused and experienced. They were here to rest and heal. Paravani sometimes flew down the hill's flanks to find them and to sit quietly or hold conversations with them. It was good that Seval was there, he thought virtually every day. Sometimes, he was gone for days, and when he returned, there were ferns or lichens stuck to his feathers. Murugan looked for him at the start of each day, initially feeling a little hurt if he was told that Paravani had been seen flying off, but slowly began to understand that the bird, as he had always done, was doing the appropriate thing. Paravani knew that Seval could deal with whatever came up, and even somehow managed to snap the lovelorn Murugan out of his moping, so work could go on smoothly. To Paravani's relief, he was also keeping a protective watch over Aambal. Every time he returned, Paravani went straight to Murugan and told him that he was back. In time, both Murugan and Paravani became easy with this shift in roles.

As for Aambal, she had begun to see that she felt differently about the readings and her work now, and this was only partly because the final reading was approaching. She was more alert, knowing that if she failed at any one of the monthly readings, she would have to wait another year to try again. That would be shameful, she did not dare to even think of what Murugan would feel. And of what she would do. But, she said to herself, she was not a repeater: she got it right when she did something, because she had already laboured over her work in her mind, finding its weaknesses and providing for them. The competition was a matter of life for her. It *was* her life: she was Murugan's poet.

The poetry that she had composed on Pothigai had caused her to reckon with her own skill: it was the first time she had accomplished so much without Murugan beside her, pushing her, looking over her work, suggesting, correcting, finessing her language, the lines and verses. As she was working, it had seemed to her that she was thinking like him, as if he had slipped into her head to make up for his physical absence. She had marvelled at the way that she had been able to see when the words were trying to trick her, pretending to be what they were not: a weighty word disguised as a light one, or a syllable that shrank on her tongue to fit the count. It seemed as if she was extra alert, as if she was possessed of two minds, her own and Murugan's.

As the final reading drew closer, Murugan became extra demanding with her. She was pleased that she rarely failed his expectations and that his praise was lavish. He lauded what was inventive about her verses as much as he censured what was stale or saggy. For Aambal, there was nothing more shameful than to have Murugan find exactly the fault that she could have avoided. When he corrected something and showed her how to make it better, that was different. She hated being told that she could easily have caught a flaw and tossed it out before it entered the line. And if this happened when Thennan—who beamed as if he was the recipient of praise when Murugan commended her—was there, she would be even more angry with herself. She made it a habit to go over her work many more times before reading it aloud for Murugan. She hadn't yet realised that, sometimes, these lapses were because her attention had wandered to Thennan as he sat humming a tune or notating it, his lean fingers delicately curled around the ornate stylus that he used, with a curved head and intricate carving, unlike the plain one that Aambal used, for she wrote at length and needed a light stylus.

Aambal looked forward to waking up in the morning, her head full of the words that she had finished the previous night. She imagined how Thennan would tune it, and as she imagined her words in his voice, Aambal walked around smiling to herself, humming under her breath. Up on the hill, Thennan woke up, eager to see the words that Aambal would have completed, and hummed the parts that they had completed the previous evening, which he had fine-tuned over and over before falling asleep. He, too, hummed to himself and walked around smiling. If Seval chanced on him, he made it a point to sharply call out Thennan's name, almost as if intending to disrupt his mood. Thennan began to notice this, and he asked himself why the bird was so rude—it was, after all, born from the eyes, ears and hair of his beloved patron, King Surapadman.

Murugan, on the other hand, woke from sleep each morning feeling like he was not in the right place. His mind went back to Mayilai and the days he had spent with Theiva. He missed her more and more each day. His mood was usually disrupted by the arrival of Seval, who called out, 'Mutthu, are you awake?' or sometimes, 'Hail Mutthukumarasami, King of Pazhani, Lord of This and That.' Or something similar. Murugan became restless in his pining for Theivanai, he began to get impatient. He wanted to do something to remind her that she had said she would send word to him when she was ready. The more he thought about her, the clearer it became to him that he had to do something. But what he could do?

Pazhani Hill basked in happiness: so much Tamizh, so much work, so much music and lyric. And so much love forming, like crystal forms, slowly, unchangeably, beautifully. Like crystal, to change, it would have to break.

4

THE WOOING OF THEIVANAI

As the triad were settling into these new rhythms, two of their old friends arrived unexpectedly. Kuyili, who had been in the service of the king of Chhedi, and Perunkadungko, who came to invite them to his wedding. It was an unexpected treat to be together like this again. But Thennan was a little discomfited by the fact that he could not be as comfortable with Murugan as the new arrivals who treated him just as they had when they were all in the kalari together. Then he saw that Aambal, too, was maintaining formality. She was apprenticed to Murugan, and he was in Murugan's employ. As if sensing this discomfort, Murugan suggested that they all go down into the valley and visit the kalari. Paravani joined them, carrying Murugan, while Kuyili and Perunkadungko took Aambal and Thennan, one each on their horses. Seval accompanied them, flying alongside the horse riders, not saying much, but his ears were perked and his eyes watchful, only he knew for what.

Aasaan was delighted to see them. As they touched his feet, he embraced each one and blessed them as he had when they were children. Something about being in the kalari made them all lighter. It would have been different if, on arriving in Pazhani, Thennan had not visited the grandfather he had remained estranged from, honouring the promise made to his mother that, as long as she lived, he would not visit her father. Now, he was transformed—he was the host here, this was his grandfather they were visiting. The equation changed, too, as if they had gone back to a time when Thennan visited the kalari every six months, and all the children viewed him with admiration and some envy because Aasaan was his grandfather.

His mood affected Aambal as well, for she was calling Murugan 'Kandhan' and laughing at him like she had before accepting him as her master. No matter how stubborn she still was or how wilful, when it came to poetry, she became pliant and accepting: for poetry, she would do anything, and Murugan's lessons were treasures that he did not give unless he wanted to. And he did not teach what he knew, but what she needed, what her craft needed. He was teaching her mastery that went beyond the limits of time and occasion into the hidden cave of the language's heart, where the wellspring ran underground, hidden, till the one who waited on it proved herself.

The four of them spent the next five days in the kalari, and as was the rule, these visitors not only ate with the children and cooked for them, but also they each taught the children one lesson. Kuyili showed them how to navigate with the eyes closed: follow the heat that came at them as they moved in any direction; still, let the breath settle, then let it stream out, wait for it to hit something and come back. Perunkadungko taught them verses that an ancestor of his had composed to the birds and the animals whose breath fell into the soil and made it kind. Aambal showed them how to compose in a metre called 'The Triple Plait', in which sound units of three were joined as the three strands of a plait are joined into one single braid. And finally, Murugan taught them a dance that the hunters who came up to Velan's Hill performed on the night of the full moon in the month of Kritika, devoted to his six Krittika mothers.

It was here that, sitting around a fire that flamed gently in the quiet breeze, with Paravani and Seval perched on tree branches, that Murugan talked of Theivanai and how he had fallen in love with her. Amidst much teasing and laughing, the friends demanded to hear the whole story. He told them about how he had first seen her and what he had felt, and how he had called her 'Theivanai' and she had almost called him 'Maharasa' instead of 'Mahasena', and of their sojourn in Mayilai. As they listened rapt, Thennan's eyes went to Aambal so many times that both Kuyili and Perunkadungko noticed and smiled at each other. Murugan was looking up at the sky as he talked, and did not notice anything. On the tree top, Seval muttered and Paravani sighed.

Murugan spoke of how Theivanai's face and her voice kept returning to his mind, and how it was becoming more and more difficult to bear her absence. Aambal thought she recognised that feeling—was it not what came over her as she left Pazhani for her home in the foothills every evening after a day's work? She glanced towards Thennan, and finding him looking at her, quickly turned away. Thennan felt warmth boring into his head from above, and looked up to see Seval's beady eyes on him. He turned away.

Kuyili said, 'Muruga, she's the one. She's right for you. What are you going to do now?'

Before Murugan could say anything, Seval's voice broke in, 'He has to do more than stand around and sigh, which is what he's been doing of late.'

This evoked a burst of laughter from Kuyili. 'Show us, Muruga,' she said, 'show us how you sigh.'

There was much laughter and clapping and cheering, at the end of which Kuyili steered the conversation back to Theivanai. She suggested that Murugan should send Theivanai messages, pointing out that asking for more time was not a prohibition of all communication. Murugan clapped delightedly as he said, 'Kuyili!

No wonder you're such a good warrior. So incisive!' He had liked and admired her from their first meeting at the kalari. Kuyili had told him then that she was going to grow up and become a warrior, and that she would be a king's bodyguard and have the sharpest sword in the kingdom, for it was not the king or the commanders who had the best swords but whoever guarded the king's life. And now here she was, strategising on how he was to woo Theivanai.

'You have to send a message while we are all here. Come on, let's write one!' Turning to her friends, Kuyili said, 'Come on, you are the bards and poets, I don't know anything of all this.' Between them, with Perunkadungko, who they found out had some experience with writing love missives, taking the lead, they composed a message to Theivanai. In it, they depicted Murugan as looking at the stars and thinking of Theivanai in Svarloka, and feeling that he had to send her a message. There were lines that spoke in exquisite Tamizh of the white birds flying homewards, their bodies like the movements of a dancer's hands, and of how Murugan's memory rose in waves and winged upwards to her. Before the following day dawned, they had Aambal stylus the lines onto a palm leaf, which was then delicately wrapped in another leaf, and it was decided that Seval would carry this missive to Theivanai. Kuyili and Perunkadungko would both stay on till he returned with a message.

It was not to be, for Seval came back without a reply. Theivanai had been busy, and while polite, clearly distracted. She had asked her companions to take the message, and to ensure that Seval ate before he returned to Bhu. She had not been excited, Seval reported, and added, 'She could have been a little more attentive to me.'

This cast a pall on the mood of the friends, but Kuyili roused them out of it with a story. The king of Chhedi, she told them, set off towards the ghats of Kashi one day. He was not yet king then, his father still ruled. He was in search of a man named Trataka who, it was rumoured, had a copy of a treatise that the prince was keen to get hold of. Trataka was a taciturn man, the prince was told, who did not think much of the human race. But the prince, well trained in the art of diplomacy, was not deterred. He soon brought in the grouchy Trataka a change of mood, and got him to agree to let a scribe copy out the treatise. But that wasn't the story that Kuyili was telling. Her story was about the prince falling in love with a woman he saw on the ghats—she had the matted locks and the ochre of a renunciate, and the fearsome trident she carried identified her as a member of the mendicants known as the 'wild ones'. They could, it was said, fell a man or woman with one hand, and think nothing of it, for death was to them as unreal as life. By this time, Trataka had taken a liking to the young man whose vast reading and general good nature he found endearing. So he warned the prince against pursuing this dangerous infatuation. But Prince Nakula was in love, and he not only dared to approach the woman, but wooed her with such perseverance that she soon began to wait for him and to imagine a life in which he was her companion. He returned home only when she had agreed to accompany him, with no other conditions on either side.

'That's what you need to do, Muruga, persevere. And woo her, woo her till she says "yes",' Kuyili said, adding with a laugh, 'Or "no".'

And so they composed another message. This time, they procured a well-cured, handsome scroll, and Perunkadungko, whose scripting was beautiful, wrote out the message in verse that they composed line by line. And once more, Seval, his feathers glowing and combed and perfumed, the comb on his head gleaming and swaying like a pennant on a windy rampart, flew off. The group of friends were disappointed again when Seval returned, for it was the same story this time too: Theivanai had asked her companions to attend to him because she was very busy. This time, he had asked for a reply, only to be told that when she had the time to read the missive, she would send a messenger with a reply. She said, Seval reported, his voice shrill with impatience, 'Don't bother to wait or come again.'

Murugan felt disoriented: what did their adventures together mean then? Had she not said that she hoped it would not be too long before they met again?

When the visitors left, Murugan, Aambal, Thennan, Paravani and Seval went back to Pazhani.

How were they to know that Theivanai had a plan? After her brief sojourn in Mayilai, before she returned to her parents' house in Svarloka, Theivanai had decided that she would keep Murugan waiting even though she had already decided that she would marry him. She knew she would not grow weary of him—curious and intelligent as he was and delighting in the many forms he took on. His delight was so like that of the manavas, amongst whom he felt the happiest. She knew he wanted to be like them, to have his heart fill and ebb with affection, to long for a lover or pine for a friend, to charm the words out of the imaginations of poets, to fill the alphabets of the scholars. He was full of the urge to immerse.

She understood that his falling in love with her was as inevitable as her falling in love with him: it was the Vast's waves that surged in them, it was the Supreme Rasa that longed to join as Murugan and Theivanai. She would say yes, but not before she had given him what he so envied: the pain of separation and the thrill of hope. She would make him court her until he was thoroughly confused, and then she would say 'yes'.

―――

As the days passed, Aambal's portfolio for the Assembly readings grew thicker, Thennan's stock of songs grew larger and Murugan's misery grew, as did his sighs and tantrums. When Paravani's wings took him high up into the skies, where no one else was watching, listening, he sang his sadness out loud. Murugan tried to lose himself in composing songs and writing riddles, he made up new metres, he checked in old tomes for intriguing studies. He asked his friends, the hunters from the mountains, to sing him their courting songs, which he got transcribed and bound into palm leaves. He sent for cloth, pearls, copies of his best books. But he did not dare send them to Theivanai. On the contrary, doing these things made him even more miserable. It made him bad-tempered, and things came to a head one day when Seval went off in a huff because Murugan had yelled at him for calling him out of a sleep in which he had been dreaming of Theivanai. It was only after days of coaxing and begging from both Murugan and Paravani that he relented and came back. After that, Murugan was careful with his temper, at least around Seval.

Finally, it was Paravani, feeling more and more sorry for the young man, who came up with an idea. But Murugan was in a mood. 'It's a stupid idea,' he snapped, 'keep it to yourself.' He stomped off, but returned soon enough, and asked, 'You think it will really work?' Paravani shook with laughter. Murugan let his shoulders slump in relief.

The idea worked. Murugan wrote a poem in which the name of the meter was hidden in the syllable count of the words. But first, the words had to be formed by separating the syllables, because the entire poem was unbroken syllables. That done, you had to figure out the line breaks, and the whole poem appeared. Then you had to find the hidden word, the name of the metre. It was difficult because first you had to locate a break in the sound pattern, and for this you had to know of the sound that is unsounded but which appears in the mind as you read. The very thing that Father and Theivanai had talked about in Mayilai. It was clever and complex, and the name of the metre was 'Theivam': her name with an extra syllable, and the last sound in one of his names, Kuzhanthai Theivam.

Theiva sent a message to him, expressing her delight in the verse and her longing to meet him, and Murugan was ecstatic and went to visit her. They walked in the gardens around her palace, and the buds on trees and shrubs and bushes burst into bloom. The gods came out of their palaces and stood around gawking at Murugan as he walked unseeing of everything except the woman he was in love with.

When he returned to Pazhani, Murugan sat down with Paravani and Seval to discuss the wedding. Paravani advised him that the wedding should be in a place that was new for him too, somewhere Theivanai and he would begin together, a place that marked the new life. Pazhani was the cave where Murugan retreated. It was his and his alone. This appealed to Murugan, who had been feeling drawn to the idea of moving closer to Madurai. In the days following Theivanai's acceptance, Murugan's imagination leapt to a future time when they were a married couple, building their love and their work hand-in-hand, and it came to him that he wanted Theivanai to take an active role in the working of the Poets' Assembly. She wanted to be taught Tamizh, but he would not teach her, he would ask Akattiyan to do so—for he knew that he would be distracted and disorderly in his excitement, unlike Akattiyan. It was important for Theivanai to learn in a way that would make it possible for her to understand the weighing and evaluating of poetry in the Assembly.

Murugan visited Aasaan, and sent word to Ganesha and his six mothers informing them of Theivanai's acceptance of his marriage proposal, and asking their blessings to find a new home. The Krittikas appeared before him on Pazhani. They blessed him, and told him of a place that he might like both to be married at and to make a home in. They held his hand and transported him to the site. It loomed high over the bustling town of Madurai. From that height, the great temple and the Assembly were both visible, their gopurams rising into the blue, blue sky. Murugan was delighted, this was like Pazhani, but also different. It was close to Madurai, but also at a little distance. It was a hill and it had caves, and when he stood there, he felt the resonance of the winds accented by the stone faces of the great hill. When his mothers took leave of Murugan and rose into the skies, Paravani appeared beside him to carry him back to Pazhani.

Murugan informed Seval that he had the blessings of all those whose approval he had desired and had also found the site he had been looking for. Seval looked like he wanted to say something, something sharp at that, but Paravani shook his head. Murugan had once decided that he would never ask his parents for anything, not even blessings. That would not change. And when news that Murugan had sought the blessings of others reached Shambhu and Parvathy, they were silent, for they knew it was the price they had to pay for having chosen creation over him.

'So are you going to tell me where this place is?' Seval asked Murugan, 'The venue for this event?'

Murugan laughed and said, 'Yes, I am.' He said no more, just stood there laughing.

And Seval was silent, knowing that it would take some doing to wrest the name from the god. He thinks he's a child, Seval thought, gnashing his beak. 'And?' he asked after some time. 'What is the place?'

'I'll give you a hint,' Murugan replied. 'It's high, it's hard and it's hollow. And it's close to the town the poets love.'

Seval's eyes widened, he gasped, 'Paramkundram? The Great Mountain? That rocky place, its sides full of the little holes that those taciturn renunciates sit inside doing their severe penance?'

'Yes,' Murugan answered, 'that's it. For too long, it's been severe. Things must change now. Like rain on hard soil, it will soften with my presence and my wedded life.' Murugan's face was still, as if he was sleeping. Then, his voice firmer, more matter of fact, he said, 'We need someone to organise everything—the wedding, the building of a home. I want a big wedding, but a small palace, intimate enough for me to always be near the one I love.' He added, 'And my best poets.' Face impassive, he asked again, 'Now, who can take charge of all this?'

Paravani burst into an uncharacteristic fit of laughter, making Seval frown. At this, Paravani said soberly, 'We don't need to waste time on that, Kandha, Seval here is the best choice.'

Seval rose up to his full hight, comb shaking with the force of his nodding, and he waited for Murugan to say something.

Murugan said, 'Hmm, I'm not so sure. I mean, Seval has no sense of propriety. He will go calling me "Mutthu" at odd times. I think maybe—'

He broke off as Seval rose into the air, his wings flapping madly and his voice, shriller than ever, calling, 'Mutthu, Mutthu, Mutthu, Muuuu-tthuuuu!' The bird pecked his ear hard enough for the god to cry out, 'Ow!' So it was that Seval had the overall charge of organising everything.

Preparations began without delay. It would be grander than any other wedding that had ever taken place, Seval said to anyone who mentioned the event. Seval consulted with Paravani and began to assign tasks to people. Murugan was too distracted to do anything. But who should be assigned the task of overseeing the many formalities of the wedding? It required, in addition to everything else, great tact to ensure that no egos were wounded and no one found any fault. And it had to be someone of great merit, the kind of merit that would please Murugan. Seval wanted this wedding to reflect the unpredictable nature of Mutthukumaran and the expansiveness of Theivanai. He explained this to Paravani, who heard him out and without a doubt said, 'King Muchukunda.' Why, Seval demanded. Why was the king worthy of such an honour? So, Paravani recounted to him the wonderful life of King Muchukunda.

Once it so happened that Muchukunda was roaming a forest on the western boundaries of his kingdom. He was seated under a tree, watching the birds and animals. For as long as he or anyone else could remember, the king had felt a deep longing to understand what other creatures were saying. He shut his eyes and imagined what it would be like if he could find a way to learn the language of the birds. Suddenly, there appeared before him a rakshasi. Her skin had the sheen of an old rock over which water flows, her eyes were fiery, her hands and legs thick like tree trunks, her long hair knotted in two rolls above her ears, her chest shining from the sparks of a sky-blue pendant.

She said to the king, 'Oh Muchukunda, I have lived in your forests a long time and I have seen you pause here, wishing you could hear the birds and bugs and creatures speak. I am the keeper of these forests, and I have seen how you neither hunt nor hurt. And I have heard your unspoken wish to know what the forest needs. Come close and let us talk.' The king took off his crown and his footwear, and praising the rakshasi, bending his head, sat down before her. She spoke to him about the forest and the laws of nature that humans broke. When she came to the part where she would explain what the forest wished for, she said to the king, 'Now listen, I cannot repeat myself, and if you hear these words, you will no longer be as you are now. Your heart will change, your seeing will change and your governance will change so that you will become not a sovereign but a servant to life. Is that what you want?'

It was what Muchukunda had wanted ever since he had heard of the Chera prince who refused to be crowned to his father's throne until he had learnt the language of every living creature in his kingdom. He said yes and the Rakshasi said, 'If you disregard these words, nothing will happen to you, for we don't hold ill will and we abhor curses, but you will lose this love you have for nature, and you will have insulted me.' The king nodded his agreement. The gods were annoyed at this turn of events because it was not right, they felt, that a human be given such knowledge. It offended their sense of order and separation. They sent the wind, Vayu, to appear there as a band of monkeys, running amok, flinging overripe fruit and seeds and flowers at the king, who ignored them by covering his head with his upper cloth and keeping his eyes shut. The Rakshasi, whose name was Suruli, Curved Breath, imparted to the king all the secrets that the king's human body and mind and heart could bear to hold. She then blessed him, invoking the Goddess Who Sends Rain and the God Who Dances on Funeral Pyres. And since then, his kingdom had been blessed with an equanimity that ran through its people, its animals, its land and waters and crops as an unseen current.

King Muchukunda was only too happy to accept Seval's invitation to help plan and organise the wedding on Paramkundram, which would be attended by beings from all fourteen worlds. Seval began his own part of the preparations by engaging the efforts of scribes from the many worlds as well as travelling news collectors to make lists of invitees—a preliminary step to Muchukunda's preparations. This was tough, because there were beings who were living hidden from sight, invisible or in other bodies, and there were those who had left their bodies in safe-keeping inside plants, rocks and the dead. In short, it was a tricky business, and only those whose work it was to track all life could be entrusted with it.

Then there was the question of how to accommodate everyone at the wedding? Who could build a hall large enough to hold so many, and still not be 'too big' for the liking of the groom, who had specified only this one thing: this home, unlike the one on Pazhani, would be small. Modest, intimate, it would be like a gentle embrace around him and his beloved. Muchukunda was wise enough to know that the question would find an answer in time.

Seval, on the other hand, was vexed. He was impatient to start work, and did not approve of the choice of this unyielding rock for a home. He could understand the temptation to move closer to Madurai, but why couldn't Mutthu live *in* Madurai? The more he thought about it, the more annoyed Seval became. Murugan left on a visit to the foothills to avoid Seval's bad temper. Kuyili would help him make a list of the children who had been with them at the kalari. This annoyed Aambal: why hadn't Murugan invited her along? He took her along to all kinds of places, even when she wanted to write, but now that he was going to Kuyili's house, he didn't want her.

Seval was pacing outside the reading room, making bad-tempered noises when he heard a little thwack from inside the room. When he got closer to the window, he could hear Aambal's voice muttering but not what she was saying. He knocked on the window pane with his beak. A startled Aambal fell backwards, causing Seval to go flapping off the ledge. Up in the air, his feathers ruffled with the sudden movement, it came to Seval how funny the whole situation was and he burst into laughter. Aambal, who had clambered to her feet and come to the window, was even angrier. This changed Seval's mood, and he decided to soothe her.

When he found out what was annoying her, he grinned and said, 'Don't be silly, Aambal. Mutthu can't like anyone better than you.'

This made Aambal smile, and she asked, 'Really?'

With a snort, Seval said, 'He wouldn't dare, he's scared of you, you bossy young woman.'

This seemed to give him such amusement that he was laughing riotously. Aambal picked up a cushion and flung it at the bird, who flew out of its reach. Seval pacified her, and began explaining to her all the difficulties of organising the wedding and getting the hill ready for Murugan to move into. For all of us to move into, he added, you and Thennan included. He watched as Aambal's face changed expression. He sighed. What games Time plays, he thought to himself.

It was Aambal from whose mouth came the suggestion that perhaps, unlike Pazhani, which was built by humans, Paramkundram should have an architect who was not of this world, immune to curses, jinxes, magic—in short, immune to the ire of the sages and mystics that had settled on the hill and made it theirs. Seval's mind went immediately to Mayasura, the architect who had built the magnificent Veeramahendrapuram.

5

PARAMKUNDRAM

So tall was Paramkundram, it appeared to reach the sky. It was so large that it took a while for the sun to cross it. From Madurai, the mountain was about two naligai if you walked, less than half of that by horse and chariot. Old words spoke of a time before, when the land had fallen away from around the hard stone of the single rock that now towered upwards from the flat landscape. The stone mountain sat like a giant creature that had slumped down there long ago, its head raised to the skies, and never got up again. The hills that stood not very far from it had rich loamy soil, and plants and creatures thrived there, unlike on stony, inhospitable Paramkundram. Here and there, a few tiny blades of grass managed to push through cracks that had filled with mud particles brought by the winds. The only creatures that lived there were birds, hundreds of them. Legend had it that when people came to the hill to do penance, they changed from their human bodies to bird shapes in order to perch in the many little crevices that dotted the hill face. There they sat unmoving, untouched by wind and rain and sun, meditating, their bodies temporarily arrested. No one dared climb up there, unless certain that they had protection against the birds that had acquired a reputation for being violent if disturbed, cursing, mutilating, sometimes even killing what disturbed them.

This is why the thought of Mayan had put Seval in a better mood. He, like all the Asuras, bore inside him such an urge to life that neither death nor disease nor harm could affect him. Seval imagined the angry renunciates getting more and more ill-tempered as their curses went shooting out of their mouths only to sputter uselessly.

When Mayan arrived at Paramkundram, although he had no fear of the sages and their powers, he did not climb up the hill for a full six days. He waited, immersed in the preparation of his insides before the starting of a work so important that he himself must be emptied to make place for it. On the seventh day, a tiny chittukuruvi flew on to Mayan's shoulder and chirped in his ear. He then climbed up the hill instead of transporting himself to the top. When he reached the summit, there stood before him ancient sages, women and men with white hair that fell to the ground, hair so wispy that, every time the wind blew, it rose up and waved like long banners, trailing back down when the gusts paused. They greeted Mayan. One of them stepped closer, and taking his hand in hers, said, 'Welcome Mayasura, the greatest of architects.'

Mayan told them of Murugan's approaching marriage and his desire to hold it here on Paramkundram and to live here afterwards, and that he had come to carry out those wishes. He had not known what to expect, but when they began to smile and laugh with abandon, he was more than mildly surprised. The same woman then explained to him that they had been waiting for this. They had, at some time, all of them, even if momentarily, been ill-natured and caused harm to a being who had unknowingly disturbed them. Time had turned those curses back on them, and they had been fated to live in the cage of their own disdain, their own joyless irascibility. To each of these seekers who had called on Time for mercy, he had said, 'Go to the Great Hill, southwest of Madurai, and when the second child born to the Parents of Creation meets one that he longs to spouse, and chooses this stony hill for a home, if he does choose it, then will you be released.' Mayan was astounded and pleased. He wondered where they would go, what did it mean to be 'released' from a cage of curses? He could not imagine why anyone would curse, for the Asuras delighted in life and the endless ways in which life grows and changes. To them, everything was worthy of a blessing.

He took their leave, and transported himself to Pazhani where, after paying his respects to Murugan, he went to meet Seval. Mayan's meeting with Murugan had been quick because the groom had only one condition: everything in the house should reflect his joy that Theivanai had accepted him and consented to come to Bhu and live with him. He wanted the wedding to be grand but the palace to be modest, intimate.

Before Mayan began his work, he stood on the top of Paramkundram and surveyed it again. To his surprise, small plants had now appeared and the sound of water could be heard, though he could not, even with his Asura sight, locate the source of the water. The ancient penance-servers were nowhere in sight. He stood there for some moments, feeling disoriented; had he imagined the previous meeting? Had he mistakenly thought that the hill was stony and disapproving? Laughter bubbled out of the little flower buds on the plants and the throats of the many-coloured butterflies, dragonflies and birds that had appeared overnight. Then he understood that everything had transformed: Murugan was joyous and so everything became joyous. The moistening of the stone's heart had transformed the accumulated ire of its inhabitants and erased the impenetrable coating that it had left on the mountain.

Mayan saw that Paramkundram leaned in the direction from which Murugan would arrive from Pazhani. The great stone head of Paramkundram inclined, bowing. No other hill or mountain in creation—not Kailasa, not Meru, nor mighty Himavan—had the glory that Pazhani did. For when the God of the Kurinji fled the home of his parents, a humiliated, naked, orphaned little boy, not yet six, it was Pazhani that had been a mother to him, the womb into which he crept, weeping, raging, silent, to be reborn. No other hill could have borne the boy god's ire. The hill loved him and he loved the hill. And all other hills envied Pazhani. Paramkundram prided itself on being chosen to house the God of Hills.

Mayan looked out over the landscape and his eyes swept over the busy town of Madurai, where the temple of the goddess rose into the skies, and then to the three hills in the shapes of elephant, snake and cow, and the green, lush hills past all of these. He considered how he would build. This was the house where Murugan and Theivanai would begin their married life, so at the heart of the house would be their room, where they would be intimate, where they would join in union. Unlike on Pazhani, the heart of the house would not be the reading room or the hall of performance, but the bedroom of the couple. That room would have light from all directions, it would have balconies that would be hidden from view, and it would have spaces where the two of them could be together, as well as separate spaces for each of them.

He planned all the furniture they would need, tables and a bed and places to sit, and when he had the entire picture clear in his head, Mayan moved on to the next circle. What would be around their room? Should it be rooms for the poets and bards? That was too close, Mayan decided, awkward for everyone. Thus it was that, between the bedroom and the rest of the household, he built an enormous room that was open to the skies, its roof and two of its walls transparent, so that everything on the hilltop was visible. The only solid wall was the one connecting to Murugan and Theivanai's quarters.

After that were reception rooms, where visitors could meet the couple. At the end of that level was a small reading room. On a lower level, were rooms for visitors, and all those in Murugan's retinue, including Aambal and Thennan, and kitchens and store rooms and the like.

Mayan sat down on the scorching stone and shut his eyes, and the entire picture came together, like scattered iron shavings to a magnet. He stayed like that till he had traversed it all, bit by bit in his head, checking for misalignments, making corrections, adjustments. When he was satisfied that everything was in place, Mayan opened his eyes and counted the time that had passed: six days and six nights. And so he descended the hill once more and sent word that he was ready to begin work, and asked that Murugan and Theivanai be present. Theivanai, Murugan, Paravani, Seval, Veerabahu and the other eight, the six Krittikas, Ganesha, Aambal and Thennan, his friend Kuyili, as well as Aasaan and Kuyili's grandmother, all arrived in Paramkundram. They were lifted up to the top in pulley-drawn baskets that Mayan had erected.

There they waited in the gentle warmth of the early morning sun, fanned by breezes that were still cool, for Mayan to begin. Just then, the sound of gurgling water came to their ears. Some of them were looking around, trying to spot the water's source. Ganesha and Paravani smiled, as did Murugan and the Krittikas. Murugan removed his bejewelled crown, and pressed his forehead to the cool stone, the sun only just coming up in the east, and said, 'Mother, bless me.' From under the stone, the gurgling accelerated until the stone cracked and there stood, in shining white brocade, her hair blowing wildly in the wind, Sarasvati, who had gone underground after she delivered the six babies to the south. She placed her hands on the head of the handsome young man and said, 'Rise, my son. May you be blessed, may wherever you go, plants and trees sprout and fruit and flower. May stony hearts become filled with moisture. May the gurgling rush of water flow in your speech in Tamizh and may your love be a mighty river that gives life.'

Those who did not know who she was looked surprised and baffled. Murugan turned to them and said, 'This is my mother, it was she who bore me to my home in the shara vana. This is the secret river Sarasvati.' Tears of joy sprang in Sarasvati's eyes, and she wept without restraint. The crack in the stone widened and water rushed forth in a stream that would never dry. This stream Murugan named 'Sarasvati'.

Then Murugan took the blessings of the Krittikas, of Ganesha, of Aasaan, of Akattiyan, who moved back in alarm as Murugan bent to touch his feet, of Kuyili's grandmother and others. Finally, Mayan sat the couple down, and asked them to join hands with each other and him as well, and to see what he had imagined as their home, to walk through and take stock, and to nod if they were happy with it. Which they did. There it was then: the magnificent palace on Paramkundram, its many rooms luxuriously appointed, its work spaces efficiently filled with implements, and beside it, the gurgling stream that was a testimony to the spirit of freedom that Murugan embodied. Sarasvati had broken free and stayed hidden, diving into the earth's dark and remaining there—nothing was too big a price to pay for freedom.

The day ended and Murugan and his people left. Only Seval stayed behind to organise other things. What of Murugan's parents, you may wonder. He had neither consulted them about the date of the wedding nor invited them to the building of Paramkundram's palace. You might think that he was being hard-hearted, but he was not, he was merely balancing the neglect that they had meted out to him, for a gesture made needed a gesture returned. There was neither anger nor a spirit of revenge here, and once this was over and they had agonised over it, it would be over. They were the first ones to whom Murugan went with the exquisite scroll in which was an invitation to his wedding. At the top, it said 'We, the six Krittikas, invite you to the wedding of Murugan, Lord of Pazhani, who will henceforth also be called Mutthukumarasami of

Paramkundram.' A new name, Murugan had thought, and a new aspect, for a new part of his life, and he had grown to like the sound of 'Mutthu'. It was a way for him to acknowledge the role that Seval played in his new life.

Paravani laughed when Murugan showed him the invite, and Murugan asked, 'Does it sound silly?'

'No,' replied Paravani, 'I was only thinking of the vain bird. He's now going to want to trumpet this in all the worlds.'

Theivanai was happy. She knew exactly what she wanted to wear for the wedding. She had already picked out her jewellery and selai in Mayilai on one of her many shopping sprees in Murugan's company. This wasn't the only one she had bought either: Seval had gone around the busy weavers' streets and examined their wares, selecting the ones he thought worthy of viewing, and also sent word to weavers outside Mayilai, even in faraway Kanchi. Murugan, excited to be making these shopping trips with her, bought much fabric and many a selai for Aambal, his mother and others too.

Theivanai loved off-white, she loved pearls and gold. Then she had heard Murugan exclaim over an indigo selai, and learnt that it was his favourite colour. She put her hand on it before Murugan bought it for Aambal as well. 'I like this one,' she had said, and he had smiled, and said to her, 'Drape it on and see how you look in it.' He had helped her make the pleats and put it over her shoulder so she could see herself in the polished bronze mirror in the store, and he had exclaimed in surprise at how well it suited her: her sandalwood complexion, her mayi-darkened eyes, the hair that she wore rolled into many little knots on her head, with a few perfumed and curled locks tumbling on to her strong neck. Theivanai had gone red with pleasure, and said that she now needed jewellery.

She had then asked for more selai in the same colour and bought more of them than the ecstatic store keeper sold in a whole season. Seval took them around to a jeweller whose craft and eye for design were the talk of Mayilai. His collection of neelam-studded jewellery made Theivanai gasp in wonder. Murugan helped Theivanai to make up her mind, with Seval piping up to say, take everything. When they got home after the day's shopping, he had handed her a little silk pouch and said, 'This is a gift for you. I hope you like it.' She had opened the pouch as soon as she was in her room and found a jewel box with a mukkuti inside it. It was in two tiers, with an enormous indigo sapphire that matched the jewellery she had bought earlier. This wasn't from any of the stores that they had visited, and if it was, then Murugan had made sure she hadn't seen it. She removed the white pearl from her nose and put on the blue mukkuti, and its dark blue rays darkened the paleness of her skin, making her wish that she had been blessed with duskier skin, like Murugan's mother, like Aambal or the women in this city by the sea. She had determined then, to wear the mukkuti and the first indigo brocade selai when she married Murugan. And that was what she wore, her entire trousseau was blue, as was her jewellery, their blue darks lightened by the pearls and yellows of the jewellery that her mother Indranai had passed on to her.

Murugan was accompanied by Seval in his shopping trips for his trousseau. His jewellery and clothes for this new life were of many, many colours. He spent a long time picking out clothes for all his friends, especially Aambal and Kuyili. For Aasaan, he would have the royal weavers bring in cotton yarn from Ponduru and weave an extra fine veshti and shoulder cloth. For his parents, Murugan had the weavers go to them and ask their preference.

Paravani tried to tell Murugan that he should, as he had done for all the others, also pick for them, but he said no. And that was that.

Aambal was excited. Kandhan and Theivanai were so well matched. She had met Theivanai at Chendur, but Murugan had talked so much about her that it felt as if she had known her forever. She found thoughts of the wedding settling her mind, for of late she had been filled with little pangs of jealousy: did Murugan like Thennan more than her, did he like Kuyili more, or Perunkadungko?

Jealousy seemed to be wafting in the air then, for Theivanai herself wondered if Murugan's friends, especially Aambal, would be closer to him than she would be. She had understood that for Murugan, Aambal was special. Aambal, Paravani, Ganesha, Akattiyan, the Krittikas were like the compartments of his heart. Would she ever be as close to him? Of Aambal, especially, she was afraid. When Murugan spoke of her, there was a note in his voice and a look in his eyes that never appeared with anyone else. And the way he was always thinking of her when he went to a new place, when he said something interesting, when he was shopping. Theivanai knew that they were best friends, and that Murugan was not in love with her, but he didn't have to be in love with her to give her a place in his heart.

Aambal's excitement at the approaching wedding and the shift to Paramkundram was palpable and enormous. Was the excitement coming from the fact that the new home would be so close to Madurai? Was it that, as an applicant to the Assembly, the proximity to the town where it was housed filled her with excitement? Or was it that she had heard Murugan say to Seval that he wanted to be in a 'more romantic place'? Pazhani was a place where people gave up their many longings and sought their own solitude. Maybe she too wanted to be in that new place? Or maybe she was just eager to be in in a place filled with the bustle and hustle of a big town? Or did she want to be where she was not living at the bottom of the hill and Thennan ... Her thoughts broke off, as they always did when they came to this matter. She did not know how to navigate such thoughts, and so she would return to her work. Now she turned her attention to the many selai and jewels that Murugan had sent her. She wanted to look her best for her best friend's wedding. Which one to wear? Kandhan liked her wearing green. He liked to tease her, saying that she looked like a speaking tree, and whenever he sent her more than one selai, there was bound to be a green. But he liked white, too and ink-blue. Unbidden, her thoughts turned to Thennan: what was his favourite colour?

On his part, Thennan had no thought of clothes or jewellery. He would wear what he had been gifted. All this talk of marriage all around made him think of his own marriage. About Aambal and marriage. Would she marry? Whom would she marry? Or would she refuse to be married? Murugan seemed to occupy almost all the space of her affections. He had seen how she glowered at Kuyili when the latter put her arms around Murugan's shoulder as they walked or slapped him on the back when he said something. Was Aambal in love with Murugan? He shook his head and turned to work, which was uncomplicated, in comparison.

The one person who had no time for any thoughts was Seval. The harried bird was flying hither and thither, checking on everything, making sure that tempers remained even and work got done with full concentration. So, when the day arrived for them to make the move to Paramkundram, it all went very neatly, because Seval had set it all up with the precision of a battle manoeuvre. That is, except for a hitch that held up the wedding for so long that the fixed 'auspicious' time passed, and the wedding took place at a time that no one bothered to check, but which could well have been 'inauspicious'.

Aambal was the cause for this delay. Aambal and Murugan's friends smiled and waited patiently, knowing why this was so, but others were annoyed and shocked. 'So careless,' very many of them said. In the end, no one at the wedding was in any doubt about two things: the relationship between Murugan and Aambal and that between Time and poetry.

When the wedding was fixed, Aambal had asked Murugan what he would like as a gift, and he had said he wanted a hundred poems describing his courtship and wooing of Theiva, up to the wedding itself. It was not an easy thing, but not beyond Aambal's skill. Yet, although she had had enough time, she was unable to finish. This was the first time in all her life with Murugan that she had failed her poetry and failed Murugan. Even on the day of wedding, she was unable to break through the wall of dullness that stood between her and the last verse. Her palm leaves were all done, threaded through, waiting to be pulled tight and bound, but the last verse was incomplete.

To be exact, the last line of the last verse just wasn't forming to perfection. Had it been someone else, perhaps they would have used a lesser line. Aambal certainly had some good lines there, but none was as perfect as the line that was dancing at the edge of her words. Aambal knew that *that* line was the one. But she had let it slip away. For two days, she had been trying to catch the fall of its step, a glimpse of its attire, something she could hold on to. She had not imagined that even on the morning of the day she had to hand over the poems to Murugan, she still would not have found the line. Lines were what she dealt in, they were what she knew best, they were what she had grown to think of as unchanging. She walked up and down, she sat, she stood, she closed her eyes, she opened them, she dipped her head into the stream. But nothing.

She had been so pleased with what she had—all ninety-nine verses had come together fluently, and the last line of the last verse was to be the crown, like 'Mutthu' was the crown of all creation.

Aambal was just picking up her stylus to press out the lines, her practiced hand steady, so immersed in her work that she didn't at first hear the voice that called out, 'Aambal, Aambal'. When her ears registered the soft, lilting voice with the inflections of the seacoast lands, a warmth passed over her. Her hand was suddenly damp, and she felt her heart pushing against her ribs. She put the stylus down and opened the door and said to Thennan, 'Come in.' He smiled at her and handed her a little leaf-wrapped bundle. She knew what was inside before she opened it because the fragrance had already filled the whole room. Taking it from him wordlessly, she looked at him, and he looked at her. It was as if they had no language, the both of them, for such an occasion. The silence stretched on. Thennan looked around the room and his eyes fell on a pile of selai on the mat. He asked, 'You have a reading today?'

Aambal didn't want to tell him that she had been trying them on. She felt something between shame and fear to think that, instead of dwelling on the sound and sense of words, she had been dwelling on images of herself in these selai. She didn't want to tell him how, in the middle of imagining the tempo of the lines, she had slipped into imagining her own feet with delicate-belled anklets. As always, when she was scared, she set her face into an impassive mask and her voice into a steady register. She told him that she had just taken them out to pick one for the wedding.

Her voice made Thennan aware of the oddness of the situation: he had seen the flowers by the roadside and stopped to buy some, thinking neither of the propriety of it, nor anything else. And when he handed it to her, he had felt as if this was the first time he was giving flowers to a woman—and that she would say or do something to indicate what she was feeling. Instead, here they were, talking about reading and the wedding of the man in whose apprenticeship and employ they were both bound. Thennan felt as if he had come to the edge of a forest, his chest thrust out and his lungs filled with bravado, but at the boundary between wilderness and scruffy forest, the sounds, the smells and the air itself was so different as to be frightening, and his lungs deflated, his footsteps slowed and his determination was gone. He felt a strange sense of relief, as he might have felt turning away from a real forest. When they were children, Kandhan and Aambal had treated the forest as if it was their backyard—neither of them was afraid.

Thennan turned towards Aambal, and saw that she was looking away. He felt sad, but also strangely relieved, and so, he took his leave of her. When his footsteps had faded away, Aambal looked at the flowers in her hand. She opened the leaf and smelt them, she held them to her chest, a smile filling her insides. She stood there, humming to herself, but when a gust of wind snatched at the palm leaf ready to be written on, she shook her head and dropped the string of flowers on the windowsill. Turning away from it, she sat down, straightened her back and picked up the stylus to write down the line she had just perfected. But she could not remember what it had been.

In the days that followed, whatever she did, the line would not return, and though she wrote down many six lines, only five of them were right. She crushed palm leaf after palm leaf onto which her stylus had reluctantly pressed down lines. With each failed attempt, she despaired. The more anxious she got, the worse her lines got. She began to think of running away. Of shutting the door of her room and never coming out. But then she recalled what Murugan had said when she asked him what he wanted from her for a gift, 'What I want is something you can give, but consider before you say yes, for if you do agree and but cannot give it, I will consider the occasion for which you're gifting it to me not meant to be.'

She had to finish, she must finish. Sweat broke and ran all over her white work clothes, she didn't even glance at the ornate selai. She closed her eyes and the image of a pale-skinned, handsome, honey-voiced man, his curly locks perfumed, his fingers elegant, rushed into her head. Should she slam her head against the windowsill or the floor? But what use would that be? Murugan's marriage would not happen, and then what?

Just then there was the rustle of wings, and Seval was in the room. 'Aambal,' he said, 'why aren't you on the hill?' Aambal burst into tears and told him everything. She looked ready to fling the entire palm leaf bundle out of the window. Seval picked it up, holding it carefully, for the thread hadn't been tightened since the last leaf still had to be added. He bent down and picked up one of the crumpled leaves and read through it. Letting out a snort, he said, 'Aambal, this is so bad. Just read it. That first line is terrible, even an untutored poet would do better. What are you doing?'

Aambal felt anger course through her. She snapped at Seval, 'Then you finish it. It's not so bad, it's just the use of *beyond hills, beyond sun, beyond sea* instead of *behind hills, beyond sun, below sea* in the line that's making it sound bad.' As she was speaking, she realised that she had just corrected the line, after days and days of unyielding labour. 'Seval,' she cried out, 'Seval, you saved my life!'

But Seval was already out of the window, calling out, 'Come on now, the wedding is waiting for your verses.'

Indeed the wedding was waiting—all the guests, Murugan's parents, the Krittikas, Theivanai, Muchukunda, Murugan's uncle and aunt, his brother, his Aasaan, his favourite disciple, the Kuru Muni, his friends. They were all there, but Murugan said, 'Wait.' Again and again. Someone asked him what he was waiting for, and those who knew him knew that, since Aambal wasn't there, it was she he was waiting for. Some of them knew why.

Theivanai began to get agitated when the auspicious time approached. Kuyili and Perunkadungko whispered to Murugan, 'The time's passing. It's becoming embarrassing.' But he said, 'No. Aambal's gift must first come. The right time is the time that the gift arrives.' And Seval, who had been caught up in a thousand last-minute things, now realised what was happening. He flew down and his suspicions were confirmed: Aambal was stuck, and the shame of her inability to devise a means to navigate past the stubborn damming of the words froze her further into her shame. And thus it was that Murugan's wedding happened past the 'auspicious' time, past the expected moment when he and Theivanai would marry. Instead, it happened when the poetry arrived.

The wise King Muchukunda said, 'The right time is the time when the poem is perfected, for this is the God of Poetry, the Patron of the Great Assembly, Mutthukumarasami of Paramkundram.'

As soon as Aambal had added the last palm leaf, with the now perfect last verse, to the other verses and bound the whole, she herself was bounding up the seemingly endless steps to the location of the wedding. So, in the end, she wore none of the many selai that she had tried on, nor the jewellery Murugan had lovingly selected for her, nor did she comb her hair or wash her face. Perhaps she hadn't even bathed that day, or the day before, but she had her gift. When Aambal rushed into the hall, Murugan heaved such a big sigh that it made the earring swing in Theivanai's earlobe. He jumped down from the dais, all but snatched the palm leaf bundle out of Aambal's outstretched hands, and turned immediately to the last one. He read it and laughed with delight. He said, 'Thank you, Aambal.' And then went back up to take his place beside Theivanai, who was not quite sure that she wasn't angry.

The ceremony was a short one, with the Krittikas giving Murugan a bangle and a ring that they had made for him to put on Theivanai's hand. Airavata handed Theivanai an exquisite ring studded with one large pearl, at the heart of which was a tiny indigo spot that cast blue rays all over the room when it caught the light, for her to put on Murugan's finger.

In all this time, Thennan had been anxious, he had no clue what had happened to Aambal. He had the suspicion that Aambal's delay had something to do with the poems she had promised

Murugan. He shook his head, *why did the writing of poems have to be so dramatic?* Then he reminded himself that he was a bard and could not fully understand the almost life-and-death nature of the energies involved in writing a poem, true of sense and sound, bound with perfect grammar and metre. He had recited verses himself on the battlefield, but those were not like this, those rushed into and out of him, impelled by forces that were beyond his control or comprehension. He was worried. Had Aambal fought with Murugan? Was she unwell? Or worse, was she secretly in love with Murugan, and couldn't bring herself to watch him marry another? The thoughts ran through his head disorderly and unbearable, and he was quite tired by the time Aambal arrived, huffing and puffing, clutching to her chest a palm-leaf bundle bound with indigo thread. He heaved a sigh and felt a smile forming in his mind, and then he noticed the sweaty dampness of her face, her hair clammy, the plainness of her clothes and her unadorned hands and neck and ears. Oh god, he thought, what was she thinking? He heard a hiss above his head and looked up to see Seval glaring at him.

The rest of the day went quickly and happily. Aambal ran to her room as soon as the ritual was over, to bathe, change and put on her jewellery. She returned to the hall just in time to join the rest of her classmates in formally wishing the couple. When it was her turn, Theivanai said, 'Ah, Aambal, Murugan tells me that I, too, am in your hundred poems. I look forward to reading them.' Aambal was happy. In that short time, Kandhan had already told Theivanai about the gift that she had given him, given them, she corrected herself, you give a couple the wedding gift, for both of them.

As the day wore on, she went over the events of the morning and shuddered at the memory of the feeling that had gripped her when she was stuck. Never again, she told herself. No distractions. No thoughts of any selai, or anklets, of flowers, or those who brought flowers, their handsome faces serious. She shuddered again. Her life was her poetry and Murugan and the Assembly. And she would let nothing get in the way of that. And then she thought of Velliveethi's poetry: the unabashed declaration of her love for the man to whom she had given her heart, the search to find that man who had wandered on, nomadic like her and unable to stop anywhere. She was one of the best poets of Tamizh, and she wrote and loved. Even when she was distracted, she wrote. But Aambal shook her head again, thinking, not for me, never. Seval was watching the expressions flit across Aambal's face, and he shook his head.

Later that evening, Theivanai picked up the palm-leaf bundle that Murugan had so carefully handed to Seval before the wedding rituals, instructing him not to let it out of his hands. She thought she would flip through and return to it later, but soon was so drawn in that she could not put it down till the last poem.

She sighed at the end of it, and understood why Murugan loved Aambal so much, understood the depth of both Aambal's love for Murugan and her skill at poetry. Theivanai envied them their friendship. She wanted Aambal to be her friend too, to be part of this friendship.

Once the excitement of the wedding passed, Murugan resumed his routines with Aambal and Thennan. He also sent word for Akattiyan to come to Paramkundram and to instruct Theivanai in Tamizh, and to reveal to her the story of how it had been reborn. 'It's better heard from one who has looked at it, long and longingly, from the outside and who looks on it as a treasure, rather than from the one who made it, unmade it and remade it.'

༄

With the wedding, everything shifted—just a little, as if all the events and people in Murugan's life had taken a measured half-step back, so that when Theivanai took her place beside their god, she would not feel cramped. The severe aloneness that sometimes slipped over Murugan like a well-fitting mantle seemed to have fallen off, as if its clasps had melted and snapped away in the heat of Theivanai's chest. On Pazhani, Murugan had once fortressed himself to burn through the version of himself that had caused him shame and humiliation and become another. Even after he was befriended by Aambal and went to the kalari and became friends with the others, the mood on Pazhani stayed the same. Those who came to see Murugan there and to seek guidance were often those that wanted to distance themselves from the world—people who wanted to turn away and track their own interiors.

Paramkundram was pliant, seduced by the spirited Vaigai, whose eddies and ripples splashed not just her banks, but moistened the very air of Madurai, which the wind carried to the mountain. The poets sang of how Vaigai slowed in her journey as she entered Madurai, to linger by her lover's side.

To all those who came to the home of Murugan and Theivanai, their hospitality had the added resonance of this love story. Murugan had grown to enjoy being companioned, and now this companion, Theivanai, would always be with him. Everywhere he once went alone, now he would go with her. Even when he thought of himself in solitude, in the belly of Pazhani Hill, he imagined Theiva by his side, quiet, with her own solitary thoughts held firm in her chest, not caring what he was thinking or feeling. With her, it was easier for him to feel at home everywhere. After the Great Battle at Chendur, it was the company of Theivanai that kept him out of that cave of solitude that was always seductive, always welcoming to him. Theivanai's arrival was like the hill winds that bring notice of an approaching season, making everything pause and prepare for the new.

Falling in love with Theiva made Murugan even more eager for this world, its little quirks, its people and all its gestures of affection.

And with Theiva, that was easy—her delight in everything made it easy for him to be delighted too.

Theivanai understood his desire to live in a body like a manava, to witness the joy that the language he had made gave those who learnt it. The endlessness of Maharasa she struggled to imagine, but when they joined, at times she felt as if she was afloat on the startracks of the universes, flowing from one path to another, and sometimes it was as if all was inside her—the endless flow of the many universes with their starways and suns and moons spinning inside her passages. When he entered into her, he made her himself. She loved Murugan, yet remained attentive to herself, and as she went from one station to another of her relationship with him, she knew that she was changing, and that he was too.

It didn't take Theivanai long to settle down. She was happy that Murugan let down his guard with her: she knew how unshakeable that guard had been. She was glad that he felt happy that this world and the people in it welcomed her as his companion. As Theivanai had expected, Murugan's sense of order and routine meant that she was coming into a household that worked and rested well.

She was very glad to have Seval around since he kept things under control. He also took her up the hill, down winding paths to show her the caves and through the big and little streets of the modest town that lay between the great hill and the bustling splendour of Madurai. There was a special bond between the two of them—perhaps in the many days that he carried messages from Murugan to Theivanai, they had developed a grudging respect for each other. Theivanai turned to Seval for advice in the way that Murugan turned to Paravani.

Theivanai had wondered how she would feel about Aambal and Murugan's closeness. Now she knew that she wanted a friend like that too. Theivanai watched with wonder, sometimes anxiety, as the serious young woman sat in front of the God of

Poetry, afraid of nothing except her own inability to bring to life poems as he visualised them. She admired Aambal's fearlessness when it came to language: she would fling herself off the cliffs of Paramkundram or lie down in the paths of storms if that was what a poem demanded.

Without a word from Murugan, Theivanai understood the feeling that held the two together: the friendship of children that became the sturdy trunk of adult friendship. Equally, she understood that Aambal's adoration was the adoration of the poet for the God of Poetry, for the Great Rasa which flowed in the language that was her life. In her ears, every syllable rang with praise of Murugan. What more could a poet ask for, and what more could the God of Poetry ask for?

Yet, Theivanai could not help feeling a pang when she saw Murugan and Aambal absorbed in another language adventure. She wanted to be part of that absorption, she wanted to sit there with them, all the worlds forgotten except the world of the sense and sound of Tamizh. She wanted Aambal to see her and Murugan as one. Theivanai wanted Aambal to want to be friends with her the way she was with Murugan. Even as she thought it, she knew that that would never be. Aambal would love only one person in all creation that way: Murugan himself, her Kandhan. But that didn't mean she couldn't be friends with Theiva. This brought an edge to Theiva's desire to understand, to know and to learn Tamizh.

Aambal liked Theivanai, but she also wondered what the arrival of a spouse to the God of Poetry would mean for his apprentice. She did not wonder what it meant for his friend: that would always be. Aambal was also caught between anxiety and eagerness at the thought of being alone with Thennan more often. She wondered if Theivanai had read the hundred poems that Murugan had demanded she write as his wedding gift. Did they read it together? What would Theivanai have thought of how she, the courtship, her testing of Murugan had appeared in Aambal's verses? What had she made of the parts that described Murugan's suffering in that time: would those verses have made her cry? Aambal had cried writing them, love is painful, she had thought, so painful. She thought of how it ate into attentiveness. As she wrote, it seemed as if she could hear Thennan's voice singing. What made her pick up her stylus and get back to work was the image of her hero Velliveethi, whose poems singed the language with the fire of her longing for her missing lover. Velliveethi became for Aambal what the Krittikas were for Murugan: always steady, always reliable, always bringing a measure of certainty.

And Thennan? The handsome bard whose face now routinely wore a flush was glad at the lessening of Murugan's attention to Aambal. He was happy for days when Murugan was busy with the wedding preparations, and after the wedding, for the times when Murugan and Theivanai were visiting or receiving visitors themselves at Paramkundram. He surprised himself by becoming more and more daring in Aambal's company: he tried new beats that were of imported metrical nature from the Vadamozhi texts that he had become familiar with on his journeys. He mixed and matched, a couple of times, he even suggested words to Aambal.

Theivanai did not sit with them when they were working, but Murugan often invited her to come and listen when something was done. She had started her lessons with Akattiyan and had begun to get a hold of the metres and the anatomy of the language, its heartbeat. Theivanai marvelled at Aambal's calm once she had herself revised a poem to her satisfaction and Murugan had gone over it with her. She appeared certain that she had tracked down the words she wanted to their varied habitats, and persuaded one or the other to nest in her verse for the season of its writing, for there was no doubting that the nesting would be fecund. But Theivanai sensed that her presence made Aambal nervous. She listened intently to Aambal's reading, sometimes exclaimed over the beauty of a line, an image, a rhyme, the rhythm, or over

Thennan's inflection. She was open, friendly and appreciative. So why was Aambal so nervous?

Aambal, too, was conscious of how tense she became when Theivanai was present. She didn't want Theivanai to see … didn't want her to see how she was stopping herself from looking at Thennan as often as she did when it was only the two of them, and sometimes, even when Murugan was there. Theivanai did see, of course. She saw the look in Aambal's eyes, the way her body registered Thennan's every move, she saw how Thennan looked at Aambal. Murugan and Seval saw too, it was clear. She sensed that neither of them would speak of it. Theivanai worried: Aambal should not, she could not fail to make it into the Assembly. She had to win every one of the examinations. She could not let Murugan down, and even more, herself. Theivanai shuddered to think of what Aambal might do if she failed. She was already one of the best younger poets of the language, and she must not let anything get in her poetry's way.

But love was in the air on Paramkundram. Theivanai and Murugan courted love, and Aambal played crocodile and monkey with it—on tip toes, always ready to leap away should the creature show signs of opening its jaws and taking a brutal snap at her. Thennan wished she would not be so watchful. He wanted her to look at him, to talk to him, sometimes, he wanted her to even— and this thought made him fearful—choose love over her work, should that choice ever become necessary. He was dizzy with the force of what he was feeling, but Aambal's stubbornness, and the ever-present fear of Murugan, tripped him out of his joyful spinning. He would then remind himself that Murugan and poetry were the most important things in Aambal's life, and that she was determined to let nothing get in the way. So Thennan was wary, careful, watchful and patient. And Seval watched Thennan, pugnacious, snarly. He made it a point to come into the reading room more often than necessary when Aambal and Thennan were alone, his sharp claws beating a staccato rhythm on the polished floors, belying the smile on his face.

6

AKATTIYAN REVEALS THE SECRET

Theivanai was interested in the work of the scholars and poets and bards, in the lives of the visitors who came to meet Murugan on Paramkundram, in the ways of the gypsies and hunters who always brought gifts that were a wonder to her. Murugan was glad when Theivanai was by his side. She accompanied him and shared his work of being judge and guide to his poets and scholars. He also hoped that Theiva would take over some of his work as the Patron of the Assembly. Murugan knew that the time had come for a big change at the Assembly, and that in times before, his father had come and done the things that were needed: a way to measure expertise and eliminate the unworthy, a way to organise and collect the poetry that was worthy. These things had brought into the Assembly a sense of discipline, but also a fear of the chaos that had reigned before. That fear became a leading principle, which pinnacled in Nakkeeran who held on to directives, rules, formats as if they were life itself, forgetting that Murugan himself had said that the best poetry came from the mouths of the hunters, untrammelled by rules, bound only to the throbbing beats inside their bellies.

Theivanai was filled with eagerness to learn about the 'old tongue', how it had been remade, made new and rebirthed by the man who was now husband and companion to her. The story of the old tongue began far away from these lands where the purple flowers waited twelve years, twice the number of heads their god once had, to burst out of the mud. It began up north, where its earliest inhabitants travelled and settled around the land's torrential many-limbed river. These people were led thatward by the call of the land, which burst like ripened seeds in their dreams and sent root tendrils into their chests. The land that had been hazy and undefined in dream became clearer as they came closer, and when they arrived, they saw that it was a welcome place: its mud soft, its trees and plants lush, its waters clear and sweet. It made them feel like they could do much, made them want to root into the mud, to hold on like the mighty trees that filled the landscape.

They brought with them knowledge of fire and of moulding and baking soft clay; they came with a tested and tried knowledge of building. The former they had discovered by simulating the strike of lightning that produced flame, by smiting together and rubbing things that were around them, wood and stone included, till they found the robust flint that flared into fire. Their ease with brick-making came from watching and following the way rain-softened clay baked under sunfire, and over time set into indissoluble hardness.

These early dwellers looked around their new land, and marked out a boundary to stand between them and the dark, dense, intimidating forest. Sometimes, when they were close to this area that lay midway between wilderness and habitation, they heard human steps, a delicate footfall, and turned towards the sound, but whoever it was had pivoted with light steps and was gone before they could even focus. They understood that whoever it was would not be sighted so easily, but at the same time, wanted to be seen. Another sound also assailed their ears. It came from deep inside the forest's belly: a roaring and bellowing that made their hair stand on end and their hearts go cold.

As the days passed, as both of these sounds became familiar, they were an enticement for the dwellers to go further and deeper into what had once been out of bounds. As they walked into the forest, their eyes grew damp, their hearts grew damp, their feet slowed, and the green, yellow, maroon, brown forest cast its spell on them. The roaring and the elusive footfalls soon became tokens of protection that they did not need to fear.

When they returned home from these outings and slept, exhausted, the nights brought dreams: a wild man, his skin ruddy, as if he was wearing the evening skies, his body covered with ash and mud, in his hands a horn that he raised to smiling lips and blew on. In his other hand, he held a little drum that he twirled constantly, holding its slender middle between his thumb and middle finger. His hair was matted and fell to his feet, his eyes were red, his lips were red, snakes wound around his chest, neck and shoulders and hung from his arms. Sometimes there were birds in his hair, and he was mounted on a bull, its neck, like his, muscled and enormous. In some of those dreams, another figure appeared—a child, his hair in curls, his mouth open in a laugh, in his hands a stick that was alive, leaves springing from little green knobs. He rode on a peacock and hailed them, looking at them, his eyes sparkling, his laughter falling into their dreams, making their hearts full.

As the days passed, these visitations became more and more insistent, barging into their sleep, and over time, the dreamers began to prepare themselves for the seeing. The days and the nights passed, and they realised that, as they slept, their bodies were mimicking what the bull-riding wild one in the dream was doing. On waking, they strove to repeat these movements, and they slowly arrived at the understanding that they were better able to accomplish this at certain times of the day. They also understood that they had to prepare their bodies—not be full-bellied, not be sleepy-headed and so on—when they made the attempt.

That was how they arrived at a preparedness, by assigning a fixed time and a fixed place near the forest for this pursuit, which demanded much energy, focus and effort. And the Bull Rider began to pause long enough for them to catch sight of him at the edge of the forest. He seemed pleased with their efforts, for he stopped and smiled, sometimes, he corrected what they were doing. He also began to show them postures that their dreams had not yet revealed to them. He sat at a distance from them and demonstrated ways to draw in and let go of the air that they breathed. Now, not only were their bodies more sprightly but so was their breath, and they became aware that their breathing was weaving in and out with the earth's breath. They felt like they had grown taller, stronger, that they had somehow more power.

The other one, the boy, neither sat still nor breathed deliberately. When he appeared, everything breathed differently—the leaves and branches, the birds and the beasts all ran around him, breathing hard and joyfully. And their own breath took up the lilt, the beat, the rhythm, the stepping of the boy's, and their mouths opened and sounds came out of them: little sounds and big sounds, fat sounds and lean, soft sounds and rough sounds, sounds that took longer than other sounds. So many, so many sounds, which made them delighted and light. He repeated the sounds they made, sometimes changing their inflection, at other times, clapping to their fall. In the course of the days that passed, they began to repeat sounds they recognised, a sound that was in the process of being breathed out of another's mouth before it came out. They soon made connections between when they produced a certain sound—what they had been looking at, what they had been hearing or touching, or what was going in and out of them—and the sound itself. Soon, there were sounds corresponding to things and actions that they all recognised, and began to use with each other and with the boy.

He was coming closer and closer, till one day, he was sitting next to them as they ate their morning meal. He pointed to the food and rubbed his belly, then his lips opened and he held his head forward. They understood that he wanted to be fed, and one of them held out a morsel, which he ate, and they gave him more and more mouthfuls. When he had had enough, he stood up and beckoned to them. He led them deep into the forest, down paths that seemed to materialise as he put step after step. The boy stopped when they reached a wall of rock. They waited, and the little one pushed aside shrubs with his stick, from which the leaves were springing thick.

Those who had followed the boy saw that there was an opening in the rock face. Without a thought, they followed him into the cave. He bent down to pick something up, then raised his arm and walked closer to the pale inner wall. His hand moved along its surface—the piece of stone that he held between fingers was red, and left a line of red on the wall. As his fingers moved, they saw that he was drawing a vine on which flowers grew and leaves grew. They laughed in delight, and he laughed with them, and held out the stone to one of them. The boy gestured to the wall, and the elderly woman who had the shale piece in her hand looked confused for a moment, but moved towards the wall and began to trace a line along it. The red line grew longer, then she stopped and looked back at those who stood behind her. The boy clapped delightedly and gestured for her to go on. She looked at the wall and them all, then shut her eyes and stood still. When her hand moved again, it became clear that she was trying to trace out leaves and flowers like the ones the boy had made. When she finished, the crowd gasped in wonder: she had drawn the same things, a vine, leaves, flowers, but it was different from the boy's. He laughed again, and raising his hands above his head, turned round and round, the staff raised high. They copied him, laughter tumbling out of their mouths. Now, someone else pushed forward and held out a hand—it was a little girl and her brother, bigger than her. He took the shale, held his sister's hand and traced something. It was not a vine, it was a stemmed flower that stood with its head raised, and there was a similar flower-face in the sky, the sun.

Others came forward, and there was much excitement and noise, and they did not notice when the boy disappeared. When they did register the absence, they fell quiet and went outside to look for him. He was nowhere to be seen that day. But he returned another day, and then again and again, and they all continued to visit the cave and pick up pieces of red stone and draw the things that filled the world around them: trees, animals, people. At first, they drew what they saw, then as they stood looking at what they had drawn, they began to try and draw what they made of these things: they drew animals that were sitting, standing, moving. They also drew them in various stages of life, they tried to draw what they did with each other: they drew people trying to strike flint for fire, they drew children running, women, men, animals, the elements of their world.

The rider on the bull continued to appear to them, usually around the times that the sun had just risen or when it was close to setting. He got off his bull and sat down on the moss-softened floor of the forest clearing, and as he twisted and bent his body and his breath, they followed along. Sometimes, when someone took too long to learn and do what he was showing them, or if someone was distracted, he roared and brandished his trident. If he was exceedingly angry, he walked away. Otherwise, he breathed and waited.

As the days passed, these people felt a change in their bodies: as they walked, they felt the earth ripple, sometimes it seemed as if their feet and bodies were being given a gentle push upwards. When more time had passed, they began to be able to feel what was waiting to happen in the air, in mud, in water and in the fire of the sky as well as in their bellies. Indeed, they knew when the rain was coming, they could hear the approach of the curling wind long before it came, and they could see things happen before they did. It gave them a feeling that they were not under the control of nature, which they had thus far feared and were in awe of. It made them walk with a spring in their step, but it also made them rush about, disregarding the lesson that nature had once imparted to them—to bend before its might, to wait and follow what it hinted at through signs like lightning, bird calls and more.

This new potence in their bodies also made them blind and deaf to the little boy. They ignored him and those who still followed him into the cave and came out feeling the delight that everything felt when he was near. Those who had chosen the boy knew that he had brought to them a slowing, a pausing in which they looked around them. They held those sights inside their bellies and then brought it out onto the cave wall and in the mud with lines that did not falter because they had gone over them so many times in their minds. It made them want to look more, to understand and then to reveal what they had understood. It had made them want to take what they saw and mix it with what was inside them and to draw that too.

One day, the boy came earlier than ever. They walked to the cave and he gestured to them to sit down. Then he began to draw: a thick vertical line ending in three prongs, and under that a seated figure, its hands folded on its lap and its legs folded across each other. He gestured to the forest and mimed riding on a bull, then sitting still and twisting the limbs into different shapes. They understood that he was telling them that this was the man who sat under the tree and showed the others from their habitation how to do what he was doing. They looked long and hard and understood that the pronged line was the tree, even if it did not look like one. He pointed to them and gestured to the wall. Many came up and stood, thinking about objects that were like what he had drawn—something that could be recognised without looking as it did.

Soon the cave wall began to fill with more pronged lines, with curved cup-like lines, with stars, with animals that were nothing like the animals that they actually saw and knew. They may or may not have seen that, in the journey from their initial scratchings on the cave walls to what they were doing now, that what they had mastered was a way to make connections between things that were physical and of the world and the intangible things that appeared in their heads. They had learnt to make groups of images that manifested something: an idea. The little boy was pleased with them, and he brought them gifts, pieces of soft stone for drawing, fruit that they had not seen, the feathers that his peacock had shed. He also danced and played music on a little gourd instrument that he held in his hand. They delighted in the strength of his steps and the lilt of the music he made and what came out of his mouth, pleasing sound units that they did not know were the units of a language.

But some among them had become enamoured of what the others had achieved with the Bull Rider: the feeling of being powerful, of knowing, with their bodies, how to control the very elements that the boy delighted in, and which he wanted them to look at, listen to and wait upon. Slowly, the numbers of those going with him into the cave reduced. He tried to get their attention back. One day, he showed them something new: he took little pebbles, then he hid some of them and pointed to the remaining stones. He touched his fingers and then etched out on the cave wall little boxes, and then, with the heel of his palm, he rubbed away some of them and touched his fingers again. This seemed to excite them, and the boy was excited too. He began to come earlier and stay later, and the cave walls became thick with lines, curves in red and black. Soon, he led them deeper into the forest and into a bigger cave. There was a sense of anticipation, an excitement that reflected on their faces and in their steps. Still, some among the group continued to leave and go to the other teacher, for they found the boy's ways to be hard. He did not show them what was to be done, only guided their own seek. Many did not have the will to try again and again or to find ways to overcome obstacles, and resented that the boy, unlike the man, would not just show them.

One day, the boy came to the clearing and saw that very few had gathered that day. His face asked the question, 'Where are they?' The people bent their heads, silent, but one among them took the boy's hand and led him to the forest clearing. There, very many people were standing on their heads. The Bull Rider was seated cross-legged under a tree. His trident stood beside him, not resting in the hand or on the tree trunk. The boy's face was calm. He saw some of the people who had been part of the group that worked in the cave looking at him sidelong, and he gestured to them—come. One or two of them got up and followed him; others refused to meet his eye.

In this way, the numbers of those in the cave grew smaller and smaller. One day, the boy arrived and found no one waiting for him, and he was enraged. But in truth, it had become difficult for them to labour over the formless, shapeless things that he required of them. As the days passed, they had moved from lines, shapes and abstract representation—what he wanted them to do was to gather all these into one, and to understand what they were shaping. These tasks seemed to send them running to the comforting solidity of their own bodies and what those bodies could do. They could spend hours and days baking bricks for the walls of storage spaces, homes or water channels, or creating round bowls and rolled beads. These things were laborious, but they found no difficulty in doing them. The way of the boy was harder, because there was nothing to touch and measure, and they could not tell if they were closer to succeeding through repetitions that never seemed to end. And so, they began to evade him, to hide away, or to join the other group. Despite this, the boy came again and again, not roaring in anger or brandishing the staff that sprouted leaves.

Then he stopped appearing, and they understood that he had gone away. At first, they were glad they did not have to watch out for his arrival and ensure he did not see where they hid.

In the course of time, it occurred to the people whom he had nurtured and taught that his way had been one of assimilating what was inside with what was outside. They also realised that the way of the Bull Rider was one of disconnection. His lessons taught them to narrow their breathing and their consciousness into flame-like intensity that disregarded everything else, day in and day out, unvarying and unwavering. They realised too late that the boy had brought endless movement and endless newness, and they understood with deep remorse that he had shown them how to make something from nothing. He had given them—no, companioned them into making—a way to express what knowledge they each had of the world. Had they heeded his calls, nay, his entreaties, they would not now be feeling as they did: hollow.

They tried to continue their old habit of drawing on the walls of the caves, but found their minds wandering, for the boy had been what animated their curiosity, what kept their attentiveness directed and what fired their imaginations. A terrible despair began to fill them. They danced and they beat their instruments and they called out into the forest and into the skies and rivers. But to no avail. Then they began to have dreams in which they saw the earth lurch and all their dwellings shudder and crumble, the animals in their pens fall dead and the people turn pale and breathless. On other days, they saw in the sky a star that appeared to descend towards them and then move southwards. Thus it was that they made a move towards the south, communicating with each other in their half-made speech. Very soon, what they had seen in their dreams came to pass: those who stayed behind perished under the onslaught of tremors that made the earth lurch and ribbon out in giant curls. But those who had left travelled on, waiting for the boy to appear, talking in their half-language—the scraps of what could have been a feast.

It had taken Akattiyan a long time to tell the story. He told it as if he had been there—the old man shook with emotion, sometimes wept or shut his eyes. When he came to the end, he heaved a great, big sigh, and so did Theivanai. Then he laughed and shook himself, as if to snap out of a spell, and said, 'The boy forgave them, and he sent a message with the Goddess of the South to enter the dream of a little man, a stubborn man, who later came to be called Kuru Muni, and goad him towards that little boy who was living on the highest mountain in creation.' Here, Akattiyan stopped and, laughing, wiped his eyes. He recounted what had happened on Kailasa, of being apprenticed to Murugan, how he came back to the south with Tamizh, and how the language had grown and flourished, enlivened by all those who spoke it, and how all its strands had been gathered under the roof of the Assembly. He spoke to her of the many poets and scholars, woman and men, who had been leaders of the Assembly. He told her about Sanmolli of Arur and Uvahai, the wandering astrologer-turned-renunciate, and the ferocious Nanmudai, who remained a warrior till the day she died—all women who had led the Assembly in earlier times.

Theivanai was struck by the twin tones in Akattiyan's voice, of nostalgia and pride and regret and dejection. She asked what it had been like when these women ran the Assembly. Akattiyan spoke with eagerness of their spontaneity and the width of their vision. They had flung open the Assembly's great door to anyone who wanted to read, perform, challenge or interpret a famous work. He said, 'Women understand Tamizh better than men, they understand the God of Tamizh, how he held it in his belly and waited till it grew strong and well-limbed, feeding it on the fire of his longing and birthed it, how he had been midwife and mother. The women, whose fire is in their bellies, in their guts, in the passages where their babies come out from, they know that it cannot be bound up and set to order and told what to speak of and what not to. They know that, to Tamizh, every subject is attractive and every form is inventive.'

He sighed and looked out of a window at the town of Madurai, visible like a cloud from the palace on top of mighty Paramkundram. 'But women, like Murugan, are wild too, they cannot bear to be confined or to have to answer to anyone. And always, it is the men who are afraid that the women are as unpredictable as the moon, with whom their bodies have a secret pact. So the men sought and still seek to bind women to promises and rules. And thus it was that women became reluctant to take on what had shrunk to the tedious chore of running the Assembly. Nanmudai was the last one, and then there was Nakkeeran, there is Nakkeeran.'

Akattiyan's tone changed as he said, 'Women need to stop dodging this responsibility. Imagine Velli or Auvvai …'

Theivanai had listened with rapt attention to the story of the 'old tongue', the unmanifest half-language that had been rebirthed into the one that had given her a new name, a softened, moist version of 'Devayani'. Her heart rushed like a mountain stream and her mind leapt. Watching her, Akattiyan smiled. He said, 'This is your work. The Patron of the Assembly, its god, will not persuade the women, or initiate the changes that really ought to happen. He will not do anything that might upset Nakkeeran, but you can. And you must.' Then he added with a chuckle, 'And I know you well enough to know that you are already thinking of what to do. Your face tells it all.'

Theivanai laughed. She asked him if he would help her in this task, and he explained that it would be inappropriate for him to, and that Theivanai was surely up to the task, but also that Aambal could help her get started.

7

THEIVANAI SENDS FOR AAMBAL

Learning with Akattiyan was like traversing the landscape of Tamizh barefoot, going from high hills that were dream-like in the embrace of mist, along shady paths through forests where fruit dropped into your hands if you paused, alongside green fields and past seashores and the barren palai lands where thorny shrubs and death lurked. Theivanai's legs grew muscular, her ears grew sharp and her hands grew tenacious, for often, she had to clutch at rock outcrops or hardy vines to keep her balance on this demanding trek. To Akattiyan, this was a mission and he laboured over it, but the labour was sweet, for he could not have found a better student. Theivanai was intelligent and humble, the only way to fully absorb anything that was taught. And she liked Akattiyan. He was a taskmaster whose joy at seeing the progress of his student spurred her on to outdo herself.

In the course of her lessons, Theivanai also began to appreciate the enormity of the Assembly's work, and the many rhythms, rhyme schemes, metres, innovations, poem cycles and editorial innovations that had come from there. She delighted in the stories that Akattiyan told of the great poets who had passed through its halls, and of the legendary poems that had come from the language of these poets, which lived on in the hearts and voices of the people and, indeed, the very air of Tamizhagam.

Over the days and weeks after that conversation, Akattiyan's subtle hints and Murugan's not-so-subtle rejoinders told Theivanai that they were nudging her to set things in motion, but also that they would not tell her in so many words. She also understood that while Murugan was impatient, Akattiyan was resigned. He had for too long put himself at the disposal of Tamizh and the Poets' Assembly, and now it was the language of nature and of the Kani on Pothigai that he wanted. Tamizh, he was happy to leave to its god and that god's poets, scholars and his very able wife.

As the days passed under the spell of Tamizh, Theivanai began to dream of things that she wished to see happen in the Assembly. It was time to do something, she decided, but what of Nakkeeran? He would be offended by mention of the need for change, and an offended Nakkeeran was something she knew that neither Akattiyan nor Murugan would deal with.

Aambal! She would ask her for advice. So, Seval was sent to Aambal with a request that that she come and meet Theivanai.

On her part, Aambal felt a nervousness that had no real basis. Theivanai had been nothing but good-natured in their dealings. But, among other things, Aambal still felt guilty about delaying the wedding.

Seval decided to ease her out of her nervousness. 'Aambal, come, wear something nice and wear some jewellery. When you go to visit the wife of the Lord of Paramkundram, it is appropriate that you don't look like, like, like you ...' A sound that was something between a squawk and a snort escaped his mouth. '... like you did at her wedding.'

Aambal's head shot up. This bird! She turned, ready to snap at him, then changed her mind. It would be easier if Seval was with her. 'What should I wear?'

Seval went to her little cupboard and scrutinised the clothes as if the chariot of Time would stop if he didn't find the correct attire for Aambal. He shook his head and muttered until he came to one the colour of the sea with silver lines, and crowed, 'Yes!' It was one of the numerous selai that Murugan had brought her from Mayilai. He added some silver jewellery, and waited for Aambal to change, then looked at her and gestured to her hair. Aambal ran a comb through it and would have rolled it all into a scraggly bun on top of her head, but Seval handed her a bright ribbon and snapped, 'Braid it.'

He liked Aambal, the way she looked at her palm leaves, as if the words were going to appear there, the way the Lord of Paramkundram looked at her, as if the words were going to appear on her face. He liked the way they looked at each other—their faces open, their eyes open, their hearts open to each other. As if they were reading their lives there.

When Aambal appeared at the palace on the High Hill, Theivanai's eyes widened and her lips spread in a smile: the poet was all dressed up! Why, she was even wearing matching jewellery—or rather, Theivanai thought, she had allowed Seval to tell her what to wear. She saw that Aambal was nervous. She greeted her warmly, rising and moving to take both of Aambal's hands in her own and then embracing her. Aambal stood stiffly, making Seval smile, and remark, 'An embrace given needs an embrace returned.' Aambal flushed and clumsily embraced Theivanai back.

Pleasantries over, Theivanai came straight to the point. She talked about her Tamizh lessons and poetry, and of the things that Akattiyan had told her about the Assembly's current competition rounds for aspiring poets. As if it was but natural, she then spoke of hearing from many sources that there was a stagnation in the Assembly, and wondered aloud why the Assembly did not have a woman leader, and that there ought to be a way to keep the leadership rotating. She saw that Aambal was embarrassed and nervous with these observations, so quickly changed the topic, asking Aambal who her favourite of the women poets was.

Aambal had sat quite still, lest her own impatience with Nakkeeran poured out—an impropriety that the Aambal of yore may not have given thought to, but now she too was part of the great Assembly, the running of which 'hinged on obedience to the rules that tradition had firmed over hundreds of years'. She thought hard: Murugan had never said anything to her about the leadership, or about the Assembly being stagnant, but he had on more than one occasion pointed her in the direction of the verses of women poets and to their ways of composition. 'Look at Ponmudiyaar,' he had said recently, 'look how her metaphors come from her gut, how her life as a woman shapes her verses.' This was something she could talk about without feeling she was betraying the trust the Assembly had placed in her, without feeling she was staining Nakkeeran's honour. To her, as to all the young poets, he was never anything other than absolutely fair in his judgement, and his love for Tamizh leapt from his eyes and tongue, flowing ahead of him, and it had become habitual to think of him as the herald-bearer of the language.

Aambal began her answer to Theivanai's many questions with the safest of them: who were the women poets she admired. Her favourite Velliveethi, a god to Aambal, and the others were all like demi-gods: Auvaiyyar, Kavarpendu, Aadimandi, Allur Nanmullaiyar, Kaakaipaadiniyaar, Kuramagal Ilaiveyni, Ponmudiyaar, Kaamakkani Pasalaiyaar, Mulliyoor Poodiyaar, Kuramagal Kuriyeyni, Nalvelliyaar. As she spoke, animated and passionate, Aambal became more at ease, surer of Theivanai, and tentatively voiced some of her reservations about the rules for the competitions for entry into the Assembly. She talked of how they sometimes had an unyielding hold that prevented the verse from soaring. Sometimes, the verses, Aambal said with an unselfconscious shudder, groaned, as if straining to burst its bonds. 'It's not that the poetry isn't good, it's just a feeling that, without such strict rules, perhaps they would have been glorious. Like the verses of Velliveethi.'

Akattiyan had said to Theivanai that many of the women elders preferred to read outside the Assembly, at festivals and informal gatherings, because these allowed them more spontaneous expression, often times as a response to the cheering and clapping and the playing on instruments and the dancing of the audiences.

Aambal sat up straight, as if some thought had jabbed her, and told Theivanai how one time, answering a question from the audience after a reading at the Assembly, Kavarpendu said that she believed in 'abandoning herself to the words, not sitting down and making deals with them'. Her voice now rising, Aambal said, 'That's the difference between what Nakkeeran wants and what the women do.'

Theivanai smiled. Aambal's agitation gave her face and body an added animation, as if they were being pulled and pushed by ideas that had been brooding inside her, waiting to burst through the shell of her reserve. As they continued to talk, Aambal's thoughts were leaping. Was Theivanai saying that the women's presence in the Assembly should become stronger, as should their voice in its running? Was she saying that, for far too long, the men—all of them 'unquestioningly committed to Tamizh'—led the hundreds of its grammarians, scholars, poets and bards with 'manly determination and vigour'? Was Theivanai saying that it was time that the Assembly itself became more 'womanly'? Was she saying that this would bring back to it Murugan's own way with the language—quick, open in spirit, melting the rules and letting them run away in little skipping rivulets?

Now Theivanai asked Aambal to tell her more about these women poets. Aambal, of course, started with Velliveethi. Nobody recalled anymore what her parents had named her because she was now known only by this other name, her poetic name, the one given to her spontaneously by those who heard her verses and repeated them. Some said the name came from her repeated use of 'venmai', whiteness, in her poetry, others said that it was because she and her lover were like the Morning Star, 'velli', and the road, 'veethi', never able to come together. The story was that Velliveethi and an unidentified man lost their hearts to each other, but the man left one day, without a word and never was seen again, and she pined for him from the depths of her heart and language, and her pining poured out of her in poems that burnt, like water stinging an open wound, they wrung the heart, like leave-taking from a beloved. By the time Aambal had begun to speak, Velli's poems were already known all over Tamizhagam, repeated so often that even children knew them. In one, Velli lamented her youth and beauty, comparing it to milk in a cow's udder, neither drunk by the calf, nor milked into a utensil, but spilling onto the ground. Her beautiful body, she said, was just like that: wasted by the pasalainoi, the dis-ease of separation from their lovers that clung as a pallor to the limbs of women.

In another poem, an excited Aambal told Theiva, reminded by others, that she is growing so thin with longing that the bangles slip off her hands, and that her body is losing lustre. Velliveethi says that she is like butter that is left on a sun-baked rock guarded by a mute man without hands who can neither scoop up the butter nor call out.

Theivanai became conscious of a strange sadness as she saw that Aambal was celebrating the elder poet's ability with words as much as her ability to abandon herself to love. There was a sharp note of anger in Aambal's voice when she said that, among the poets and bards, it was agreed that Velliveethi's lover may have left her because he was so in awe of her that he feared she might find him limited. 'She was like that! So independent, flaring like the mid-day sun's rays.' Theivanai knew from all that she had heard from Akattiyan and Murugan, and from what she had read, that

Velliveethi was fearless with herself and the world. Without a doubt one of the best poets of Tamizh, she was equally passionate about poetry and about love, and that Nakkeeran, Akattiyan and Murugan admired and paid heed to her in all matters of the Assembly and poetry. She would not take part in competitions, though, because she found them limiting. The last one she had participated in was the one for her own admittance into the Assembly. Even that was done under the insistence of her master, also Nakkeeran's and Auvvai's master, Tolkappiyan, who had once been apprenticed to Akattiyan himself.

'My favourite poem of Velliveethiyar,' Aambal was saying, her eyes far away, her voice full, resonant, 'is the one in which she tells the world that her man may have left, but she is going to find him. Do you know what she says?'

Theiva did know the poem, but she wanted to hear it from Aambal, so she said, 'What? Recite it.'

Aambal closed her eyes, and hands clasped, she declaimed with perfect intonation and rhythm Velliveethi's most celebrated poem: '*Nilam thottu pugaar, vaanam eraar*'. As Aambal's strong voice rang out, it seemed as if for the moment, the young poet had become inhabited by the elder one, proclaiming to the world that her man could neither slip into the earth, ascend to the skies, nor tread on the seas, therefore, he was alive somewhere, and she would go from village to village, from tribe to tribe, from house to house and find him.

'Such words,' Aambal exclaimed, 'such words!'

Theiva was gripped by the look in Aambal's eyes, the urgency in her voice. She said to Aambal, 'Love of a man is like the sea. It makes you want to row further and further in. And the further you go, the more you want that sea to toss you out of your boat.' She paused as Aambal's eyes fluttered and came to a rest on her face. Then, emboldened by the moment, Theivanai asked, 'Have you known such a love?'

Aambal's eyes grew wide. She gasped and said, 'Kandhan and I are friends.'

This made Theiva laugh. 'I know.'

Aambal looked confused, her eyes turned away from Theiva, her shoulders hunched a little and she answered, 'I don't know.'

Once again, Theiva felt as if she was on the periphery, the momentary closeness with Aambal was gone, like the water jewel snapped back into the pond from the lotus leaf by the slap of a leaping fish or the kick of a frog.

Seval, who had witnessed the whole thing, felt his eyes mist up. The truthfulness of the poet, he thought.

Theivanai smiled and said to Aambal, almost as if she was duty-bound to complete what she had started, 'You will know when you do. And if ever you need a friend to plot and plan, I am always here.'

Aambal's confusion increased. What was she saying, Kandhan's wife? Did she see something? Did she know?

When Aambal left Theivanai, the whole morning had passed. On another day, she would have resented the loss of writing time, but not today. The morning had been exhilarating, it had stirred her thoughts into a ferment. She felt enlivened and expectant. More women's poetry, women's anthologies, a women's poetry festival, more women in the Assembly, a woman at the head of the Assembly! The very idea of a change in the somewhat phlegmatic Assembly—which was meant to be the mother tree, the maternal breast poets drew nourishment from—was thrilling in its ambition and scale. Aambal was too restless to be confined to her room, and as if her feet recognised this, they skipped and leapt down the steps that led from the palace down into the town, past the laughing Vaigai.

As the moments passed, her steps slowed and the last thing Theivanai had said came back into her mind. The Vaigai too slowed, as it always did when the sun reached the top of the sky and paused to draw breath. To Aambal, it seemed as if the beautiful river was telling her to slow, too. To take pause, to wait, to remind herself of what she was doing, where she was and where she was headed. And most of all, whose she was. As the water gurgled past her, it seemed as if the ripples were calling out to her, 'Murugan's poet, Murugan's poet'. She felt the sun's heat now, and made her way back to the looming mountain, and back to her room, her styluses, inks, parchments and palm leaves. And to her words, her Tamizh. She was Murugan's poet and she was competing to get into the Assembly. She would get in, and she would stay there until, one day, she was the one leading it, wisely, strongly, with all her womanly grit and inventiveness, Kandhan's favourite quality.

⊰⊱

Theivanai was ready to meet those she had identified as the twelve most able and important of the women poets, Velliveethi, Auvaiyyar, Kavarpendu, Aadimandi, Allur Nanmullaiyar, Kaakaipaadiniyaar, Kuramagal Ilaiveyni, Ponmudiyaar, Kaamakkani Pasalaiyaar, Mulliyoor Poodiyaar, Kuramagal Kuriyeyni, Nalvelliyaar.

She knew that Aambal had no real standing in the Assembly, or in the company of its poets, and it would be improper to send her, a sapling not even fully branched, to the seasoned women poets who were mighty trees spreading into the skies. Theivanai also began to think of how she could invite the women to the palace discreetly. She did not want this meeting to become the topic of gossip, but she wanted the meeting. As Murugan's wife, she was aware that she would be given the utmost respect, but at least some of them would find a way to get out of the meeting, which like all meetings made them restless and feel out of place. Theivanai wanted to make them want to come.

She imagined the women in her home, climbing up the stone steps, all in poets' whites, their bodies fit with years of traversing the land, going from recitation to recitation, competition to competition, judging, performing, reading. What women! What verses! If one of them took over the leadership from Nakkeeran, there would be a stir, and a new spark would light up Tamizh. Theivanai determined that something must change, and soon. A change of leadership might take longer, but surely gathering of the work of the women poets, a women's poetry festival, these were things that did not need to wait.

For too long, these women had chosen to keep away for the Assembly because it made them feel constricted. So many of them were wanderers, they could not sit still and keep order, unlike many of the men, especially Nakkeeran, who seemed to be driven by the homely desire to keep the house of poetry well ordered. Perhaps with a change in leadership, more women might be willing to temper their wanderlust and their travels to stay and participate in the work that would revive the Assembly. Perhaps there could be groups that could divide the work. Theivanai's brain was on fire, and she was excited to go to the next session of readings at the Assembly.

She imagined Nakkeeran's reaction when he found out that she was organising ... hmm, what *was* she organising? A rebellion in the ranks of stylus-wielding poets? An image of the women poets rising up, their palm leaf bundles and styluses held aloft, waving them in the air like weapons, made her giggle, and Seval shook his head. 'Mad like the husband.'

Murugan was delighted by Theiva's plans for the Assembly. He told her that the next gathering of poets and the next round of readings, at which Aambal would be reciting, would be a good time for Theiva to speak to the women. They would all be present because they never missed sessions in the selection of new poets. He had been wanting to go and rest on Pothigai and this would be a good time to do that, Murugan chuckled. Staying out of Nakkeeran's way, Theivanai thought.

So, on the day of the reading, the last of the two remaining before Aambal's final reading, Theivanai appeared at the door of the Assembly, and smiled at Nakkeeran, saying, 'Greetings, sir.' She said that Murugan had asked her to take his place. Nakkeeran was taken aback and annoyed. But, of course, he had no choice, and he reminded himself that Theivanai had finished her training under Akattiyan's incomparable tutelage. Murugan would never do this unless he trusted her completely. When Theivanai told Nakkeeran, with a smile that would have charmed even the grumpy Durvasa, that she was leaving the judging to him as she had no experience or expertise for that, he reluctantly admitted that it wasn't so bad after all.

Theivanai sat in Murugan's place and did what Murugan himself did: listened with rapt attention and mentally made note of the things that were admirable and those that needed correcting. She made a note of the poets who excelled, and was glad that Aambal was among them, and of what the judges were saying. She asked questions of the women poets that Aambal had mentioned by name in order to hear them speak. Theivanai noticed that Akattiyan himself often turned to Velliveethi for comments. She waited eagerly for the end of the readings of the novice poets, so she could hear the elders read, as was the custom. Not all of them would read, and Theivanai held her breath and hoped that Velliveethi would, and she did.

When the readings were over, Theivanai went up to Velliveethi and invited her to Paramkundram. She requested elder poet to bring as many of the women poets as were free to attend. Velliveethi was gracious in her reply, but said that she did not know what her plans were, and it was clear she was only being polite. Theivanai smiled to herself, what else could she expect from this fiery one? She quickly thought of something that would make it impossible for the poet to refuse. She said to Velliveethi that Murugan had expressed a desire for her to meet with these elder women, and get their blessings and that he had assured her they were loving and would not refuse. Velliveethi could not now refuse. And when she assured Theivanai that she and those others who did not have urgent engagements would be there, Theivanai knew that she meant what she said.

So, on a day not too far from that one, a group of them appeared at the palace on the hill. Theivanai awaited them at the entrance in her colourful finery, and watched as the women, all clad in poet's white, moved up the hill. They looked like a slow-moving, majestic cloud sailing along, exchanging greetings with the ancient rock mountain. Theivanai had asked Aambal to come and help her with the arrangements. Aambal could not contain her excitement, and Theiva laughed to see the otherwise reticent Aambal all agog. These were her heroes! The women were breathtaking, their sturdy bodies, their rich skin, the way they held and conducted themselves, and Theivanai understood what Murugan had meant when he said to her that no other women, anywhere in the universes could compare to the women of his home, here in the south, on Bhu. They are like the rock, seasoned by sun, wind and rain, he had said, and as generous as salt, their voices as inviting as the wind, and they themselves as loving as Tamizh.

Theivanai's eyes went to them one by one: Velliveethi, so tall, it seemed as if she would have to bend to pass under the doorway, her body like a hunter's, her face tawny, its expression searching, her long, dark eyes darting to every tiny sound that appeared, as if she expected it to be her lover. Her hair was coiled on the top of her head, her neck, hands and ankles sparkled with beads and stones. Then there was Kaakaipaadiniyaar from the sea coast, another tall woman with the glowing skin of the south. Auvaiyyar, her soft round body that seemed full of the laughter which often tripped out of her mouth, filling the ears of those around her, making them smile. So many women, so many different faces, bodies, ornaments, make-up, but all of them clad in the white that set them apart. All of them committed to poetry and devoted to the God of Tamizh, who appeared sometimes in their dreams to leave them instructions.

They treated Theivanai with care. She was the wife of their patron and god, but also they knew of her tremendous scholarship. They held her hands and spoke words of welcome to their land like a mother-in-law might welcome her son's wife. They touched her head and her shoulders, and blessed her with happiness, with grammar and with the unending love of the God of Paramkundram.

They turned to Aambal, whose awe was writ large in her eyes, and they said, 'Child, why are you holding back? You're one of us' or 'Oh ho, little poet, is this what you do when you should be practising your verses?' or 'Look who's here, our little poet who's going to make us proud.' Aambal began to see herself in a new light in their company. Everything Kandhan said to her seemed to resound in their words. They were right, she was of this land, she was of the home of Murugan. It was her place to stand next to Theivanai and help her to settle into the conversation. But she would not sit with them, that would be improper. She ran around, leading the women to seats that were arranged in a half circle.

Seval entered and called out loud greetings to the women who laughed and greeted him back. Everybody knows Seval, everybody becomes jovial in his presence, Theiva thought.

They sat down, with Aambal hovering, and no matter what they said to her, she would not sit with them. Once everyone was settled, Theiva began explaining why she had wanted to meet with them. She spoke with respect and moderation, and the women admired this, for they could sense that Theivanai's feelings were really far stronger than she was letting them see, and they also knew that the voice of their patron, their god, resounded silently in what she said.

The women could not but like her, and as the conversation grew, a change came over them. They began to admit that what Theivanai was proposing was something they had themselves sometimes imagined. As the conversation progressed, the ideas that she had presented no longer seemed too big or too difficult.

Aambal was in a strange state: she felt as if the words and the intentions of the women had latched on to her body and turned into wings. She wanted to go to a window and leap out, shake her wings and fly over the lands where Tamizh reigned. She felt at home in the company of all these women. Here, she could make mistakes. Like Murugan, they would consider a mistake a sign of life. Murugan's name made Aambal start, a fit of guilt taking hold of her gut and squeezing. She hadn't thought of him till now. What would he say? Would he be angry? Would he be angry with her? What if he said, 'You can go find another master'? She heard a snort from behind, and turned to see Seval watching her. 'No,' he was saying to Aambal, 'of course he won't. Mutthu knows a good deal. And you're the best apprentice he can hope to find.' As the panic seeped away, Aambal thought, of course, how silly it was of her to think that anything to do with Tamizh could have happened without Kandhan's knowing. He had gone away on purpose, to let this meeting happen without Nakkeeran blaming him.

8

NAKKEERAN AND THE 'PLOT'

Nakkeeran did blame him, though. He had been hearing whispers of the 'women's plans' too often for him to dismiss them as mere fancies or malicious gossip. He had, by now, understood that it was Theivanai whose will was driving the whole thing, and that she had got Aambal to help her. Also, he knew that neither of these things could happen without Murugan's approval and support. It had not escaped Nakkeeran's attention that Murugan was going off to Pothigai far too often, and that, as if he had something to hide, Akattiyan no longer automatically came by the Assembly when he visited Paramkundram. Or as if he was ensuring that he would not be implicated in whatever was to come.

In the beginning, Nakkeeran had felt affronted and wounded, but as the days passed and things began to fall into place, he was furious. He had been there the day that Theivanai had first invited the women poets to her home. Nakkeeran had not thought much of it then, considering it customary for a new bride to want women around her, especially the elder women with their rituals of blessing.

Then the rumours had amplified: a big group of the women poets were meeting repeatedly at the palace; there were plots for the women to take over the Assembly; Theivanai, the Lord's wife and therefore also a patron of the Poets' Assembly, was hell bent on seeing this come true. It was clear to Nakkeeran that Theivanai was gathering the women poets together for a reason. He wondered what it was, and many possibilities ran through his head, but not even in his dreams could he have imagined the extent of what she and the women were proposing.

It was Theivanai who took the matter into her hands, telling Murugan of all that had transpired in these days. He said nothing, but his smile was a bit pensive, and for a moment, Theiva felt a pang of regret. Why did he say nothing? Surely he could see that it was time. Surely he could see that this was the right way. But he turned to her and said, 'I'm certain you will do what you think is right,' and added with a laugh that he would go to Pothigai so as to 'not get in anyone's way', and Theivanai felt that quick sting of unexpected happiness.

She knew, of course, that Murugan could not bear to face Nakkeeran's hurt and anger. He loved the old man for his perseverance and the dedication with which he had tended to the Assembly, its training, assessing and rewarding of poets. To Murugan, Nakkeeran was no less dear than Akattiyan, but he could not tell the former, like he could the latter, to 'be still' and not do anything. Nakkeeran's world was one of formal procedures and of an etiquette that would always be part of his relationship with Murugan: to Nakkeeran, Murugan was the patron, respected and venerated, to whose will he always surrendered. While Murugan coddled Akattiyan like a grandmother would her first grandchild, and never refused him anything, he gave Nakkeeran the utmost respect and courtesy, but never did anything he did not want to.

Theivanai sent word to Velliveethi and the others that it was time. They were to come to the Assembly in Madurai on the eve of the new moon just before the season of falling leaves ended. She also sent word, through Seval, to Nakkeeran that she would be honoured if he would grant her and a group of elder women poets some time so they could present an idea to him. Nakkeeran's heart skipped a few beats, then calmed down into its unhurried step. Whatever he feared, it was better that he knew what was happening rather than imagine and brood. He sent a reply that held no hint of his feelings, but merely said in gracious words that he would consider it an honour to be allowed to spend time with her and the poets.

Among the women, conversations had become more animated, less guarded. Theivanai's eagerness was contagious, and they had all become more ambitious in their wishing, their foreseeing, their plans: a women's poetry festival, a collection of the poetry read at the festival, an anthology of the poetry written by women in the past year, a touring women's group, women standing for more elections at the Assembly and so on and more.

There was much in the following days that filled them with excitement, but for many of them, the possibility that the working of the Assembly could become less tedious was the thing they felt most animated by. They had turned away from its lumbering insistence on set rules, making up whatever discipline they needed for their own work as they went along, rules that changed with what the work demanded of them.

This often disqualified them from competitive readings or being included in the official anthologies of the Assembly. But they were still composing, and their verses were far from languishing. The women travelled and read their poems to gatherings far and wide, and these verses would be copied by scribes and distributed or committed to memory and passed from mouth to mouth, and even with the variations that crept in with these transmissions, their poetry soared, like victory flags planted on flagpoles and the ramparts of forts. Many of the women poets preferred a nomadic life spent with ever-new groups of people, and the thrill of audiences standing up and cheering, dancing and playing their instruments as they recited. Such a life also assured them of an endless variety of lovers whom they could forget about when they moved on, and whom they could welcome with warmth if they ran into them again somewhere. For those with husbands and children, the nomadic life meant that they were not expected to keep house or conduct themselves according to the seasons of the family's traditions. There were also many women poets who neither travelled, nor performed anywhere other than the Assembly and other assemblies like it. Some of them officiated in the highest positions. And there were those who enjoyed being in their homes with their families and neighbours, bound by unspoken rules that to them were neither burdensome nor disagreeable.

It was not easy to get some of them, so used to wandering, to commit to staying put in the city for the many months that it would take for their plans to fruition. Once Velli and the other eleven had assented to the meeting, Theivanai broached the topic of who would actually do the speaking. She felt that one of the older women would be ideal, for they would have known Nakkeeran when they were beginning their poetic lives and their relationship with him would be stronger and more easy than the formal one the younger poets had with him. Theiva suggested that Velli, Auvvai or Kaakaipaadiniyaar should speak on behalf of all of them, because she knew that the three of them and Nakkeeran had been apprentices together under Master Tolkappiyan. In a time now lost, they had all been great friends. But they were quick to refuse this suggestion, and said that Theiva should do it, for she was the wife of the God of Tamizh, the one that the Assembly's patron had thought fit to stand in for him. Knowing that it would be a waste of time to argue this, Theivanai assented. In any case, once a conversation started, none of them would be able to contain their ideas.

Thus it was that Theivanai, accompanied by Seval, arrived in Madurai and headed straight for the Assembly, which that day would remain inaccessible to all others. Its great doors would be half closed, indicating that something official was going on inside. Nakkeeran had arranged for the group to meet in one of the smaller reading rooms, a rectangular room with windows that looked out on to the lotus pond of the Temple of the Fish-eyed Goddess and her spouse, the Handsome God.

He greeted all the women with folded hands and a smile that belied the impatience he had been feeling since he received Theivanai's message. Velliveethi, Auvvai and Kaakaipaadiniyaar, the oldest of the women, each took Nakkeeran's hands in their own, holding them for a moment, before raising them to their lips and whispering, 'To Tamizh, you and I, alphabet by alphabet. Dear one, in love always with Tamizh.' It was the old chant that they had learnt and repeated every day in the years that they had been apprenticed to their master. Nakkeeran's eyes dewed, as they did every time he heard these words, and he spoke them back, taking in turn the hands that had held his own, and bending his head to kiss them. His voice seemed unaware of his turmoil, the bitterness that he had been feeling, for it was sweet and light.

They sat on rich mats arranged in two rows facing each other. Theivanai settled at the end of a mat on which Velliveethi and some others also sat, and Nakkeeran sat on the other one, next to Auvvai and the remaining poets.

Nakkeeran heard out all that Theivanai said. The other women did not speak. They had told Theiva that, for years, they had only spoken their verses, and had not, in any way, contributed to the running of the Assembly, letting Nakkeeran struggle through it all by himself, that they had settled into that pattern and now would not step out of it. Truth be told, like Murugan, they too could not bear to see Nakkeeran suffer, though sometimes, like Murugan, they too wished he would let go, let himself go. Theiva knew that the women had not agreed to the meeting only out of respect for her and out of the regard they had for Tamizh and the Assembly, but also because what she was proposing excited them, and this gave her speech a flourish that made even Nakkeeran forget himself and his ire and be carried away.

She described their plans, and there were nods and smiles not only from the other women, but from Nakkeeran himself. At the end, Theivanai brought up the suggestion that a woman be chosen to lead the Assembly, at which Nakkeeran's eyes went automatically to Velliveethi, who looked back at him calmly.

After the women left, it was as if the spell cast by their presence and their words had snapped, and all of Nakkeeran's indignation came roaring back into his head like a horde of hungry beasts. How could they have met without him? How could they have gone behind his back? How could they have made plans for Tamizh without him? How could they have thought that anyone could be a better leader than he? He was like clockwork. He kept the rules, made sure that nothing spilt out. What gave them the right, the courage to suggest these alterations?

As these thoughts invaded his mind, the echo of Theivanai's gentle suggestions to him at an earlier time, in the presence of the God of Tamizh, rang in his memory. He recalled now the smile that had flickered on Murugan's lips, which he quickly bit back when he caught Nakkeeran's eye. So that was it! This was all his doing. Nakkeeran began to seethe. How could he! Was this how Murugan paid back loyalty? He had spent all his life in the service of Tamizh and the Assembly. He rushed to Pothigai to find Murugan, only to be told by Akattiyan, who greeted him with warmth, that Murugan had just then left for Paramkundram on urgent work, and led him instead to Ganesha.

Always gentle, even when he was provoked, almost never did Ganesha lose his temper, and so Nakkeeran did not stop to think before bursting out with a tirade against Murugan and a litany of complaints against the women. Ganesha listened quietly, his face impassive, his hands resting on his belly. 'It's not right. He's not a child now,' Nakkeeran squeaked with indignation. 'Does the young man not understand that the Assembly is a serious place? If he can't behave himself, he should stay out.' A movement from Ganesha made him stop.

'What did Murugan do?' Ganesha asked. The slight jiggling of his tummy was the only sign that he was laughing.

Nakkeeran noticed neither the shaking of Ganesha's belly, nor the smile on Akattiyan's face, and went on and on about how improper Murugan was, that he should know better, he had, after all, been at the helm of the Assembly for so long.

Ganesha stopped the disgruntled old man with a slight grunt and sat up to quote a verse that he said was from the manual written on the day the Assembly had been inaugurated: 'In every assembly, will come The Youth/ scanty of age, abounding in Tamizh/ who will be like the wind/ When the learned ones want to go this way/ he will compel them that way/ When they want to sit firm, he will shake them/ and when they make stacks, he will strike it all down.'

Nakkeeran knew everything there was to know about the Assembly: its history, its rules, the crises it had gone through, every poet who had made a mark, every event of celebration, every collection, every little thing connected to it. He had immersed himself in that work, only coming up for small gulps of air. No such verse had ever been written, he began to protest, and there wasn't even a manual. But one look at Ganesha's face told him the god was not going to chide his brother—he himself was already committed to what the younger sibling desired. In that moment, Nakkeeran felt let down as never before. He had expected loyalty from both the Patron of the Assembly as well as the Elder God. He had expected indulgence from Ganesha, for Ganesha was an indulgent god, a kind one, a gentle, maternal god who guided the lost with light words that were like an accurately placed stone protecting the flame of a lamp in the wide open. Where was the indulgence? The kindness?

As these feelings took Nakkeeran in their grasp and proceeded to squash him, the winds on Pothigai blew at him with their vetiver breath. Slowly, his thoughts settled. His seething mind stilled. His heart shrugged off its rancour and returned to a sweeter beat. Nakkeeran realised that perhaps Ganesha was telling him there was no way out, no way around this. And perhaps he wanted Nakkeeran to see why it was that Murugan wanted this, and why he was avoiding him. He sighed. Murugan had never been able to look him in the face and deny him anything, but he had done it without speaking, without looking. Murugan is an indulgent god, he has indulged me time and again. The old man felt as if a sack that had been pressing into his shoulder blades, a sack filled with hundreds of palm-leaf bundles, had been taken down. His shoulders slumped and he sighed again. Ganesha and Akattiyan looked at each other and smiled.

Nakkeeran sat down. He was grateful when Akattiyan patted him on the shoulder and said, 'Nakkeeran, why don't you stay here for some time?' He did not see the grin that crossed Ganesha's and Akattiyan's faces at the words 'some time'. Nakkeeran would have been alarmed. He would have thought it was a trick. It was a trick indeed, which was that nothing mattered on Pothigai. When the winds blew through the giant trees, and the calls of birds filtered through the net of their thick branches, it undid all grammars and literatures. All actions and reactions hummed with the wordless exultation of the Rasa, the Great Rasa that was the life in everything, and which was everything in life.

Already Nakkeeran's eyes were relaxing, his ears were allowing themselves to become unfocused. He was rooting into Pothigai's easefulness. For the first time in many, many years, he could think of a life where he was not constantly on guard, protecting Tamizh, taking care of the Assembly. He wanted to lie back against a rock, and be warmed by the soothing, tree-strained sunlight and sleep. The sounds of nature were washing his ears out, he felt, emptying them, filling them with silence. Nakkeeran lay there and imagined that Tamizh was going back into the rib cage that his flesh covered, and it lay there like a jewel inside the pods of a clam. He felt as he had when he was a boy, as if inside him there were veins of a treasure that needed to be dug up, smelted, polished and displayed. As it had, indeed. He recalled his own years of apprenticeship, the learning, the testing, the awards, the accomplishments, his own glory, and he lay there, his limbs relaxing, his heart slowing, his mind curled up and resting.

Nakkeeran slept long and deep, there were no sounds to the images that walked in his dream: high hills covered in purpling flowers, a peacock as big as a cloud on whose back sat a young boy, his head covered in thick curls, his face shining with a smile as white as the skin of his face was black, in his hand a staff of what he knew even in the dream to be akil, its rough surface sprouting little knobs of green. He was smiling in his sleep, and the Kani who passed him by as they went about their chores smiled with him. They knew who it was that brought this kind of smile to the lips of people and animals, and made the trees and clouds lurch madly.

※

When he returned to Madurai, Nakkeeran felt lighter, easier about what his feelings were doing, bringing to his mind a reminder of how carefree he had once been, especially during the years of apprenticeship with friends who had been life itself to each other. Velli, in particular; how deep and full had been their friendship. How she would insist that he meet all the many men she seemed to never tire of, her many lovers. Nakkeeran smiled at the memory, and random lines from one of Velli's poems came to his lips. How wonderfully her writing had evolved, how well she had aged, how well she had held herself through the years of intense suffering caused by the separation from the last of her lovers. But how distant she had grown from him. How distant they had all grown from him. He felt saddened, but then the thought of Pothigai and the invitation to return made him smile again.

As did the thought of the poems that he would hear at the next reading, now approaching quickly, the last round before the final. He was filled with excitement. The poems for this round would be some of the best that the participants would write, for it was the last round in which their masters oversaw their work.

Then he remembered that one of those masters was Murugan, and in the moment, he envied Aambal. And fleetingly, the old resentment about the unfair advantage that she had in the person of her master came back to him. The moment passed surprisingly quickly, and he felt with certainty that there was no advantage, for Murugan would not give Aambal skills she had not worked at herself, apprenticeship to him meant only a daily, disciplined and rigorous honing. He felt a strange movement in his heart: he liked Aambal. He had always liked her. She was **the most consistently sincere, the most hardworking of all the participants.** She reminded him of Velli, the same seriousness, the same intensity, the same determination to labour over her writing. She would be like Velli too, in suffering, would she not, if ever she loved and lost a man? But he would not wish away such a suffering, for that suffering, if it brought forth verses like Velli's, would be worth much. He caught himself and placed his hand over his heart and silently wished, may the child not suffer.

Back at the Assembly, the place that he had never thought of as anything but home, Nakkeeran surprised the women, and himself, by sending them a message in which he praised their ideas and plans and offered them his cooperation. He ended with a request for a meeting with Theivanai and Murugan and the twelve women poets. Murugan declined the invitation, saying that what Theivanai had started, she would take forward and that he was happy to go along with anything that came with the approval of all concerned. The meeting took place, and everybody was delighted with the outcome: Nakkeeran expressed his admiration of all their plans, including the one for an election to the post of the leader from among the women with such open enthusiasm that it almost seemed as if their earlier meeting hadn't taken place at all. His good cheer seemed to draw everyone else into its embrace. When it was time to take their leave of him, his friends Velli, Kaakai and Auvvai came up, and he embraced each of them and they put their arms around his waist and held him close, and they stood like that for a while, as they had done so often in the days when their poetic skill was being whetted.

When the news reached Aambal, she was filled with uncontrollable delight. She slipped away to her quarters, shut herself in and ran around the small room waving her stylus in the air. She laughed and hummed under her breath lines that she made up on the spot, something, something, something, Velli, Velli something, Assembly something, leader, leader. From the time Theivanai had asked for her cooperation, Aambal had begun to feel that she had also contributed to the poetic status quo by not questioning it, by not resisting it. Now she felt that she had made up for that lapse. She felt proud, as if she herself was one of those twelve. Aambal imagined Velliveethi in the places where Nakkeeran customarily stood: taller by far than Nakkeeran, her face as calm as a lily leaf on water. She was also relieved to not have to face Nakkeeran's disapproving glare when she joined the Assembly.

Aambal imagined herself passing round after round of the selection processes, she saw herself standing up and speaking, her eyes on Murugan and his on her, proud, a little nervous, beaming when she finished. She imagined Theiva smiling at both of them, and the twelve women looking at her with affection and pride. She thought of Nakkeeran delivering judgement of her work, always incisive and fair, and imagined Velliveethi in his place, and Aambal would be proud, eager for the next reading, the next round of selections, her achievements and expertise growing until she was in the Elders' Council, the little group of poets that advised, guided and censured the leader. Then her imagination leapt further, and she saw herself at the head of the Assembly, standing tall, her spine held firm by the authority of Tamizh. She saw herself delivering judgement to aspiring poets, novices working their way through the tests to get into the Assembly. She was wearing white, and had on the silver jewellery that Kandhan had given her when she first read at the Assembly. She saw herself reading, and lines came rushing into her head. In her room now, Aambal recited them loudly, excitement giving them an extra flourish. In her mind, she heard applause, and expressions of delight, and imagined the look on Kandhan's face, on Theiva's face, on other faces, Paravani, Seval ...

Suddenly she stopped, clutching her chest, trying to still her racing, dancing heart. The Aambal in her mind was now wearing not white but kanakambaram, the favourite colour of the man whose face filled her eyes: long, light eyes, thick curls of perfumed hair cascading to slender shoulders. It seemed to Aambal that the image came alive and walked towards her, took her by the waist and drew her close to him. Rooted to the spot, she shut her eyes and let herself be kissed, gathered close in an embrace. She saw the two of them walking hand-in-hand, she saw them in a ceremonious procession, going to their own wedding, she saw a house, a child, no, two children. She would name the boy Kandhan and the girl would be Velli.

At the thought of Velli's name, panic gripped Aambal: she had forgotten entirely the enchanting lines that she had only just recited. Shaking her head, she tried to call it back, but to no avail. Not again, she thought, desperately. She sat down and tried to speak it back, but it had gone. Her verse had left without trace, as if in protest that she had let something displace it, stalking off, punishing her. Despair assailed her. And anger. How could she have let this happen? Again? Was she so foolish that she hadn't learnt from the last time? That should have taught her never to turn away from a poem that had come uninvited, grace-filled, demanding nothing but to be pressed on to the smooth surface of a palm leaf. Aambal slumped down on to the floor, her eyes dry, her lips unmoving, no tears, no sobs—everything was frozen, inside and outside her, caught in the cursed immobility of inattentiveness.

This was not for her. She was a poet and words always came first. And last. The face and body, the arms that had a moment before filled her head were gone, and she gave it not even a passing thought. She sat up, shut her eyes, picked up her stylus and a single palm leaf. Holding them between her hands, she waited. Her hands grew warm after some time and the warmth spread through her body, rising into her head, pressing against her eyelids. Aambal remained still, all her attention gathered into the darkness of her closed eyes, and slowly, her ears began to catch faint sounds, and she heard her own voice, getting louder and louder, as if approaching closer. She caught a word here, a word there, then a line and another and after what seemed like a very long time, she had the entire verse ringing through her, as if her verse had returned and was running through all the rooms in its home: her body. Aambal quickly stylused the verse on to the palm leaf.

However, later in the day, when the dread left and she was calmer, questions rose in her mind.

Why should she have to dismiss every thought to attend to her work? Why couldn't she do both? Why couldn't she learn how to do both? What was she to do with these feelings and the images that they brought? Had not other women poets done both? Loved, and also written poetry so exquisite that the entire land had the lines on their lips? Had not Velli? Auvvai? Do they not love and write well? If they could do it, why couldn't she? Love! Had she said 'love'? Was this love, and was it always going to be so demanding?

Aambal was often ambushed by these thoughts as the days marched towards her last reading before the final. Murugan became stricter than ever with practice sessions, readings, suggestions and rework. The final was as much a test of the master's expertise as the student's, for the performance was proof of the teaching. Aambal had been confident and relaxed about her reading, but shaken by the recent bout of what she thought of as neglect, she had become anxious. She set herself a strict system to not lose focus, of not letting thoughts of bards and kanakambaram-coloured selai and babies get in the way of her work. Seval, as if he knew what she was experiencing, appeared frequently at Aambal's window, squawking, or called out to her as she walked to and from the reading room: 'Aambal, Aambal, keep your head clear.'

Unknown to everybody, Nakkeeran set himself a test for this round. He wanted to go through the day that would start at dawn and continue till dusk without feeling rancour, regret, resentment or dejection. He wished, nay, prayed that something would take hold of the current that had begun to flow in him on holy Pothigai and churn it into a river that looped around him, its ripples knocking at his ankles, tripping him into its flow and carrying him far along till he was washed free of history. Up on the balcony of his room, Murugan smiled. He could see the stars in the sky. As always, before a turning point, his six mothers shone so bright that their warmth fell on his shoulders like a garland, and in the dark he glowed, bejewelled with gems that not even night could dim.

9

EVERYBODY PREPARES

Every year, the round just before the final qualifying one drew large crowds. Those gathered liked to guess who might make it and who might not. People came from near and far. All the poets who were members in the Assembly were present: court poets, travelling bards, gypsy singers, the hunters with their own versions of Tamizh, they would all be there. Grammarians, scholars, scribes, students at advanced stages of their own training in the many kalaris of Tamizhagam, they too would all be there. From Ilangkai and Veeramahendrapuram, and from across the Vindhyas, too, they would come. Murugan and Aambal's friend, Cheraman Perunkadungko would be there. As would Akattiyan and Murugan and Theiva, of course.

On the day, Paravani accompanied Aambal. Seval got there moments before Theiva and Murugan, and announced their arrival with the shrill piping of his horn. He perched momentarily on the backrest of Murugan's ornate seat, his comb an eye-catching banner.

Aambal was anxious. As the readings progressed, poets usually became more confident. The initial terror, of standing up and reading aloud with a hall full of people sitting in silent judgement and stern Nakkeeran looming, slowly passed. But Aambal had never been as nervous as she was today. What if she forgot a line? What if she lost words? What if, what if. She was annoyed with herself, and wondered what Kandhan thought of her discomfort.

She wished that he had said more to her than, 'Aambal, do your best. That is the best.' She wished that he would speak about her almost-lost lines and the reason they had almost been lost, even though she would do anything to hide it from him. She wished that he would tap her head with the akil dandam and assure her that it would never happen again. He was a god, after all. But no, he never would do that. He would say something like, 'Language will protect you.' Where was he? He would not even be looking at her now that he was in the seat of the Patron of the Assembly, would he? Her eyes went to Murugan.

He was looking straight at her, and nodded and smiled. No matter how much Aambal might tell herself that she was a grown woman, who was expert enough to reach this far, she needed Kandhan's reassurance when she had her rare moments of doubt. She wished that he would come up and stand with her, hold her hand, but of course he could not, he would not, for he was the Patron, bound to impartiality in gesture as much as judgement. Aambal looked at him and was filled with the thought that, for her, he was the measure for everything. He had her loyalty always: that was her life. He was her life. Poetry was her life, nothing would come in the way of that. Aambal was still looking at Murugan, but her eyes glazed over, for another image had swam into them. She shivered. No, no! Not this again, not now. She did not want to see his face. Or think of him. All she wanted were her words. Only this mattered: getting into the Assembly ... Aambal started as her name resounded in her ears, and she turned to see the old man, leader of the Poets' Assembly, glaring. 'One more call and you would have lost your chance,' he told her, rapping his golden staff on the floor in impatience.

Aambal's hands trembled, her chest was tight and would not let the breath pass, waves of shame assailed her as she stood frozen. Then she heard another rapping sound, a sound that she had heard from the time she first met him, the sound of the akil staff, musical, gentle, alive. It gambolled across the room and ran all over Aambal like a swarm of butterflies, their wing flaps blowing everything but language out of her body. It ran through her veins and tugged at her hands and pushed her feet. She felt as if she had just bathed in the cool stream that ran past their kalari, its water warmed by the sun. She walked towards Nakkeeran, her head high and her face impassive. Bowing her head, she apologised. She looked at Murugan. Was he angry with her? Aambal dreaded seeing that slight frown on his face, which others would not see, but she would know by the slightest pursing of his lips. And that was worse for her than when he was angry and chided her. She did not want to look, but knew that if she didn't, it would weigh on her during the recitation, and she would lose time, lagging or rushing and ruining the metre. Her eyes went to his lips, and to her surprise, there was no tightening. He was smiling at her as he might have done when they were in the kalari, a smile of shared secrets. She did not smile back, but proceeded to greet the audience and then the various judges and dignitaries. Then she began the long recitation. It was a series of linked verses, in the metre of 'Wind's Eager Lips Kiss the Yellow Leaves'.

The judges listened carefully. Nakkeeran sat looking severe, his head resting on the golden head of the stout staff that he also used as a walking stick. His expression did not change, but as Aambal recited, Velliveethi smiled, and from the audience there came sounds of appreciation. Several voices identified the metre and the places where she had cleverly interworked another metrical thread to mark the complexity of the emotion expressed there. She felt lighter as the confusion left her body, and those who were listening to her and watching her felt the change in her tone, her posture and her voice, and they responded with louder cheering. This was her life, Aambal thought. This was where she wanted her whole self to be. This was the one place that she wanted to be in positions of power. Even at the court, at poets' gatherings across Tamizhagam, Aambal rarely felt like she wanted to be up front, or be in a position to say, let's do this, let's do it this way. But here. Ah, here, she did. As she stood there, she once more acknowledged her ambition: to head the Assembly one day. And when she was reciting, her voice soaring upwards to the arena seats, one above the other, a voice in her chest said, 'And I will.'

Murugan sighed. How he loved Aambal. He wanted to walk up to the front and say to all the crowds in the audience, 'This is Aambal, she is my best friend and my best poet. You wait and see. One day ...' Ah, but he could not, could he?

※

Nakkeeran was feeling strange. He had been feeling odd since the visit to Pothigai, and during the time that Aambal was called to read and as she began reading, it seemed to collect itself and become more evident. It was like nothing he had felt before—it was, he might think afterwards, as if he was melting. He had found it difficult to take his eyes off Aambal's face as she was reading. To most, it just looked serious, her attention gripped by her poem. To Nakkeeran's poet's eye, it had looked like a sky full of clouds poised between thunder, lightning and pouring. What was the child thinking?

Aambal's head was held straight, which was unusual, for when she was attentive, it tended to be tilted. He registered with a start that this little one, as Akattiyan still referred to her, despite the fact that she was old enough to bear children, had changed. There was something new about her. In all the years, since their first meeting at the kalari, when she and Murugan had been children, and in all the times that she had come to the Assembly to read, during all the times that he was at Paramkundram, there had always been about her a certain firmness—as if her will was a solid thing that she wore like armour. Now he noticed her eyes half-closed, her lips trembling ever so slightly, sweat forming on her forehead and her head unmoving, as if her thoughts had warned it to not be weak. She looked vulnerable. No, she had allowed herself to be vulnerable, Nakkeeran corrected himself.

As he looked at her standing there, stone-like, he recognised the look on her face, the look of her body: it was a look that poets had described again and again. It was one of the many looks of a kizhathi, a heroine, in the grip of one of many the moods that poetry had defined, moods that took hold of and transformed everything about her: the way she sat, the way her eyes changed contour, the way her hands were placed, even the way she breathed. Nakkeeran sighed, and that sigh took with it what remained of his sternness, and he let himself finally allow free flow to the deep affection he had come to feel for the girl, till now dammed behind his resentment of what he thought of as Murugan's blind love for her. He admitted to himself that, along with his resentment of her, his harshness with her, his demanding restrictions and his jealousy, he had all along known that she was a model novice poet. She had never once, in readings, preparations, apprenticeship sessions, behaved with anything other than the utmost attentiveness, humility, respect and sincerity. He also finally admitted to himself that he was proud of her, proud of her potential, proud of what the Assembly had contributed to her evolution. He was proud for another reason. A startling thought had come to him, a thought that pleased him: she could, when the time came, be where he was, play the role he had played.

Nakkeeran felt light. He felt as if a hand was at his neck steering him, and he felt a strange yearning: he wanted to climb up the Great Hill, stand atop it and call out to Madurai town and announce his retirement: he wanted to say, I am ready to become light. These thoughts seemed to be moving through him, unknotting old knots, releasing his limbs, breath, and gestures, making his body ripple with ease. He felt as if he was swimming in a stream of affection that connected him to Aambal, Murugan, Theivanai and to his fellow poets. His eyes skipped over them all and settled on Velliveethi, and stayed there. She was majestic. Her hair, wound up on the top of her head, looked to him like a crown. Her eyes were half-shut, as if all that she had seen and knew wanted to stay homed there. He wanted to go up to her and hold her hands and to say to her, 'Velliveethi, you must take my place.' This is right, he thought, she should take my place. Not because I am unworthy or incapable, but it is time for me to be lightened and for new ways in the Assembly.

He felt happy and he did not bite down his smile, as he was wont to do if ever a smile came to his lips during sessions. Now it was so wide that those who looked on it felt as if his whole face had become someone else's. Murugan was grinning, Nakkeeran saw, the same grin that he had worn when he first came there to pronounce judgement on three poetic works. A little laugh escaped his lips, making those near to him look at each other in puzzlement. Nakkeeran was recalling the blindfold over Murugan's eyes, the cork in his ears and the way he had kept his mouth clamped shut on that occasion. What an imp, he thought. Still.

His straying attention came back to Aambal's voice, and as he listened, Nakkeeran knew that something had also changed in his hearing, and it would affect the way he delivered his judgement, the feedback he would give. Not the way he measured a poem's worth, that would never change, his training had been scrupulous, and his inner ear and outer ears would never be imbalanced. No matter what he thought of a poet, he could only think of a poem in one way: full-heartedly. But he was no longer the same. His heart's transformation made these young poets and their experiences clearer to him, dearer to him, and that made it seem possible for the severe rules that he had long felt responsible for housing to be sent to find lodgings elsewhere. It is the poetry that's important, his own voice whispered to him.

How long was it since he had composed anything in that spirit? He laid the golden staff down across his lap. Ah! His fingers felt happy, he felt his head clear, into it came words … his fingers were moving, twitching, they were itching to hold a stylus. Murugan's eyes were on him, and he smiled. Nakkeeran had no awareness of what his body was doing: his lips had uncurled from their stern clasp of each other, his fingers had uncurled from the gold staff of authority. He is freed, thought Murugan, he is finally freed of himself. Now things will change. Nakkeeran had returned to himself, for he remembered that he too once worked 'like women work'.

Murugan felt Theivanai's eyes on him. She must have been alerted by his breathing, her acute sense of rhythm would let nothing escape her. He smiled at her. He admired her broad shoulders, the strength of the arm that moved closer to his own, and in that moment, he felt a bashfulness wash over him. The heat rose in his face, and he felt a longing for her to embrace him, to hold him as he rested against her firm chest on which her delightful breasts burgeoned, and inside which her heartbeat sounded steadily.

10

THE SELECTION

Then it was time for the final selection. On the day, as every day, Murugan woke up in the morning to the sound of Seval's little horn. Beside him, Theiva was already awake—she woke before the kuyil arrived and lay there waiting for them to start their concordant calls. She smiled at him and said, 'You're nervous.' He said nothing, and she continued, 'So many things hanging in the balance today: Aambal's selection, Nakkeeran's decision. The women's decision.'

Murugan looked out of the window, it was still black outside, but soon the sun would light up the clouds and the stone slopes that rose beyond the palace. It would fall into the room where Aambal, his poet—Murugan's poet—would be at her chowki, perhaps going over her poems, perhaps checking the knots on the palm leaves, ensuring that they were not so tight that she would not be able to flip them fully, or so loose that they flopped. The sun's warmth would also fall, a far distance away, on their friend, the long-eyed, pale-skinned young man with the voice that could still make Aambal and him forget everything. It would fall on the woman and two children who lay asleep near him. Might it pierce through his chest, urging him to change his mind? He shook his head. Watching him, Theivanai said, 'I wonder what will happen today. I wonder what Nakkeeran will say. I wonder what Auvvai, Kaakai and Velli will say.'

Murugan smiled at her. 'I expect Velli to say yes.' And he thought, Aambal, what will she say? He didn't expect her to say yes.

Theiva did not ask Murugan what he was thinking. She knew he was anxious about Aambal, and that it was not about her poems. Aambal wrote and rewrote till her verses had the edge of a warrior's sword: the choicest metal, refined over, smelted, strained, kept molten, poured into a hollowed iron block, beaten, removed, heated, cooled, beaten again and again till all its aberrations were smoothed out. Then to be put through the cutting and shaping and be melded into its strong and exquisite handle, taking at least a full moon's cycle to attain that form. Such a sword, like Aambal's verse, rang with spirals of resonance that those who knew such things counted in their minds. There was no cause to worry about Aambal's writing.

Seval's voice called out, 'Coming in!' and then he was inside, busily moving about the room, his red-and-black feathers bright with dew. He said, 'I will lay out your clothes now, for I want to go down and help Aambal get ready.' With his characteristic half-sneer, he asked, 'What does your grace feel like wearing today?' Theiva giggled, but Murugan wasn't amused. 'You decide,' he said and walked out to the balcony. Theiva turned to Seval, and was surprised to see him looking so sombre. What did he know that she didn't? She raised her eyebrows, and he silently mouthed something, glancing furtively at the balcony. Whatever it was, it made Theivanai sigh and say, 'Poor thing.' She went to join Murugan on the balcony, and Seval smiled to see them stand there, looking eastwards, waiting for the sun that would make the stone slopes of their home shimmer.

When he reached Aambal's house, she was awake, of course, and surprised to see him. Had Murugan sent more clothes?

Already she had a stack of selai that he had got woven for her final reading. The previous evening, she had stood looking at them, and her eyes had settled immediately on the only off-white—stitched through with dull golden leaves and little knobs of rain-grey, the entire stretch of cloth shot through with threads of gold. Then the blue one caught her eye, and a red, a green, till she shook her head and shut her eyes. The off-white, her favourite colour, wasn't that a suitable colour for the most important event of her poetic life? Instead, her eyes had finally settled on a selai the colour of the flower that had been present the very first time she met Murugan. The flower that was someone else's favourite too.

Aambal had trembled a little then and her eyes had shot open. She reached out to hold the windowsill, as if she expected to be knocked off balance. It was a relief that Seval was there, she wished he would say something sharp, sarcastic, biting, and so she asked, laughing, 'Has the reading been cancelled?'

Seval snorted. 'Don't be silly, girl. I've come to help you get ready.'

Aambal didn't snap at him, didn't say she was old enough to choose her own clothes, because she didn't want to look at those selai. She didn't want to pick, to decide. In any case, Seval's sense of style was better than hers—even Murugan had no quarrel with his choices—and Aambal wanted to look her best today. The hall would be packed, and everybody would be wearing their finest clothes. And he would be there too. He had promised to come back in time for the reading.

Seval watched her face as expressions rippled across it. He caught himself when he felt his mood changing to one that he didn't want, and quickly said, 'Come on, Aambal. I don't have all day. Let's choose your clothes and jewellery.' He went up to the pile of selai, muttering about Aambal not putting them away. 'Bah, if they were scrolls, or palm leaves, or styluses, ink wells, ink urns,' he said to her, 'you would have wrapped them and put them away the day they arrived.'

Aambal looked at the multi-coloured selai and blouses. How many were there? She hadn't counted, but now she realised that there were more than she remembered.

Seval was looking through them. As he picked up each one, he exclaimed, 'Beautiful!' or 'Lovely!' or 'Gorgeous!' till he came to the last one, and his breath came out in a long *aah*. 'This one,' he said. It was the pale saffron of kanakambaram, its weave lighter than a silk selai would have been, Seval knew, for he had been there when the Lord of Pazhani had instructed the weavers to mix cotton and silk, with the count of the silk threads less than the cotton. So much attention to these little things, Seval thought crossly, but when it comes to the matter of her life … His thoughts broke off as he opened out the selai and the intricate embroidery became visible. 'Incredible,' he gasped, 'this is so incredibly beautiful—it's almost as if Mutthu knew that you would wear this! Look,' he said, voice even higher with excitement, 'look at this. Who else but he would have thought of white for the munthanai?' He was glad that Aambal didn't need to make this decision to wear Thennan's favourite colour, and also glad that it really was the most beautiful of the selai. He was not glad to think that Murugan had spent more attention on this one, even ensuring that the bard's white was blended into the orange. Had he wanted her to wear it?

Aambal was glad for Seval's presence. She hadn't known how to get ready for the reading—her head had been full of the poems, with thoughts of Murugan and what he would think of the new work, thoughts of Velli, Auvvai, Kaakai and the other women, and of Nakkeeran. She tried to crowd her mind with thoughts that would leave no room for Thennan and the force of her longing for him to look at her in the kanakambaram-coloured selai. She remembered his eyes lingering on other occasions when he had looked at her. The memory shook her. She feared her longing for

Thennan. It disrupted her sense of time. Of place. Of language. Seval's presence calmed her.

She was happy to let him choose the blouse to go with the kanakambaram, she would have picked the sandalwood, or even a blue, but he selected the purple with silver threadwork. He helped her with her hair and adjusted the folds of her selai. He told her to darken her kanmayi a little more and to make her pottu with the crimson kungumam. Then he stood back and said, 'Ah! Aambal, you look like the winning poem,' making her giggle. Seval handed her a vial of perfume, the likes of which she had only smelt on Murugan. 'Is this Murugan's?' she asked, and he laughed and said, 'Now it's yours.' They both giggled at the tone in which he said that, and at the image of him taking it from Murugan's cupboard.

If Aambal had been asked to wear perfume at another time, she would have scoffed. But today she was glad, her face was flushed as she followed Seval's instructions, 'There, behind your ears, on your wrists, underarms, on the back of your neck.' Aambal's head was filling with images that rushed in, like the slew from a dam: Thennan's eyes, his head bending towards her neck, his lips at her ears, her wrists. And her hands reaching out ... She shook her head, her hands were meant for poetry, for palm leaf and stylus. To Seval, she said, 'Shall we leave now?' His heart filling with affection for this young woman whom everyone knew, but whose heart was visible only to a few, Seval saw that she wanted to be told that she looked good enough for Murugan's approval, but was too stubborn to ask, and so he said, 'Aambal, you look more lovely than I have ever seen you,' making her go warm and look away. He was happy that she was pleased.

They went to the Assembly together, walking in through the magnificent doors towards Nakkeeran, who smiled and held out his hands to her. When she put her palm-leaf bundle into them, he pressed them to his eyes and said to her, 'May the words hear you. May you hear the words.' Aambal looked toward the elder poets and bowed, and then went to Velliveethi and stood before her, not doing anything, not saying anything. The elder stood up, embraced the young woman, placed her hand on her head and softly recited the little verse that she herself said every day, several times a day, 'In my time, and in Time/ in step with His steps/ syllable, word, sentence, verse and language/ All breathing with His breath/ all speaking with His speech/ May the God of Tamizh lead my words.' Aambal felt as if she was standing on one of the many slopes of Pazhani Hill, a gentle wind blowing over her, over her turmoil and anxiety, and when she sat down in the place reserved for the twelve participants, she was no longer holding herself as if she was trying to keep from coming undone.

Some of the participants had not arrived yet, but they all knew each other from previous readings, and so there was some conversation, questions about family, about how they had travelled up to Madurai, about their masters, of how they were feeling. Aambal suddenly seemed to recall something and looked around. There was no sign of Thennan. She was eager to begin, and at the same time, she didn't want the time to pass. What if Thennan didn't make it in time? What if the doors shut before he managed to get in?

Aambal heard her name being called, and looked up to see Velliveethi, who had come to wish all the participants. 'Aambal,' she said, 'you were far away.' She recognised the look in Aambal's eyes and her heart went out to the young woman. There was a sudden bustle as Nakkeeran stood up and went to the enormous twin doors, standing just outside, his gold-covered staff in one hand. And then Paravani's wings could be heard, and Murugan and Theivanai entered. Musical instruments sounded together, but no flowers were strewn as Murugan hated that. The couple entered, looking like the sun and moon and stars had come and settled on them, and behind them, Paravani looked like an incandescent rainbow. They were greeted by the elders, including the judges.

Murugan looked at Aambal, she looked back at him—neither of them smiled, but both felt as if the other had said, *here you are*. She sighed. Kandhan was here, now everything would be fine.

༄

Nakkeeran was happy. He was always happy when the Assembly was full like this—especially when the hill tribes and hunters and visitors from other lands, other worlds were present—and when it was this time of the cycle of days, time for the final selection that would mean six new poets for the Assembly. Nakkeeran's ears buzzed with eagerness to hear what they each had to read. His chest swelled, this was his Assembly, these were his fellow poets, this was his seat, his place of honour, this was his day to deliver the final judgement. He felt his face stirring with the warmth of these thoughts, and his eyes traversed the huge hall, settling on Murugan, who raised an eyebrow and smiled. Nakkeeran's eyes could move no further, they were like thirsting mud that had felt the first drop of rain, like fish in a parched waterhole filling with rain, like a poet who has arrived at the font of language. His hands sought each other and saluted the young god; his eyes waited for acknowledgement, and when it came in the form of a blinding smile, Nakkeeran's eyes momentarily shut.

Behind the curtain of his eyelids, he saw the God of Tamizh, his feet reaching down to the last of the worlds, past the stem, past where the Great Snake sat, to his head that rose above Kailasa. Behind him, the giant wings of Paravani spread in a fabulous fan. On his shoulder, Seval stood, crest rippling. From the mouth of the rooster poured out the alphabets of the language to which he and all those present in the hall were enslaved to. அ ஆ இ ஈ உ ஊ எ ஏ ஐ ஒ ஓ ஔ க ங ச ஞ ஜ ட ண த ந ப ம ய ர ல வ ழ ள ற ன.

They fell on Murugan, gathered into a garland of red kadamba buds. Nakkeeran's eyes popped open. This is all his, he thought.

Like me, I too am his. He felt as if someone had reached inside and taken his heart, ripped it open, cleared its hardened doorways and channels and set it beating anew. He felt different, like he stood on Murugan's shoulders, unabashedly calling aloud with rooster-like abandon the letters of the beloved language. He bowed deeply to his god, who smiled at him and waved with his akil dandam, much like he had on that memorable first visit.

All the participants had arrived and were seated in their places. Some of them were nervously clutching their palm leaf bundles, others sat, smiling and talking. Aambal's eyes stretched over the endless rows of the Assembly, to the doorway. Where was he? He had said he would be here. Why hadn't he come? Did he think it was a waste of his time to come and listen to her when he had all those commissions from Murugan to complete? But this was her most important reading, wasn't it? Either she made it into the Assembly, or, or … She didn't want to think about it. Her mouth was beginning to go dry and her hands were sweaty. Aambal shook her head, she would not fail. She had worked hard. Murugan had worked alongside her and he had tested and criticised and overseen her work. She would not, could not fail—she knew how good she was. No matter how much Nakkeeran disapproved of her, he was nothing but fair in his judgement of her work, and of the work of all those who stood before him in the Assembly over which he presided. Her thoughts ran wild, like deer scattering at the approach of a leopard, but her eyes were single-minded in their focus, unbudging from the entrance. Her mother and grandmother looked at Aambal and at the door—they knew that look on her face, in her eyes, and they waited to see who would walk through and cause her to take a breath and relax.

Aambal's face is like an aambal, Murugan thought, watching her. When she was impassioned, with anger or inspiration or, as now, anxiously longing for a beloved, it darkened and closed a little. Where is the man, Murugan wondered. Had he decided to not come? He will come, Murugan decided. He had seen the way Thennan looked at Aambal, his eyes stretched with longing, darkened with the thin film of love's oil, the skin of his face alive, leaping towards Aambal's. Thennan was in love with Aambal. Maybe no one really knew, Murugan thought, but surely many suspected it. He knew, he knew these two friends better than they would let themselves know their own natures. With Aambal, he had been aware of her shifting moods: Murugan had known that she longed to be near Thennan, but feared it, feared the effect it would have on her work. Aambal's feelings for Thennan did affect her writing, but not in the way she dreaded. It didn't weaken it or distract her, rather it deepened her reach into the reservoir of words, love propelling her further and further.

Murugan smiled, thinking of how he had asked for love poems, knowing that they were forming inside her, and that, left to herself, she might never have given voice to them. Two sets of a hundred each, that's how many she had composed in the time between the return to Pazhani and the move to Paramkundram, in between the poems for the Assembly. He had let her think that he wanted them because he himself was in love with Theiva. He had, after all, first asked Aambal to write a love song to be tuned and sung for the woman he was trying to court, and she had had no trouble representing the emotions of an eager lover and neither had Thennan any trouble setting them to tune and singing them. Murugan's thoughts were broken when he saw Aambal's face changing and her shoulders relaxing, and he turned to where her eyes were and saw that Thennan had just run in, panting and sweating.

Aambal's eyes fluttered and her face relaxed, as did her hands, which she may not have realised were clenched. Her mother and grandmother looked at each other. The grandmother whispered something to her daughter, which neither her husband, her son-in-law nor her grandchildren heard. Theiva, Paravani and Seval were also watching Aambal. Paravani sighed when Thennan entered, and Seval frowned and muttered under his breath. Theivanai's face clouded over, and she touched Murugan's arm. He was lost in thought and did not respond. Theivanai sighed. When he's looking at Aambal, he can't see anything else!

***

From his distant home in Tanjai, where the brimming Kaviri separated into the Pudhaaru, the Vadavaaru and the Vennaaru, as if one of her was not enough to fill the thirst of this land of crops, Thennan set out two days before the reading. That was the time it would take the bard to walk there, but he hoped that farmers, landowners and merchants riding in their bullock carts towards Madurai or other towns would allow him to ride with them. That was indeed how it worked out.

As the train of carts moved past the fallowing fields and orchards, full of bird, animal and insect movements, and proceeded southwards, the landscape became bare. Thennan was filled with an anxiety, the slight fear that accompanied travellers through this stretch of barren land. He also knew from experience that these caravans were unhurried, they carried grains that had been dried and carefully stored, their goods would not spoil, and there was no fear of rains at this time. After a season of labour, whole families made these journeys, treating it as an outing, a treat to celebrate a season of work well done. And so there was no hurry to get to their destination. When Thennan's anxiety became noticeable, they asked him what the matter was, and when he told them that he had to be in Madurai at a certain time, or else his whole journey would be wasted, they suggested that he walk towards a crossroads and he would surely meet a soldier or messenger riding that way. They noticed his little bard's tudi and they asked if he had a performance or a competition to attend, and he said that it was not he but another who did.

Thennan's companions smiled at the way his pale face turned red. Someone whispered, kizhathi, lady love. It made Thennan's heart race to hear this. He had not yet put words to what he was feeling. But now hearing them say the word, he felt his body go cool, then warm as he imagined them as lovers: Aambal and Thennan—kizhathi and kizhavan.

These words brought Murugan to mind, he was Kurinji Kizhavan, the Hero of the Kurinji. Always the First Hero when you thought of romance; young, handsome and charming. And the lovely and intelligent Devayani was the ideal kizhathi. He recalled seeing Theivanai for the first time on the beaches of Chendur. She stood next to Murugan after the battle. When Murugan was present, all eyes were on him, mantled in a cover of stillness. When Theivanai stood next to him, it was as if she had always been there, her golden-skinned face seeming to turn the ebony of Murugan's incandescent. That's what a heroine and hero were like, he thought.

He didn't feel like a hero, he didn't think that Aambal thought of him as one either. Did he think of her as a heroine? Unbidden, her appearance in the gathering at Murugan's wedding came to mind: dishevelled, hair awry, clothes of rough, ink-stained kora, sweaty, unadorned and ungainly. He shook his head and another image appeared before him: Aambal, her eyes bright, her voice soft, silky in a way that he hadn't heard before, as she sat reading the love poems that Murugan had asked her to write. 'Vela,' they each began, 'if you want me to,' and then continued to make deals with the god, saying that if he wanted her to do something for him, like take messages to Theivanai, then he had to return the favour, do something for her, like turn the stony heart of 'he who I have lost my heart to' into a page with her poetry on it.

Thennan was certain that the 'he' was he, Thennan, childhood friend, now the man her heart had run off with. The man who loved her. She must love him, why else would she blush as she did, why else would she look at him like that, why would her breath change gait when he was near? His own breathing grew heavier as he thought these things. His thoughts were in full flow now, and his head was filling up with images, images that he sent away when he was in Pazhani and in Paramkundram for fear of Murugan, for fear that Aambal would rebuke him, for fear that Seval would mock him. For fear that if he let them be, he would blurt out his feelings. But now they came swarming in: Aambal and he together, hand-in-hand, climbing to the top of Pazhani Hill, the two of them by the river, her tawny face cradled to his pale-skinned chest, her riotous hair, smelling of palm leaf, dye, inks and of the hill, spread all over his face. Her fingers in his, her lips on his, her waist against his. Thennan started at how vivid his thoughts of Aambal were. He thought back to the change that came over her in the months that they had spent working together—the way she looked at him when she thought he wasn't looking, the way she had begun to wear brighter clothes, the way she drew her eyes darker and the way her lips trembled sometimes. These poems were proof of what she was feeling. They were statements of her desire. In the poems, they were lovers.

She loved him, he was certain of it. His heart was certain. He would tell her today, he would beg her to tell him if she returned his feelings. First, he would hear her reciting. But he must tell her today, he thought to himself, looking at the sky. Would he make it in time? Or would he be late and have to stand outside the bolted doors of the Assembly? Those giant doors that took twelve people to pull shut would close at the exact time announced. He wasn't certain of reaching the town in time to find a room to bathe and change. He would be smelling by the time they reached Madurai.

Into his head, darting through all these thoughts, there swam in images of the people he had left behind: Jvala, Maran, Senitha. A wave of regret hit him, but he shook it off like the monkey, climbing a tree after it rains, shakes off the drip from its leaves, his eyes on the fruit hanging from branches above him. All he wanted now was to tell Aambal and to hear her response. His heart beat faster as his mind leapt past all the in-between steps to the conclusion of a courtship that had not even begun. Did Murugan know, Thennan wondered. Of course he knew. He was a god, and even if he wasn't, he would still know.

Thennan had to wait at the crossroads for longer than he had hoped to before a party of horse riders came that way. One of them, a woman named Arthi who was going home to Chera lands from the Vindhyas, where she had offered her martial services, said to him, 'Jump on!' When Thennan told her that he had to make it to Madurai in time for the reading, she laughed and said, 'Hold on tight,' and galloped at wind-whistling speed. In Madurai, it was as Thennan had feared. All the inns were occupied. He rushed around to a public bath house, washed and changed and ran to the Assembly, barely slipping in as the doors began to shut.

⚬⚭⚬

The imposing figure of Nakkeeran drew admiring looks. He was standing in the bare stretch that ran from one enormous door to the one on the opposite side. This space cut the room in two, and was always left empty. It was where the elders sometimes stood to speak, where the participants to competitions or those receiving honours stood before the patron who sat in the first of the many rows that stretched to the back wall. Accompanied by the rapping of his walking stick, Nakkeeran called the names of the twelve readers, asking for them to come forward and greet Murugan, the God of Tamizh, and his consort and co-patron of the Great

Poets' Assembly, the scholar Theivanai. The twelve young women and men rose from their seats and came to stand in a row facing Murugan, who sat unsmiling, and Theivanai beside him, smiling. Seval stood on Theivanai's side and Paravani on the other. Seval stepped forward and blew a pippiri-pip-pippiri-pip-pip-pip on his horn, and the audience went silent.

In one half of the circular room, seats ran in arcs of widening rows, rising in tiers to the end. The fluted wooden walls on either side were dotted with strategically placed knobs of brass, bell-metal and cured wood that had been hollowed and filled with lime and sand to catch and hold the sounds and ensure that they did not echo or crash into each other, but resonated naturally, the ring of each sound rising, spreading outwards, then regathering and sinking into silence. The ceiling was panelled, with wood of varying textures and thickness, and unseen to all but expert eyes, embedded in these panels were conch shells, their surfaces darkened, and these took the voices of the poets and filled them with resonance and then sent them out. In this way, no matter where anyone was sitting, they could hear the poetry clearly.

The first row contained two seats, one of these was Murugan's and the other Theivanai's. Had Akattiyan or Ganesha been present, they would have sat here too. Nakkeeran and the other judges had seats in the other half of the room, curving along the front left of Murugan, and to the right was the curved seating for the competing poets. In the middle of that half circle was the little pulpit for those who were speaking. The judges were twelve, including the leader Nakkeeran: Velliveethiyar, Auvaiyyar, Kaakaipaadiniyaar, Kuramagal Ilaiveyni, Kapilar, Paranar, Sathanar, Vankanar, all of them seniors in the Assembly, and three scholar-poets from at large, Kaniyan Pungundranar, Manakkudavar and Cheraman Perunkadungko.

Nakkeeran walked up into the pulpit, raised his staff towards the sky, bent his head and touched his heart. He called on the

Great Goddess, the bringer of rain, Mari, and her companion, the one who held an udukkai in his hands and was accompanied by dogs, and hailed them as Word and Meaning, the parents of all. He turned to Murugan and Theivanai, and spoke words of welcome and invited Murugan to address the Assembly.

Murugan's indigo attire and the sapphire that adorned his chest, neck, ears, hands, waist, anklets and fingers invoked an inkwell full of ink, its blue-black muted, sombre. As he took his place at the pulpit, Paravani spread out his wings and stood behind the god, and Seval rose up into the air, blowing quick notes on the shrill horn, which seemed to spin in listeners' ears, making the silence when it came scintillating. Murugan called for the blessings of the Lord of Beginnings, he hailed Nakkeeran and the other eleven judges by name and then all twelve of the participants, of whom only half would be chosen. He wished everyone luck and returned to his place. He smiled at Theivanai, whose smile was broad, and turned to Aambal, who looked nervous. Strangely, all the anxiety he had been feeling earlier had dissipated. She had become masterful; he had trained her unsparingly and she had driven herself just as unsparingly. When she stood in her turn, everything else would go out of her mind and only the words would remain, too full to leave space for anything else. Or anyone else.

Velliveethi approached the participants and spoke to them, one at a time. She wished them luck and urged them to be relaxed. The competition would take three days to finish, four readings each day—the twelve competitors would read a set of three poems: an introductory poem, describing their poetic journey with Tamizh, their masters and their training, and the theme of their main poem, then the main poem itself, and finally the last one, in which the poet gives thanks and dedicates the poem to someone, the reasoning for that dedication made clear to the audience by the two earlier poems. The time for recitation, for questions and answers was all defined, and would not spill over, except on the rare occasion when the judges or someone from the audience wasn't convinced by the poets' answers or wanted explication on something a poet said, or found the poets' answers so interesting, they wanted to hear more.

Aambal's reading was in the second half of the third day, the last person reading on that day was the bhikku, Naninda. The judges, who by now knew the quirks of the twelve participants, gave them spots in accordance with their temperaments: first spot to the one who got anxious waiting, and last to the one who was always composed and who composed verses that were benign and fell into the ears of listeners like a blessing. Aambal was happy that she was not first or last, she was also happy that the one to go after her was Naninda—neither his verse nor he himself would overwhelm her or her verse. The participants knew the order in which they were reading, but not the audience, who played a game of guess-who's-next each time.

Velliveethi called out the name of the first participant, Triveni, who walked to the podium to the accompaniment of clapping and cheering. Saluting Murugan and Theivanai, the judges and everybody else, she began, 'I am Triveni, come from lands northward of the mighty Vindhya. My master is my mother, Charvi.' She recited in well-balanced verses the first poem, which talked of how her mother had come to learn Tamizh and what her training had been, then went on to describe how she herself had been trained. The lines of the poem listed the pleasures of learning this melodious language and of the challenges. Triveni's words held the airiness of the northern mountains and her voice had a slight twang that was foreign to the south. But her diction, enunciation, the metaphors and measures of time were faultless, and the other competitors watched in admiration, their fingers tapping along, their lips open in wonder, or repeating to themselves a catchy phrase or a new usage. Triveni finished her recitation with a verse identifying herself and the person to whom the verse was dedicated, 'I am Triveni, of the three rivers; my parents are one a herder, the other a poet; my brother a trader; my grandfathers a healer, and a trader, my grandmothers a mathematician, and a farmer, and my sister commander of the royal troops of Avanti. I dedicate this work to my master, my mother, who, to me, is the womb of my language.'

The entire hall burst into applause and some stood up. The bands of travelling gypsies and hunters whose steps turned towards Madurai every year at this time, like honeybees that swarmed up into the hills when the wild jackfruit and atthi began to flower, shook their kanjiras and blew on their hunting horns. The city dwellers called out praise, and the judges clapped, the God of Tamizh laughed in delight and raised his dandam. This was a place where everybody delighted in the sound of the hardy language made by the son of parents described as Word and Meaning.

Next was the young man Teshana, come from the island kingdom of Ilangkai. His verses spoke of the goddess who appeared on the dark wings of rain clouds, and responded to their calls to her with the sound of the manifold water creatures that lived in the island's waters. He spoke of glorious King Dashagriva Ravana and of his son, Indrajit, who ruled wisely and sang so well that beings from other worlds came to listen. He spoke also of the God of the Vel, who came to the Vedda hunters living deep in the forests of Kebilitha. His poem was quick-paced, flying up and down the scale in its soundscape. When he ended, his poem turned out to be dedicated to the Vedda chief's daughter, Valli, She Who is Dark as Moss, who is like the forest. When she walks, fish leap in the streams and flowers spring open and peacocks spread their wings and dance as if she were a rain cloud. Murugan's face split into a big smile. Cheers and applause broke out once again.

In this way, the recitation went on: on the first day, four poets read, on the second, another four, and each one was subjected to a series of questions by members of the judging committee, and one question from the audience. On the third day, the first poet to read was Navira, who had travelled up to Madurai from the tail end of the land, the place that marked the southern boundary of this mass of land that Himavan stood guard over. After her came Thayalan of Paramkundram and Aithu, the youngest. And then it was Aambal's turn. She looked out across the rows to her mother, her mother's mother, her father, her two grandfathers and her siblings. Then she turned to Murugan and Theiva, and out of the corner of her eyes, glanced at Thennan. Murugan's eyes followed hers, and for a moment, he looked grim. Aambal's gaze settled on Nakkeeran after all her salutations. She no longer felt uncomfortable with him, but she was surprised to see how warm the old man's smile was and at his gesture of blessing. Though he had done the same for all participants, she felt special, because nothing she did had made him smile like this at her before.

Aambal looked composed, but when she spoke, Thennan's trained musician's ears heard the tremor, and his hands clenched, Oh god, he thought, please let her win, please let her want to win. Murugan's hands were sweating, but Theiva was composed. She knew that Aambal's devotion to the language would guard her words.

'I am Aambal,' she began, 'and my Master is Mutthukumarasami, Lord of Paramkundram. I learnt to be a poet through his rough guidance. My lineage goes back as long as Tamizh has been, my ancestors, like all of yours, have adored it and sung it, composed and written it.' She went on to recite verses that linked internally one to another in metrical loops, where meaning depended on the sound and vice versa.

As she recited, her voice grew stronger, and Theiva saw Murugan's hands open and his fingers tapping, counting; his body relaxed, and his face shone, his poet was singing of him. How he loves her, thought Theiva, and she, how she loves him. Once again, she wished she had a friend like this. Her eyes followed the line of Aambal's eyes, and saw how, sweeping over the audience, they fleetingly paused on Thennan, so delicately that you could miss it. Theiva recalled a poem in the rough language of the northern lands, in which the speaker tells a man who wonders whether the woman loves him or not that she, in order not to be caught out, looks adoringly at the whole world, so that her actual adoration of him would not stand out. Aambal's eyes ran, as if looking at everybody, to the one she was looking for, and at.

Theiva shuddered slightly. Poor girl, she thought to herself, poor, poor girl. Murugan didn't seem bothered, and for a moment, she felt anger course through her: is this what you did to a friend? And then it cooled just as quickly: what had he done? As with everything else, his presence had only warmed what was there already, urging it to flower, like the kurinji. She suddenly felt sorry for the man who sat next to her, watching his favourite poet, his best friend, and she noticed that his hands clenched every time Aambal and Thennan looked at each other, though the smile stayed on his face. Maharasa, Theiva repeated silently. Maharasa: the Supreme Rasa that makes no distinctions between things, that impels everything towards fullness. She reached out and put her hand on Murugan's, and felt the warmth emanating from the ring with the single pearl that he wore—the only thing she had gifted him when she married him and came to live with him.

Aambal's main poem was about transformation: she described the way that sounds alchemised into syllables and syllables rooted into words, fed on grammar, grew lush and sprouted. The verses led up to the discovery that she had arrived at in the final days of composing this main poem: that the God of Tamizh was also the God of Love and the making of language was like the making of love. Poets and lovers fervently sought grammar, meaning and rhythm, knowing full well that it was not these that would determine what became of the poetry and of the love. Her poem ended with a line that made many in the audience leap up and clap and cheer. It made Velliveethi smile broadly, and made tears slip out of Murugan's eyes and tremble on his cheek: 'Love and language are stubborn rock, till Murugan sets foot there and turns it fruitful, like the big hill to which he said, "You are the Fruit of Knowledge—pazham nee".'

Aambal, who had been afraid to turn her eyes towards Murugan, saw the two translucent beads slip from his dark eyes, and make their way towards his fiery cheek and evaporate, and heaved a sigh of relief. She saw that Theiva was smiling, as were her parents and grandparents. She glanced at Thennan, whose face was red, as if the words had entered his slender frame and run there, making him pant and redden with the exertion.

Like those before her, Aambal too answered questions from the judges and one from the audience and then returned to her place to the sound of applause and cheers. Murugan was still smiling broadly. She smiled back. Her hands wiped her forehead and upper lip over which beads of sweat lingered. Then she turned to Thennan, and this time, looked him fully in the face. His eyes were shining, his lips trembling, and he gazed at her, hand touching his chest. What did he mean by the gesture, she wondered. Murugan watched the whole exchange and the smile left his face, though neither Aambal nor Thennan were aware of anyone else at that point. Theiva, watching the whole drama unfold, felt again the sadness that the man she had spoused was feeling, though he was god and he needn't.

She reached over and touched Murugan's hand, and he turned towards her, face serious. 'It's not your fault.'

Murugan's eyes widened, and he took her hand in his, and said, 'I know, but it is Aambal.'

After Aambal, the monk Naninda read, and as she and the judges had expected, the reading was gentle, a fitting ending. It had the gentleness of one who has been trained to stand in the middle, the place where vigour and repose, where sense and chaos all start from and return to; the place where what is and what waits to become, meet and converse.

Then it was all over, the judges asked for a break during which they would make their decision, and the crowds dispersed to go out into the open, to stretch and to walk, to expel the tension that had seeped into their bodies, and which would only be fully gone after the announcements. When proceedings resumed, Nakkeeran stood up and praised the participants and their masters, and he spoke words of appreciation that surprised everyone with their unusual warmth and unguarded affection. He then thanked all the judges and spoke a few words about each one of them, finally thanking the audience and the patron and his spouse. Nakkeeran stood in silence for a few moments, then turning towards the judges, he asked their permission to make an announcement before the results of the selection.

'I bow to the Assembly,' he said, 'to the place that has nurtured, tested and enlivened Tamizh for so many hundreds of years. I salute its patron, the God of Tamizh, Mutthukumarasami, Lord of Paramkundram, and Akattiyan, the Mother of Tamizh, who is here in spirit, if not in body.' He paused and drew a breath. 'I salute all those who have loved and strengthened, those who have spoken, recited and sung and guided the path of this language for so many years. I salute all those who have come to this great place, to listen, to appreciate, to applaud and censure and suggest.' Again, he paused, as if he had to dislodge the words physically from somewhere inside him. He leaned on his cane and it was surprising how old he looked, this man whose energy had never seemed to dull.

Nakkeeran straightened up, and he was again the pillar-like leader they were all familiar with. He said that, for as long as he could remember, all he had wanted was to be at the helm of the Assembly, and that he had led it and guided its work for so long that it was home to him. He said that now the time had come for a change, and he agreed with Akattiyan that, for too long, the women poets had run away from the position of the leader of the Assembly of Poets, not because they were incapable, but because they treasured their freedom. It was time, he said, that the Assembly became freer to lure them back, for a woman's ways are different from a man's and it was time some of that womanly spirit of abandon returned to the Assembly. It was time, he said, that a woman again led the Assembly.

The uproar in the audience was as much in appreciation as in protest, and it took a while to die down. A smiling Nakkeeran said, 'I have heard the words of the women poets here in the Assembly, and I know them to be different from those of the men. The wife of our patron, Theivanai, who has learned Tamizh from none other than Akattiyan, has suggested to me that we host a festival of women's poetry, and I wholeheartedly support this.' Again, there were cheers and clapping. Finally, he invited Velliveethi, Auvaiyyar and Kaakaipaadiniyaar to stand for election to the post he was taking leave of. 'Enough of that. Now on to what we have all been waiting for.' He announced the names of the six who had been chosen, and bade the other six to make another attempt.

Aambal had made it, and so had Naninda the monk, and Triveni, Navira and Teshana, and Thayalan of Paramkundram. None of the participants were surprised for, along with composing, they had all been trained in listening with discrimination.

The announcements brought wild cheering, clapping, blowing of horns, shaking of kanjira, dancing, comments called out loud. Members of the audience rushed up to the participants, to shower them all with words of praise, to pat their backs, even to press little gifts, tokens of their regard, into hands clammy with the relief of the end of a year of waiting and preparing. The families and masters of the participants too came up to embrace their children and their apprentices, and to have a word with the judges. People swarmed around Murugan and Theivanai, and the elder poets. It seemed everybody had something to say.

In all this, only Seval noticed that Thennan had come up to Aambal, whispered something in her ear and left.

11

CONFESSIONS

It was a while before Aambal went to meet Thennan. After the post-announcement flurry died down, all twelve of the participants gathered together, going over the days' events and taking leave of each other. Aambal waited to meet Murugan and Theiva. Aambal's family had departed, proud of her achievement. Her grandmother had patted Aambal's face and commented to her daughter about how well Aambal wore the glow of achievement. Murugan and Theivanai were to leave for Paramkundram after partaking of a meal with Nakkeeran and the judges.

After expressing his delight to all the poets for their poems and their spirited recitation, Murugan came up to Aambal, held both her hands and said, 'You were at your best. I will take leave of you now. It may be a while before I see you, and who knows how we will be then.' She was puzzled, but before she could say anything, he had raised her hand to his chest, and held it against his heart, her hand pulsed to its drumming, growing warm with its warmth. Then he was gone.

Finally, she set out to meet Thennan. Aambal wanted to run, to dash towards the spot, see him and hear what he had to say. Her steps quickened recalling the look in his eyes as she had looked at him after her readings. Now she wanted to say something to him, tell him how she felt. She had recognised the feeling even when she didn't want to, and after her test was done and she had succeeded, she was no longer afraid. Couldn't she too love and work? She felt that she could dive deep into the muscular currents of love and her lungs would strain to hold on to her breath, but she also knew that she could hold that breath and break through the current into the land and air of language. She *could* write and love. And she would do both with abandon.

Aambal slowed her breath and her steps. When she arrived at the spot where Thennan was waiting, he said, 'Let's walk.' They walked along the streets slowly, as if there was nothing special about this evening, nothing unusual in Thennan asking Aambal to meet him alone. Her hand felt the soft glide of the kanakambaram-coloured selai that she was wearing. As if it were yesterday, that day was clear in her mind: in a children's game, when asked to name a favourite flower, Thennan had said, 'Kanakambaram'. People recognised them and hailed them by name. Aambal smiled and nodded, but Thennan neither smiled nor greeted anyone back. His steps gathered pace every time someone called out to them, as if he was running from recognition. When they reached the gate to the walled section that held the great hall of the Assembly, he turned in there. Though surprised, Aambal followed. Thennan steered her towards the far end of the courtyard, empty at this time. He gestured for Aambal to sit down, and then himself sat.

Thennan was silent, and Aambal was too. She knew that this was different from all the other times they had met, that things would never be the same now. They say that poets can see through the veils of time when they are in the throes of composing. It is true that they can, but almost as if in payment for this extra sense, poets, it is said they have been rendered blind and deaf to their own life's progression. Aambal, however, began to feel a sense of dread. She said, 'Thennan, what is it?'

He rose and said again, 'Come, let's walk.' They walked aimlessly, it seemed, until they reached the row of pavalamalli that were in full bloom, coral-hearted flowers dotting the little trees. Aambal imagined the whole thing as a selai, green and coral, she imagined drawing it around her, tucking, making the folds of the front and tossing the end over her shoulder. 'Aambal,' Thennan's voice stopped her thoughts, the ornate munthanai of the imaginary selai hung mid-drop. She turned to him, the wind stirred and a few flowers dropped down onto the earth. Thennan reached up and plucked one of the tiny flowers, their cool white petals fiery with the ring of coral, and made as if to tuck it into Aambal's hair. But she moved and instead stretched out her hand and took the flower. She held it in the palm of a hand that was trembling, as if abashed to be holding a flower rather than a stylus. Thennan reached forward, clutched her hand and pulled it to his chest. She stood absolutely still, she tried to still the voice inside her head that was saying, 'This is a draft, it will be revised.'

Aambal was at a loss. She had imagined being with Thennan, but now she realised that her imagination had all been in words. Thennan would confess in perfectly worded sentences his love for her, and how those words would fly into her ears and fill her chest like swarms of the bees that descended from the hills when spring arrived. She had imagined how his words—which were her words, words that she had given to him, in her imagination—would run through her from head to toe and she would tremble with delight.

'I love you,' Thennan was saying, 'I have loved you for a long time.' Aambal shivered, she loved him too, despite having tried so hard to not love. She had barely managed to keep the distraction of it from getting in the way of her work. But now, now that she had been selected, she felt her overdrawn energy filling up again. Now she could spend time on love, she thought. Followed immediately by another thought: love's grammar would have time to settle before the next round of selections. She felt capable. A sense of her own expertise reassured her, though the unknown dread would not be banished. Her thoughts rose and filled her mind, like smoke from a fire, and she only heard Thennan's voice as a faint hum in the background. She shook her head to clear its clamour, and the bard's voice sounded clear, 'They live in Nellai.' He was saying, 'I never meant to hide it from you.'

'Who lives in Nellai?' Aambal asked.

Thennan's head, which had been downcast, rose up with a snap. Had she heard nothing? The blood rushed to his face, tinging his pale skin with a deep blush, his eyes widened and his hand dropped hers. 'My wife and children,' he said, voice atremble.

Aambal felt as if a strong wind had spun around her and lifted her up into the sky, and she was looking down at this scene. She said nothing. Thennan was married? Thennan had a wife? And children? And they lived in Nellai? And he had just said that he loved her. She loved him too. Almost as much, she thought, as she loved her words and the language and the god that had made the language. But he had a family. Was he telling her he loved her, and revoking that confession by saying he had a family? Did he not want to love her? What did he want? What was he saying? Again, his words made her mentally put them aside for rework. He had no way with words. She shuddered. If Veerabahu, who had once said that poetry was distracting and not to be trusted, had hit her, she might have felt a force equal to this, shaking the words out of her.

She shut her eyes, and scrambled in her head for words, like she always did when she was distressed or confused, but the only ones that came were Thennan's 'I love you.' What was she going to do with those words, with that love? She had loved Thennan from the time she saw him on the battlefield at Chendur, that love had been growing, sprouting leaves and buds. Why had he waited till that creeper had burst into bloom, till her love was fully blossomed, to fling a thoughtless blade at its trunk. Had he told her all this before, she would have trimmed its leaves, plucked the buds and sent them floating in the many streams on the Holy Hill. But he was telling her now that he loved her. Now? What did he expect her to do? He had a wife, whose place was beside him. He had children. What was he asking of her? That she be the 'other' wife? Would she be happy being another wife? Could a man love two women equally? Maybe, she thought. But could Thennan? Or is that not what he meant? What did he mean? He had children! Was he asking her to be another wife and another mother? Aambal, another wife to Thennan. Aambal, another mother to Thennan's children. What about Aambal, beloved? Aambal, poet? Aambal, apprentice to Murugan, future leader of the Poets' Assembly? She couldn't play so many roles, but wait, was that not what he was offering? Had he calculated and decided that she could not play such a big role, was he asking her to do less? Was he saying he wanted them to love in secret, in hiding?

Aambal's thoughts were ambushing her, and recognising this, she shook her head to knock them down. What did she want, she asked herself. Did she want to be a second wife, to stand on one side of Thennan, while his first one stood on the other? Could she be a second wife? Could she be a second mother to Thennan's children? Could she be a secret lover? No! She wanted, like Velli and Auvvai, to shout out her love in perfect verses, to proclaim to the world that she loved Thennan the bard, who loved her back. Aambal's head cleared. Her body stopped shivering, she took a step back from Thennan, she wasn't falling anymore.

Anger coursed through her body, firming her spine and her flopping tongue, recalling the words that had run from her, and she looked at Thennan and said to him, 'You, who know that the gati of words is everything, because that is what keeps it in time, how could you go so amiss with the timing here?' Thennan said nothing, and Aambal continued, her eyes not looking at him. 'You could have told me this a long time ago and saved me from this useless love.' Even as she was speaking, Aambal realised how untruthful that was—regardless of what she knew about him, she would still have fallen in love with him. She also understood what Murugan meant when he had said it is never about who or what the other person is, when love blossomed, it sprung up, like the lily she was named for, thrusting out of its green sepals, shoving aside the water that seeks to hold it down, stretching its roots, extending its stem till it broke through the restraining sheet of water, raising its head towards the waiting moon that was leaning down to kiss it. There was nothing anyone could do to stop it, except to pluck it, kill it. Nothing she could have done, nothing Kandhan could have done.

But Thennan could have chosen a better time. He could have chosen not to speak. The loud chiming of the bells from the temple made Aambal wonder: what was the fish-eyed goddess saying? Aambal thought how everybody knew, everybody knew all this while and no one had said anything to her. Why had they let this happen? Then she recalled the conversations with Theivanai, this daughter of the heavens, she who had learned Tamizh. She had tried to tell Aambal to acknowledge what she was feeling. Would that have helped? If she had spoken of it, if she had confided in someone, would she have not been standing here, listening to a confession that she had longed for, but which now drove her to despair?

Fury bubbled up and steamed through Aambal. Her anger was with Thennan, with Thennan's words, with Kandhan and his lack of words on the matter. And she was furious with herself, for too many words, for too many thoughts, all the images of days on which she had sat or walked with thoughts of Thennan filling her head, her heart filling with images of him, pushing the words away. What had she been thinking? Did she not value her words at all? Had she not lived all her life not answerable to anything other than language? What had possessed her? Why had the words to which her whole life been in service not come to her rescue? Why had language, which she had always thought of as life-breath, deserted her? Did she mean nothing to them, the syllable families, the word tribes, the kingdoms of sense, the world of language? She staggered. Without words, nothing meant anything. Without words, nothing could mean. But that was what she wanted, she thought. Nothing. She wished she was back in that cave on the mountain top that had once hailed her as 'Kandhan's Poet'. If she could, she would begin again from there. And not come to this place where she was nothing. Where she meant nothing.

She turned from Thennan and began to walk away. He followed her, called to her, but she would not even look at him. When it became awkward and people were staring, Thennan said, 'Aambal. I am sorry. I should have told you before. I just couldn't. I thought about all this, and I didn't want to tell you. I wasn't going to, I wasn't going to, really. I don't know what came over me.' He was babbling, his face red, his heart thumping as it had when he was rushing towards the Assembly earlier. 'It was your last reading before I went home, the love poems that Kandhan asked you to write, those words bursting with longing as you recited. I couldn't stop myself, every day that I was at home, your voice brooded in my heart, and it built a nest full of longing for you till it became unbearable and I had to tell you. I knew that you were writing about me. I felt your love in those poems.'

The poetry! He was blaming the poetry. If she had not written those verses, if he had not heard those words and let them fling him into love's deep current, then none of this would have happened. Is that what he was saying? Was that true? Was it the poetry? Those verses, which had been different from everything else she wrote, which burst, like the kurinji, sudden, all at once, its colour and fragrance everywhere. She remembered their tug at her heart, at her feet, and how they had brought a lingering slowness to the gait of her words and to her own footfall—as if love had made each step, each word so pleasurable that they needed more time. When he saw her pause, Thennan's courage returned and he reached out and took Aambal's hand. Aambal stopped. His beautiful fingers that had invaded her thoughts on many an occasion now seemed like an iron band, a shackle. How did he dare? After all this, to take hold of her writing hand! She shook it free of his fingers. It was the poetry, the cursed poetry. Why had she listened to the voice of her heart? Why couldn't she have resisted its call? Why couldn't she have been more ... more what? They all wrote from their hearts, didn't they? Velli, Auvvai? She said only this: 'Thennan, I want to go home. Let me leave in peace.'

He understood that she was determined not to hear him, that she had built a wall in her head that would keep out everything now. Thennan stopped where he was, as if his legs had turned to roots and the earth had closed in around them.

12

IN THE AFTERMATH

Aambal didn't want to see anyone, but did not know where to go. She looked blindly into the distance. All the roads would be crowded. Where was she to head? Just then she heard a familiar sound, the sound of giant wings, and Paravani was in front of her. He said, 'Aambal, come, I will take you wherever you want to go.' At the sound of the voice of this bird, who had been friend, guide, mentor and guardian, Aambal's face finally crumpled and she sobbed uncontrollably. With his wings wrapped around her, Paravani felt as if he was back there, so many years ago, when the king of Paramkundram, the Patron of Poets, had been a little boy of five. His eyes ran over. Poor Aambal. He wished he could take her home to her mother and grandmother, but he knew Aambal would not go there. She would go perhaps to Pothigai, to Akattiyan and the gentle Kani. Aambal said, 'Take me away from here.'

How was Paravani there? Had he known? Had Murugan known? Had Seval known—was that the explanation for his disapproval of Thennan? Perhaps they had, or rather they certainly had all known, but they could not have stopped the love that was fated, neither could they have stopped this moment, for it was fated to take whatever turn the hearts of the two dictated. They could only know what was intended for Aambal, not what she would do, for a person's heart is her own, and not even Fate or Time can enter there to direct where it went.

Paravani rose up into the sky and Aambal said, 'Take me to Velan's Hill.' Down below, everything stood as it had always had, the temple, the town, the lakes, the river, the hills. Only Aambal's heart was changed. It had turned from a tumultuous sea to a barren tract of palai, where the only things that grew were thorny, leafless trees with milk that brought death.

Aambal set foot on one of the most sacred hills in the land, and her whole life passed before her eyes. In everything she had done, Kandhan had always been there. She had never been alone, not even after Kandhan was married. But now she was alone. She said to Paravani, 'Please go, Paravani, I will be alone. I will climb up'.

Paravani held her in the embrace of his wings. His heart went out to the serious young woman, but it was the sturdy, sharp-witted little girl he was seeing, the girl who had sat on his back with her best friend, the God of Tamizh, and had dared to call him 'a little fool'. 'Aambal, come home with me, come back to Pazhani, or let me take you to Pothigai or to Chendur.'

But she refused, pulling herself free and walking away. Paravani stood there, thinking of the other hill and the other person who had been just as hurt and angry. Paravani's eyes filled and he said, 'Poor child. Poor thing.' He wasn't sure who he meant: the little unhomed boy striding up Pazhani Hill, or the young woman who was now making her way up this one, where it was believed the God of Pazhani was always present.

Aambal climbed on and on, holding neither the roots nor vines, nor using a staff on the steep winding paths. It was if her fury kept her feet sure, her footholds unerring, refusing to let her fall. She came to the point on the hill beyond which no one dared to go without a sign in a dream or from an oracle, and always bearing a gift. Only Velan's oracle and Velan himself came unbidden. Aambal had no gifts and she had not been given a sign, she had not been sent word for, nobody had given her permission, nobody waited there to lead her further in. But she strode on, and the forest did not close up and hide its path. Aambal climbed, unseeing. It took her a long time to reach the very top from where you could see the valleys spread away. The mists would rise up soon and cover everything. She was still, her eyes were dry. No thoughts came to her mind, no words, no memories. Neither did thoughts of the hill, or of the god whose hill this was, or of herself or her life or the love that had spread its roots into the fertile soil of her heart.

She stood like that for a long time, the winds rushing around a body so still they might have mistaken it for a tree. Finally, she moved, reaching for her slender bag of skin in which there was always stylus, inkwell, new palm leaves, thread, and completed verses. She took out the palm leaf bundle from which she had read at the Assembly, and lifting her arm high, flung it over the edge of the cliff. The bundle rose in an arc, its leaves flapping open, but restrained by the indigo thread, crashed downwards, hitting the slope and tumbling furiously into the precipice. Her hand grabbed unbound palm leaves from the bag and tossed them away. Then she took the inkwell, opened the latch that kept its cork pressed into the neck of the bottle and upturned it, holding it high above her. Streams of the indigo ink drifted back against her face and fell over her clothes, the grand selai that Kandhan had given her, in which she had triumphed. The kanakambaram that was Thennan's favourite colour, his favourite flower, was now speckled with blue ink. Her ink seemed to take on a life of its own, its strands stayed in the air and continued to fall far longer than they should have. She flung the little inkwell too into the evening-coloured air. It caught the sun and sparkled before crashing into the depths of the unseen gorge. Then she took out her styluses, and held them against her chest for a moment, tears flowing, and then flung them, one by one, away from her. One of them slipped and dropped near her. She bent to pick it up, she shivered, and her mouth opened in a scream. The hill, the trees and the clouds sailing past, all shook, as they would have under the force of a good poem. Aambal flung away that stylus. The scream that had ripped through her chest and out of her mouth died, and then another one started and another. When her body eventually stilled, Aambal drew herself up and said, 'Kandha, when I need you, you are not here.'

She looked up into the sky, then down into the valleys. The world was dimmed, for the mist that all poets feared had slipped over her eyes, a veil between her and everything. Every time she had heard the warning about the mist, hadn't she smiled? She was so sure that her eyes would never be covered over with the film of disconnection: when there was no feeling to connect the poet to the world, and thereby, to the word. How wrong she had been. Without that connection, she could not see the word-river, the stormy ocean of language. She shut and opened her eyes again and again and looked around her. The mist had settled, they had chosen their home and now would not leave.

Her feet pressed down, the toes gripping the moist, grass-covered mud at the peak of Velan's Hill, and her arms were spread wide, the fingers of her empty hands uncurled. Aambal let go, flying off the hillside to where her palm leaves, her ink, her inkwell and her stylus had gone before her. The hill's trees, grasses, its creatures, streams, hot rock faces stood mute witnesses. The wind rushed towards the body that had dared to obstruct its evening gambolling, flinging her here and there. Aambal's belly heaved, her guts twisted in her chest, her voice thrashed about in agony. No words came into Aambal's head, no lines stirred under her poet's tongue. If she could not compose, she was dead. Wasn't that what Aasaan had said? Wasn't that what Kandhan had said? Wasn't that what she had said, again and again? Without words, nothing mattered. Not even Kandhan. Not even Kandhan? Aambal's eyes sprung open, she turned to the grey mist, the hateful thing that had robbed her of her only wealth—she did not turn away.

Instead, she gathered what strength was left in her, to move her lips. They opened and her faint voice called, Kandha. She was still plunging downward, so swiftly that the wind was no more than a passing whisper, a barely audible hiss. Aambal's hands pressed her belly down for it felt like her guts would rip through. Her ears stung, not with the cold but because her call was not immediately met with Kandhan's voice calling, 'Aambal'. As it always had. As it should now, as it should always. She was his best friend. His best apprentice. His favourite poet-in-the-making.

Poetry! Aambal's body spasmed, her spine, like a riled-up snake shivering out of its coil, drawing venom into fangs, grew taut. Poetry! Language. Tamizh. Murugan's Tamizh. Her Tamizh, her verses. She remembered the earlier time when she had been on the brink of letting go, of discarding everything. Hadn't her heart lurched to think of discarding Tamizh and poetry? Hadn't she been unable to even consider such a thing? Now too! How could she think that she would die just like that? She did not want to die. She wanted to live, to compose and recite. She wanted to sit in front of her master and watch his face as it opened under the burn of her verses. She wanted to return to the Assembly. Why should she die? She had poems to write, prizes to win. Didn't she want one day to stand at the head of the Assembly to greet its patron, the Lord of Paramkundram? To deliver the welcome to aspiring poets awaiting selection? And to announce the results of every selection? Didn't she want to be there when Velliveethi took over from Nakkeeran? Didn't she want to be at the women's poetry festival? There was so much she wanted to do. So much to look forward to.

Her eyes stung with hot tears. She was falling fast to her death. It was too late now. Much too late. But was it? For one who was Time itself and who lay coiled inside everything, the Supreme Rasa, *late* and *early* were all the same. Where and when He was, that was the right time. As the thought passed into her mind, her mouth opened and her throat belched up with the force of a hundred tongues her favourite word, 'Kandha'.

As if in response, there came a shrill voice wrapped in the rush of the wind. 'Child,' it said, 'didn't I warn you, not to miss the step?'

Aambal's eyes closed, she sighed in relief. As she dropped, a laugh pushed up her clogged throat: if the Old One was here, could her god be far away?

ACKNOWLEDGEMENTS

To begin with, I'd like to acknowledge the origins of the three poems that are attributed to the character Velliveethi on pages 207 and 208 of this book. The first two paraphrase and the third is a quote from poems composed by Velliveethiyar, one of the most accomplished and well-loved of the Sangam poets.

I'm grateful to more people than I can thank here! Parents, siblings, niece and nephews, teachers, colleagues, students, and the many strangers who led me, sometimes back to cornerstones, sometimes astray, but always enlivened the stream of language: you all have my gratitude. And as for friends—the time of the writing of this book has been one of exhilarating new friendships and invigorated old ones: Prasanna Chandrasekharan, Siddan Chandra, Ravi Vaithees, Naval Sabharwal, Balamurugan, and Anita Singh and my Sacred Hearts' girl gang, in particular.

I am beholden to three people, who, in different ways, affected me especially during the writing of *Theivanai*:

To my dear friend Kusum Dhar, who has been an Elder to me, over many years and events—much gratitude for the generosity with which she guided me through the unsettle of my life, and for ever-renewing friendship and affection.

To my analyst, Dr Amrita Narayanan, appreciation for her expertise and empathy, and the (sometimes wicked) good humour that pervades our sessions. And gratitude for turning me towards tracking down, dusting off and re-costuming a more extroverted, even flamboyant version of myself that fell wounded by the wayside, somewhere between childhood and adult life.

To my friend Sai, many thanks for scolding me out of errant writing blocks; for nudging me towards extroversion; for useful lessons on life and for affection.

To my brother's wife, Smitha, many thanks for opening her home, and its guest room for me to retreat into and write in.

To my editors, V.K. Karthika and Ajitha G.S., as always admiration, thanks and affection for their keen reading, sharp editing and warmth.

As always, to my children—Sathyavak, Gauri and Paru—I am thankful for life itself. And to Totoro, the master of our household, for the anchor of unvarying affection.

Last, but never least, I am eternally grateful to Tamizh, which gives me life in ways that I cannot comprehend, and to the God of Tamizh, whose grammar is also love and the valour that love demands.

Bangalore
22 December 2023

VALLI

PART THREE OF THE MURUGAN TRILOGY

PROLOGUE

Ganesha wished that, like the manava, he too could fill with a resentment that would speed through his body, settle in and make it insensible to everything but its own dissatisfaction. He wished he could vomit, spew out this feeling. He wished he could lie curled in the dark of a hollow, inside a cave, as the animals did. Anything, but what he was called on to do. *Was it really necessary? Was it necessary for him to watch, to bear witness? Why did he have to be all-knowing, all too conscious of the grammars of life?* He sighed. He was Kandhan's brother, elder and guardian, and who else but he could be witness? And companion.

As for what was happening. It had to happen. Of course, it had to, this turn in Aambal's life, the transition marking what had been her life before and after Thennan. The start of the next chapter in her life. He leant back and shut his eyes. *Ready to bear witness.*

Aambal's body plunged downwards, through the chill evening air, towards the dark ravine, numb to the sting of the cold and the slap of the wind. She had not heard the birds' alarmed calls, nor see the clouds frothing, she had not tasted or smelt the bile spewing out of her mouth. But now she could feel something against her ears—a drumming so loud it seemed to batter down the barricades of her ears.

The sound boomed. So close, it made her flesh tingle. It enveloped her, breached the walls of her body and rushed in. It attacked every part of her insensate body, causing pain. She did not want to keep it out: this sound was hers, and she wanted to hear every beat, she wanted it to fill her ears, her head. Its thrum grew quicker, fuller. Then a sound burst from her. It ran out of her mouth and rang. The name that gave life to Aambal, to the dark-blue flower that she was named after, as well as the coral kadamba, the purple kurinji and to the syllables and alphabets of Tamizh: 'Vela!'

On top of Velan's Hill, the ancient one, her jata swinging in a circle as wide as the wheel of bullock cart, spun round and round, her ebony staff raised up to the skies. Her eyes were wide and unseeing, her mouth wide open, calling over and over, 'Vela, Vela, Vela.'

www.ingramcontent.com/pod-product-compliance
Lightning Source LLC
LaVergne TN
LVHW010311070526
838199LV00065B/5525